Praise for *Sing the Truth*

"As the editor of the groundbreaking journal *Kweli*, Laura Pegram has introduced us to many of the finest writers of the contemporary literary landscape. In this new, monumental anthology, Pegram has gathered several of these writers, welcoming us to a luminous community in the word."

—Honorée Fanonne Jeffers, author of
The Love Songs of W.E.B. Du Bois

SING THE TRUTH

The Kweli Journal Short Story Collection

• • •

Edited by
LAURA PEGRAM

Foreword by
EDWIDGE DANTICAT

Authors Equity
1123 Broadway, Suite 1008
New York, New York 10010

Cover design by Jaya Miceli
Cover art: Shutterstock/Dmitry Kovalchuk and Shutterstock/Kaananac
Book design by Scribe Inc.

Most Authors Equity books are available at a discount when purchased
in quantity for sales promotions or corporate use. Special editions, which
include personalized covers, excerpts, and corporate imprints, can be created when purchased in large quantities. For more information, please email
info@authorsequity.com.

Library of Congress Control Number: 2025931655
Print ISBN 9798893310252
Ebook ISBN 9798893310344

Printed in the United States of America
First printing

www.authorsequity.com

For my grandmother Dicey Slade;
my mother, Phyllis Mae Slade;
and my second mother and mentor, June Jordan

CONTENTS

FOREWORD
Edwidge Danticat

I have always enjoyed stories. I grew up in a family of lively storytellers who recounted their days encounter by encounter and even voiced the people they'd met as though they were characters in a play. The elders in my life were also very fond of folktales, myths, and fables, which were great narrative models for a budding writer. Stories are gifts offered to us to help deepen our understanding of the human experience and make better sense of our lives. Stories, I once read somewhere, are like the type of paintings or photographs you find yourself fully absorbed in. You know something happened before and after the image you're looking at, but you wholly fall into it while taking it in.

Unlike reading a novel, there's a natural stop-and-go feel to reading a collection of stories, an experience akin to entering a great big house inhabited by many different people who are eager to share their memories with you and how they are living or have lived. At times, it will be hard to leave one person or group behind and move on to the next. Still, the joy of reading a collection of stories like this one is also in the accumulation of encounters, which in the case of this anthology all center on the short story and Kweli—"truth" in Swahili—the organization that has been nurturing BIPOC writers through mentorships, fellowships, writing retreats, workshops, an annual festival, and *The Kweli Journal*, which was the first to publish many of the writers in this collection.

In a keynote at Kweli's International Literary Festival in July 2019, novelist, short story writer, and National Book Award finalist Kali Fajardo-Anstine praised Kweli's guidance and support to Indigenous writers and writers of color for fostering, as she said, "a newfound understanding of craft and camaraderie." Early in her writing life, she added, editors at *The Kweli Journal* recognized the strength of her stories when few others would.

Kweli was founded in 2009 by author, educator, jazz vocalist, and painter Laura Pegram. Pegram was facing health challenges and needed the kind of comfort and solace that only stories offer. One day, she woke up on the med-surg floor of New York Presbyterian Hospital in pain and unable to move her left leg. After her discharge, two months later, she decided to create *The Kweli Journal* with a community of friends, former students, and volunteers. Stories first published in the journal have become part of award-winning novels, as it was for Naima Coster's "Cold" and her sopho-more book, *What's Mine and Yours*. JP Infante's "Without a Big One," which appeared in *The Kweli Journal* in 2018, received the 2019 PEN / Robert J. Dau Short Story Prize for Emerging Writers.

Evoking a June 2004 tribute to Nina Simone at Carnegie Hall entitled "Sing the Truth," Pegram realized that writ-ers, including Nobel laureate Toni Morrison, who opened the event, also "sing the truth" in their own way, on the page. *The Kweli Journal* has been encouraging fiction and nonfiction writers to do this for fifteen years. In *The Kweli Journal*, one finds, as the journal's editors have noted, "Our many stories. Our shared histories. Our creative play with language. Here, our memories are wrapped inside the music of the Muscogee, the blues songs of the South, the clipped patois of the Caribbean."

Indeed, all of these voices and more are here. The stories in this collection serve as windows into diverse communities while inviting readers of all backgrounds to engage with and appreciate the richness of our cultures. Reem Kassis's "Farradiyya" depicts a family's longing for return after the Nakba, the forced displacement of close to a million Palestinians during the establishment of the state of Israel. DéLana R. A. Dameron's "Work" revolves around a precocious young woman whose life circumstances propel her formidable entrepreneurial spirit. The clash between cultural identity and familial expectations is also faced by immigrants and first- and second-generation Americans. JP Infante's "Without a Big One" portrays a young man's coming-of-age through struggles with ill-health and abuse. "Panagbenga" by Daphne Palasi Andreades describes a Filipina girl, Seya, navigating a challenging move to New York City. Seya's recollection of her homeland, in contrast to a cold and isolating new life, is reminiscent of many immigrant stories, including my own, in which all that remains of this type of journey after a while are treasured stories.

"Magic City Relic" by Jennine Capó Crucet engages a similar theme through Lizet, a young Cuban American woman navigating her return to her Cuban family and community after her first semester away at a predominately white university. "Cold" by Naima Coster shows the effects of poverty as a young woman and her family struggle to acquire basic necessities like heating and food. LaToya Watkins's

"Straight Dollars or Loose Change" explores the strained bonds between family members across generations. Ivelisse Rodriguez's "La Hija de Changó" introduces Santería, an Afro-Caribbean religion practiced by descendants of enslaved Africans forcibly brought to the Americas. Xaviera, the spiritual daughter of the orisha or deity Changó, seems to be speaking for many of the characters in the stories in this collection, or even for many of us, her readers, when she declares, "I want to be a shining star. . . . I want that pounding of the heart that I'm sure somebody promised me when I was young."

In K-Ming Chang's "Jenny's Dollar Store," we see the narrator wrestling with cultural assimilation, mixed with queer desire, as she searches for a self-determined identity in a new place. "Cleaning Lentils" by Susan Muaddi Darraj shows a young woman grappling with cultural displacement and body image. Nicole Dennis-Benn—who, like Kassis, Dameron, Infante, Coster, and Watkins, was first published in *The Kweli Journal*—offers us "What's for Sale," a story about a determined vendor at a Jamaican craft market. Delores charms tourists into buying her handmade crafts but crosses a line with her budding artist daughter. "Emperor of the Universe" by Kaitlyn Greenidge follows a grief-stricken woman who finds an unconventional way to live with her dead husband. In "A Hard Bed" by Princess Joy L. Perry, the protagonist, Joh, attempts to rebuild his life bit by difficult bit, day by day. In "Angry Blood" by Estella Gonzalez, a mother and daughter must find a way to love each other against a background of systemic racism and generational trauma.

The stories in this collection exquisitely and painstakingly explore complex family relationships, grief and loss, migration and diaspora, displacement and assimilation, mass incarceration and the carceral state, socioeconomic disparities, classism, and racism, but also hope, resilience, and joy. I am a longtime reader of *Kweli* and have participated in many Kweli festivals in person and online. *Kweli*'s presence on the literary landscape for the past fifteen years is a boon to readers and writers, as is this beautiful collection. I hope these stories will move and impress you just as they have enlightened and astounded me. As with all the pieces published in *The Kweli Journal*, these stories offer us a bridge across distance and time, a literary home. Crossroads are considered sacred in many African diaspora religions, like Santeria and Vodou. This book is a kind of crossroad reached after fifteen fruitful and empowering years. This book is also a portal, a pathway leading to new stories, ones we can—and sometimes must—write ourselves.

In the poem "To You," the poet, short story writer, novelist, playwright, and bard of Harlem Langston Hughes writes,

> To sit and dream, to sit and read,
> To sit and learn about the world
> Outside our world of here and now—
>   Our problem world—
> To dream of vast horizons of the soul
> Through dreams made whole,
> Unfettered, free—help me!

Help me, dear reader, celebrate Kweli and *The Kweli Journal*, this amazing dream made whole. Help me celebrate this remarkable book.

INTRODUCTION
SINGING OUR TRUTHS
Laura Pegram

I am the founding editor and publisher of *The Kweli Journal*, yet I rarely share *Kweli*'s origin story in public spaces. But for the publication of this commemorative book, I will try to follow Jesmyn Ward's example and "tell it straight."

In the winter of 2007, I sat in my wheelchair at my living room window and dreamed about *the before time*—when I could walk unassisted without stumbling. I had been diagnosed with an autoimmune disorder after college and was newly disabled, living in a fifth-floor walk-up in New York City. I missed so many things about my former life, my students at the Frederick Douglass Creative Arts Center, where I had volunteered for over ten years, most of all. The center, and especially my students, had taught me so much. But it was $200 a pop—each way—to leave my apartment via the Windsor Ambulette Service, and so I wasn't sure if (or when) I could continue teaching; the only time I left home was when I was carried to and from New York Presbyterian Hospital for medical appointments. Teaching the Art of the Short Story Workshop and the Art of Children's Literature at the community center had been two of my greatest joys, but the joy of connecting with the larger world—about books, literature, music, and all the things I loved—seemed completely out of reach.

My prognosis was uncertain. My diagnosis kept changing, from systemic sclerosis one year to lupus the next. Doctors told me that I had "mixed connective tissue disease," a rare autoimmune disorder. (It would cause me to lose the ability to swallow, recurring bouts of pericarditis and stabbing chest pain, and a host of other complications.) I was lonely and afraid. I tried to distract myself from the head pain my illness caused by singing things like "Lean On Me" by Bill Withers—but I was too weak to belt out the song the way I used to back in the day. Watching Nollywood films with my home care assistant and laughing at the bad jokes my kind and loving in-home physical therapist would tell were welcome distractions.

I vividly remember one summer afternoon four months after I had been discharged from the hospital. My doctors still didn't have any definitive answers about what caused the inflammation in my brain and when I would walk again. The opera *Margaret Garner*, based on an 1856 newspaper article that inspired the novel *Beloved* by Toni Morrison and the libretto, was scheduled to premiere at Lincoln Center in September, and all I knew was that I wouldn't be in the room to experience its music and power. It had "snatches of jazz, of gospel, of blues, of classical." I was wrecked. I wanted my life back, the music of it back too—but the path forward was murky.

Yet I was raised to make a way out of no way, like my mother, Phyllis Mae Slade, and my grandmother Dicey Slade had before me; I had faith that the answers would come.

That humid afternoon, I was at that same window listening to secondhand accounts from friends about the arts world that was now in my rearview mirror when suddenly, I realized that—and how—it didn't have to be behind me. With a loaner laptop, I could teach the Art of the Short Story Workshop online and maybe, just maybe, create from home.

The Kweli Journal was born, feet first, two years later.

We had our first board meeting in a Harlem brownstone in January 2009, with donated food and space, wholly owning our vision for a multicultural literary community. Three of our founding board members were colleagues from the Frederick Douglass Creative Arts Center, and our two readers were former workshop students. We launched as an online biannual journal on December 3, 2009, with short stories by Princess Joy L. Perry and Ivelisse Rodriguez—our Reading and Conversation Series with Edward P. Jones was born on April 14, 2011. From the beginning, we set out to invest in the artistic and professional growth of emerging BIPOC authors and provide them with a platform for publication. Before *Kweli*, original and brave and beautiful stories that reflected our complexity and full humanity had all too often been overlooked and passed over. We gave these stories and essays and poems a home. Often, this was the first place where works by these writers were published.

Since our humble beginnings, Kweli has grown into a multifaceted community organization with nine programs that offer writing, mentorship, and educational opportunities for underrepresented writers, including the Color of Children's Literature Conference (the preeminent gathering of BIPOC creators of children's and young adults' books), the International Literary Festival (designed as an intimate multiweek hybrid event featuring virtual and in-person readings and conversations with debut and award-winning BIPOC writers, master classes, craft talks, and multisession workshops), our Fellowship Program (a yearlong writing intensive for early career vocational writers in New York City that includes editorial support, admission-free participation in our International Literary Festival, and an all-expenses-paid writing retreat hosted at Akwaaba [see *Kweli*'s website for more information about retreats], a bed-and-breakfast/inn owned by Monique Greenwood, the former editor in chief of *Essence* magazine), the Sing the Truth! Mentorship Program (an extension of the Kweli Color of Children's Literature Conference where writers receive mentorship for a full year or more [see *Kweli*'s website for more information about conferences]), the free monthly Reading and Conversation Series (special multimedia events where, in addition to reading and conversation, there are also original dance interpretations of the works), multisession writing workshops and master classes, and curated writing retreats at Akwaaba. Last year, we launched The Third Eye on Instagram Live, a free craft series I host with *Kweli* contributing writers on the art of revision and the editorial process.

Sing the Truth celebrates our fifteenth anniversary. This book arrives as the result of all the people who have worked with me and us over the years, largely as volunteers. For it was the contributors to *The Kweli Journal* who also became volunteer readers, editors, and mentors. Publishing their fiction, nonfiction, poetry, and interviews has been a true gift.

The narratives included in this anthology explore the devastation of leaving home and the struggle to adapt to reimagined lives, lost loves, distant families, and buried pasts. Wives search for their husbands, and sons for their fathers. Mothers make difficult—sometimes terrible—decisions to ensure their families' survival. And as DéLana R. A. Dameron writes in her short story "Work," "So many folks only just take take take take from you." The characters found in this collection show us both the tragedy of invisibility and the triumph of finally being seen. These stories reflect the truth of so many BIPOC histories, along with the endless possibilities of their futures.

It was quite difficult to choose the pieces within this collection, drawn as they were from many years of literary contributions across the country and the world. Going back over the work we had published was a journey unto itself; every couple of days, I would circle back to the team working on what we would include and submit two or three more favorites. We had to whittle down from what we kept calling a "final" list to the fourteen stories here.

In selecting stories for online publication in *Kweli*, I was looking for pieces that surprised me. Good storytellers know how to surprise. And good musicians know how to listen. As a singer, I found myself listening to the sound of every sentence as I looked for writing that was aware of its music. I leaned into deeply layered work with complicated characters that provided a new perspective or a new way of seeing. Multiple storylines often within a single narrative. For example, look at the ideas of love, immigration, and freedom within "Without Inspection" by Edwidge Danticat or family, power, and religion within "Old Boys, Old Girls" by Edward P. Jones. These two brilliant short stories are on the required reading list of the multisession Art of the

Short Story Workshop I teach online each month. I see something new in each and every close and critical reading of these layered works of art, and that is true for each of the stories collected in this volume. It could be a single, beautifully compressed line of dialogue like *Bottom, top, it's all the same ship* from "Old Boys, Old Girls" by Edward P. Jones, which reminds the reader at once that slavery and mass incarceration are cousins. Or it could be the sudden revelation that *there are loves that outlive lovers* from "Without Inspection" by Edwidge Danticat, which allows anyone who has known loss intimately to carry grief. Or it could be a detailed description from "Magic City Relic" by Jennine Capó Crucet, which reveals as much about the observer as it does the person being observed, as in the following passage: *Tío Fito stood up, placing the bottle on the tile by his spot on the couch, and staggered over to me for a hug. He was shirtless and—aside from the preponderance of gray chest hair, the broken little veins sprawling over his cheeks, and the deep lines on his forehead that spelled out the eleven years he had on Papi—looked pretty much like an alcohol-drenched version of my dad, down to the goatee and the heavy eyelashes.* Or we can see the contradictions of character in "What's for Sale" by Nicole Dennis-Benn: *The man pulled out a wad of cash and began to count it in front of Delores. Delores counted six hundred-dollar bills. She was blinking so fast that her eyes grew tired from the rapid movement. She had never seen so much money in her life. The crispness of the bills and the scent of newness, which Delores thought wealth would smell like—the possibility of moving her family out of River Bank; affording her children's school fees, books, and uniforms; buying a telephone and a landline for her to call people whenever she liked instead of waiting to use the neighbor's phone. All these possibilities were too much to swallow all at once. They made her stutter her next response. "Sah—but she—she's only fourteen."* And we can see complex and complicated characters in "Jenny's Dollar Store" by K-Ming Chang: *Back in Taiwan, she told me, she lived next to an old abandoned prison with a wishbone-shaped river behind it, and the water tasted like blood, not the rusty old kind of blood, but the kind so fresh it feigns being sweet. She told me the Nationalists used to build prisons next to rivers because it made it easy to get rid of bodies: The prisoners were shot on the banks so they'd fold into the water and be recycled out to sea.* Easy, *she said.* Practical, that's what those people are. *You didn't even waste bullets, she told me. String all the prisoners together, and shoot just one of them. Then they'll all fall into the water and drown. Nothing wasted. This was how Jenny justified selling expired cans of soup and boxes of frozen pizzas that the dogs gnawed through.*

Nothing wasted. Every word has weight.

The poet June Jordan was the first writer to teach me about the weight of every word, precise and powerful language, and the musicality in a line. I was introduced to books that sing in hospital beds and (English) lit college classrooms, from *Their Eyes Were Watching God* by Zora Neale Hurston to *Song of Solomon* by Toni Morrison. I was a shy, eighteen-year-old college student at Stony Brook University with a good ear; June became both a mentor and a second mother, editing my first short stories and coproducing a Lady Day Nite program, where I would sing for the first time publicly. When June opened those books and worlds to me, I was moved and astonished to see myself on the page, to see our interior lives made visible. Our authentic voices singing.

In *the before time*, I would perform here and there, singing in various venues—from a small jazz club in New York City to the modest home of an Algerian friend who lived in the fourteenth arrondissement in Paris. My repertoire included compositions by artists like Nina Simone and Billie Holiday who were known for singing the truth about the times we live in and what we survive—if not whole, then in part. Powerful female vocals, raspy and direct. Lyrics from Simone's first protest song, "Mississippi Goddam," are deeply relevant in today's challenging world where police dogs are still weapons of racial terror: "Hound dogs on my trail // Schoolchildren sitting in jail // Black cat cross my path // I think every day's gonna be my last."

Like Simone and Holiday, the contributors to *Sing the Truth* each summoned the weight of memory to create powerful art, taking the reader, as if in one held breath, from Molly and Joh—newlyweds who were "less husband and wife than trembling children"—living on a Black-owned farm in a small town in Virginia in 1939, and in the next held breath, to Hiba, a Palestinian American girl "coming off her own humiliation" while living with her grandparents Sits and Seeda in present-day Baltimore.

Princess Joy L. Perry searches the memories of her grandmother and parents in Windsor, North Carolina, a segregated cotton and tobacco town. She wants to discover how they stayed afloat and kept patience and faith as poor, uneducated Blacks who were stubbornly alive. The questions she raises about their lives are answered in the heart-wrenching story that came out of her, "A Hard Bed."

"Farradiyya" by Reem Kassis is based on a family friend's history of dispossession in 1948. The story's twelve-year-old narrator remembers his stone home in Farradiyya, a Palestinian Arab village of 670 located eight kilometers (five miles) southwest of Safad. He remembers the olive groves, kite flying with his brothers, his love of school, and his gift for numbers. "Just watch, he'll be running his own business one day," his father boasts. But home and school soon become distant memories when his Baba falls ill, and he must step up and support his family. His math book now sits idle in his rucksack as he works in a Dabbah butcher shop in Rameh "tossing fat and scrap meat into gray plastic pails outside and chasing stray cats with the thistle broom." I fell in love with the lyric in these lines and remain haunted by the dreams deferred.

Memory for Kassis is laced throughout the lyrics, if you will, found not just in this but in each short story in this collection.

In her essay "The Site of Memory," Toni Morrison writes, "The act of imagination is bound up with memory. You know, they straightened out the Mississippi River in places, to make room for houses and livable acreage. Occasionally the river floods these places." Remembering *the before time*. "Writers are like that: remembering where we were, what valley we ran through, what the banks were like, the light that was there and the route back to our original place. It is emotional memory," she writes; for me, it's one that calls back all the notes of an imagined life, the hardship, but also the hope.

So come: Sit with us on the bank and listen to our music.

SING
THE
TRUTH

A HARD BED

Princess Joy L. Perry

Nineteen-year-old Joh Pember careened down the center of Freeman Farm Road spinning whorls of dust and spitting gravel. He wheeled the ten-year-old 1929 wood-sided Model A like it was stolen and new, like anything oncoming would give way. He was on the road to Clyde Adock's Feed and Seed to pick up corn for hogs he hated. Gluttonous beasts, they broke through the electric fence almost weekly. Always the one to fetch them, Joh found pigs in the peanuts or sweet potato mounds, rooting up a week's worth of sweat and backache. He drove them home with a stout club. If they dawdled, he landed a hard kick.

But that morning, the hogs were securely in their pen. Joh was alone in the truck and, with a little money in his pocket besides what he needed for feed, headed to town. The sun was shoulder-high over the drab and green fields, and as he swept past, the light skated and slid, played coy and reappeared, a bright warm spot on the seat beside him, a slender beam bending across his face.

It was in that new-sprung, flirty light that Joh saw her, yellow skirt swinging around her brown muscled calves and bouncing up the back of her thighs as she jumped hopscotch. The sight of her hit him like his first drunk—a sweet, surprising, full-body flush—just like the half a bottle of communion wine, stolen when he was twelve years old. He forgot the near-empty feed troughs and that Namon, his older brother, had warned him what would happen if the hogs broke free again. He tooted the horn, a bright frivolous sound, and steered the truck to the side of the road.

"I know you," he said as he leaned out of the window, his red "PURE" motor oil cap matching his red-and-khaki-checkered shirt. "Your mama sing in the choir. Y'all live down Blackrock. What you doing all the way out here?"

She nodded toward the bush of goldenrod, just budding, flanking the path home. "I stay here now with my Aunt 'Melia. You Joh. How come you don't come to church no more?"

"Cause I didn't know you was out of nursery worshipping with the grown folks," he said.

She smiled. "I bet you don't even remember my name, if you ever knowed it."

Joh turned his face to the windshield as if he might find her name magically there, then back to her, admitting, "You right, you right. I don't. But I'll pay for the privilege with a ride to wherever you going."

"School."

"School! You still in school? How old you?"

"Fifteen."

"Fifteen! Most folks I know *been* left school! You trying to learn it all, ain't you?"

"I'm gon' be a nurse."

"A colored nurse? 'Round here?"

"There's other places 'cept 'round here."

"Is there? Why don't you climb in here and tell me 'bout some of 'em." He reached to the passenger side and loosened the wire that held the door shut.

"Thank you," she said. "I'll wait for the bus."

Joh shrugged, shut the door. "Suit yourself." He looked up the empty road. "Sometime the school bus come. Sometime it don't. Depends on if they got a full load of white. Depends on if they feel like driving down here."

"I got legs for more than hopscotch."

Joh smiled as he slid the gearshift into first. "That's what I know," he said. "That's what I know."

He came back any morning when he and his brother worked separate corners of the farm and whenever Namon left the truck unattended. She traded her name, Molly, for sweet talk and bars of candy—almonds, coconut, chocolate—that had cost the biggest portion of Joh's spending change. But still it took weeks to get her into the truck, and weeks more before Molly abandoned her schoolbooks under the flowering cover of her aunt's lemon-gold hedge and let Joh teach her all else those strong brown legs were good for.

• • •

Molly grasped the dashboard and tried to keep her seat as the truck bounced in and out of potholes. They were finally headed home, to the farm Joh and his brother owned. As the landscape had grown more and more familiar, they'd talked less and less. Miles ago, the complaints of the truck began to fill the space left by their voices. Molly scooted forward at the turnoff to Aunt Amelia's, now flanked by the laden boughs of Bradford pear trees. A breeze volleyed the leaves like flags of welcome.

"We ought to live with your aunt," Joh said quietly.

Molly watched as the pear trees shrank then disappeared. The yearning in her gaze altered as it settled upon Joh. He looked small inside his blue-checkered shirt—narrow chest and charcoal skin, nineteen years old—a skinny Black boy, not a husband. But they were married. A letter signed by her mother. A half hour at the courthouse. Afterward they drove to the Outer Banks. With no money for a room, they'd left Hargraves', the only place where coloreds could drink and dance, to sleep in the bed of the truck. Her honeymoon night, but Molly did not want to make love. Grudgingly, Joh let her be. But his hand, moist and heavy, settled against her bare belly. When he fell asleep, Molly rolled away.

"She ain't gon' want nothing to do with me for a while," Molly said. "You said your brother will let us stay."

"He will."

"Then why you talking 'bout living with Aunt 'Melia?"

Joh drew his lips tightly over his teeth as if to hold in a mouthful of things. He looked toward the road. "Namon gon' be mad I kept the truck, is all."

• • •

The house was stark. Wood, brick, glass. It was nothing like the home Molly left behind, Aunt Amelia's, where there were so many potted plants on the stoop it was hard to gain the door, and the yard burst with every flowering bush imaginable: royal purple hydrangea, lavender-pink Josee lilacs, white-turned-golden fountain grass, the pale raspberry of Paree peonies. In Joh and Namon's yard, there was not even the promise of a bud; even the grass had been chewed by the tire treads and buried in the ruts.

Joh cut the motor. Namon Pember, out front cleaving stove wood, waited with the ax hanging at his side. He was tall, hard-muscled, profoundly Black. Up close, Molly found her new brother-in-law to be as severe as his house. He switched the ax from hand to hand. "Where you been?" he demanded.

"Out to Duck," Joh answered. "Hargraves. I'm married." Clipped words hid the quaver of his voice. Molly stopped herself in the act of reaching for Joh's hand.

"She gon' have a baby," Namon said flatly.

"Yeah."

Namon's gaze hardened as it moved from Joh's quaking bravado to Molly's shamed face.

"Goddamn!" he said, his words for both of them. "God-damn if you ain't the stupidest—" Namon raised the ax high above his head and brought it arcing down. Biting wood chips flew at Joh and Molly.

They did not step back or even cover their faces. Defenseless, wordless, Molly and Joh stood guilty before Namon, less husband and wife than trembling children.

. . .

Molly watched dollops of sweetened cornmeal batter spread in hot lard as she stirred ham hocks, mustard greens, and white potatoes with a splintered wood spoon. She heard Joh outside washing up at the pump. Namon already sat at the kitchen table. "You forgot the ice water" was all he'd said since walking through the door. His broad hand spread over *Pathways in Science and Learning About Our World*, a much-mended schoolbook Molly had set aside to make supper. He pushed the pages back and forth. "Whenever I see your aunt down to the store, she bragging on you," he said. "She always saying how smart you is. How far you come in school. You ain't so smart after all, is you?"

Molly flipped the bread. She took a pitcher of water from the icebox and set it on the table. Her hands shook.

"What was you gon' be? A schoolteacher?"

"Is gon' be," Molly said, voice trembling like her hands, "a nurse."

"*Gon' be?* There was already three marks against you. Poor. Colored. Girl. Now you married. Gon' have a baby."

"Nothing to say I still can't be a nurse."

Namon snorted.

Joh rushed through the door with his cap off and his hair and face still damp. "It ain't on the plates yet, Molly?"

"Feed them hogs?" Namon asked.

"Joh, get my book," Molly said as she turned toward the table with a plate in each hand.

Absently, Namon grabbed the book and dropped it to the floor. "You setting to this table and them hogs ain't ate?"

"I been—" Joh began to explain as the plates clattered to the table. Molly stooped to retrieve her fragile book. Dismayed and angry, she looked up at Namon.

"I got to take care'a that! Miss Bond won't let me borrow no more if I tear it up!"

"What you need a book for?" Namon asked as he pulled a plate forward.

"I'm going back."

Again, Namon snorted. He turned to Joh. "What I tell you gon' happen if them hogs get out again?"

Molly stood. "Ain't I going back to school, Joh?"

Joh looked from his brother to his wife. He pulled a plate forward. "Hush, Molly," he said.

"Ain't that what we said?"

"Hush!" Joh ordered. "I can't taste my food for all this foolishness!"

Molly took a step toward Joh. "We said—"

"School is out," Namon spoke firmly. "What you look like sitting up in a schoolroom full of children when you got one in your belly? You married now. There's work for you 'round here." He picked up his fork.

Standing beside the table, Molly clutched her book. She watched Namon and Joh bend their heads over greens she had picked clean and boiled. Their white teeth tore her cornbread. They chewed and drank and swallowed as if the matter were settled.

• • •

Namon Pember waited in Clyde Adock's store to buy a pack of Chesterfields. He stood aside at the long wood-and-glass counter while Adock talked to Roy Gilliam, an extension agent and a sometime cotton ginner. It was Roy's job to travel Bertie County, bringing word of better farm equipment and pest control to farmers. Somehow, though, he never managed to make it to the coloreds and poor whites. In harvest season, when farmers had little time or attention to spare, Gilliam once in a while ginned cotton, his skillful extra hands allowing the overrun gin owner to stretch the workday from early morning until late in the night.

Commonplace except for his job, Gilliam was born of the peasant farmers who bartered and sold at Adock's.

Nowadays, with a buzz cut that showed a clean pink scalp
and starched khaki shirts with "*Gilliam*" sewn in heavy-
grade, dark-blue thread over the breast pocket, he was better
off. Still, on his rounds from big farm to big farm, he always
stopped at Adock's for the time it took to win a game of
checkers and drink a beer.

At the counter, he debated crop quotas and government
price supports, brushing off Adock's reluctance to argue
and efforts to wait on Namon. The checker players got fed
up. "Gilliam!" one called. "I got a crop to bring in in 'bout
three months. You be ready to play by then?"

Gilliam slapped the counter. "You gon' see, Clyde!" he
said backing away. "You gon' see that Roosevelt ain't nothing but one'a them socialists!" He took another step, and
his heel clipped an open bag of feed. "Damn it!" he said as
he looked down at the flow of spilled grain. Then, as easy
as shoving a suitcase at a bellhop, he gestured to Namon.
"Pick that up."

Clyde Adock was already coming from behind the counter with a dustpan and broom. "I got it, Roy."

"He'll get it," Roy said as he reached deep into a barrel
of ice for a bottle of beer.

Namon stood stiff as a cooling board. This was not his
first run-in with a man like Gilliam. It wasn't his second.
Perhaps Namon understood better than Roy Gilliam himself
why he so despised colored people and beggared whites.
Gilliam was all but one of them. A favor or a phone call
from a rich white man, and Gilliam had been lifted from
the status of poor white trash. Now he had a job that put
him on speaking terms with men of historic names and
Confederate deeds. They might offer him a whiskey or a

cigar in return for exclusive information. But he had the same chance as Namon to sit at their tables or be introduced to their daughters. Namon said, "I wasn't nowhere near that bag."

With his hand on the cap of the amber glass bottle, Roy Gilliam tensed.

There rose in the store the atmosphere of a cockfight—strutting, speckled birds with razors fastened to their feet—calming only when one rooster tore the head from another. Clyde Adock surveyed the room. The white men who played checkers and ate sardines and cheese in his store had a lot in common with Namon Pember. Their farms were always at the mercy of animal disease and crop blight. Like Namon, they were passed over for loans while big acreage "farmers" who rarely touched dirt reaped subsidy checks. All in the same leaky boat, Adock had extended credit to every one of them to a man. Sometimes they called this to mind. Adock had seen them trade remedies, tools, and sometimes a cigarette with Namon. Yet these were the years of Scottsboro, when good white citizens marveled that a gang of Black boys jailed for raping white women had lived long enough to deny it in court. They straightened from the board. The gaze of every white man was on Namon, and Adock. Gilliam's hand slid down the neck of the unopened bottle. He gripped it like a hammer.

"Roy," Adock said, "there ain't got to be none of that. Namon gon' do what I say. How he gon' feed his animals and fertilize his cotton he don't?" Adock spoke coldly to Namon. "Nobody asked where you was. Do what he said."

Namon scanned the room. The only other colored in the store was Irving, the thirty-five-year-old stock "boy."

High up on a ladder, dusting the red-labeled cans of mackerel, he didn't even look down. There were five whites. Adock wouldn't pile on, but Irving wouldn't help. Namon had a new crop in the field. He couldn't work if they beat him badly. Joh could not do the work alone.

On knees that bent as if they were bit by bit breaking, Namon knelt and scraped the floor clean. But before he did, he looked into the eyes of Roy Gilliam—as if he were not outnumbered and surrounded—with the white-hot fury of any other man.

• • •

With a hand still coated in grain dust and floor grit, Namon reached into his shirt pocket for a cigarette. Nothing.

"Goddamn!" he said, bringing his attention back to the road just as a sow and three shoats trotted across. He slammed the truck to a stop, fishtailing in the road.

As fast as the truck and the narrow dirt lane would let him, Namon sped home. He found his brother in the hog pen kneeling among the slack fencing. Just as Joh looked over his shoulder to explain, Namon drew back his foot. Full weight and full of rage, he kicked Joh.

"Find," he said, "those goddamned pigs."

• • •

Molly's Aunt Amelia squatted by a whitewashed tractor tire filled with dirt. She was setting out the plant clippings that usually crowded her windowsills. Beneath a fraying straw hat, she hummed "The Old Sheep Know the Road," breaking her melody only to murmur, "Root for me now, hear?" as she lifted plants from jars, tangled roots dripping, and arranged them in the soil. Around each plant she poured murky water from its own jar so the strange new home would feel familiar.

"*Aunt 'Melia*," Molly said.

Her name spoken in a misery voice, and Amelia was yanked from her only peace. She studied her full hands for the briefest moment, then looked up. "Well, what happened?"

"I ain't going back to school."

Amelia studied the girl's woeful expression. This was news, it seemed, but only to Molly. "Why?"

"Joh's brother say I can't."

"What Joh say?"

"Nothing."

Amelia studied the hydrangea cuttings, then gazed about her yard. In some patches and corners, weeds had gotten ahead of her flowers. Amelia kept gardens for a few women in Windsor whose husbands were still wealthy enough to pay, and she came home in the evenings with her back aching and her inspiration spent. She was late putting her own garden into the ground. Maybe the plants would root and she'd have "snowballs" bordering the walk to her privy, their white petals carpeting the ground. But all of this could be for nothing. Thrive or shrivel. One was just as likely as the other. So it was with this girl. All of that hard work and hope gone to nothing.

When Molly said she wanted to be a nurse, Amelia had begun holding back a portion of her tithes to pay for schooling. She had envisioned introducing the girl: "This my niece. She a nurse," meaning, "She educated. You can't do her like you do me." Now she understood the enormity of her sin, the arrogance of her dream. When Molly turned up pregnant, Amelia said, "That's what come of robbing God."

"Aunt 'Melia?"

"I said don't let that boy turn your head." Amelia gouged a hole in the dirt. "Go to school. Get your lesson. You wouldn't listen. You wanted to be *grown*. Thought you was grown when you was sneaking off with that boy. *That* didn't make you no woman." She paused. She could almost see the rebuke, the reality, spreading through the girl like that dark water taken up by the roots. "What you feeling right now," Amelia said sadly, "*that* make you woman."

Molly finally spoke, her voice diminished like the third sounding of an echo. "What am I gon' do?"

Amelia might have told the girl to go home to her ma, but there were still four hungry mouths to feed at Odell's. Molly's mama didn't need a grown girl coming back with a baby. She might have, again, taken Molly, but hard times were turning desperate. City whites were moving back to take field jobs, and what they didn't take, cotton picking machines did. Hoot, her husband, hadn't worked steady in weeks, and weeks were all it took for the notes on the stove and furniture to fall behind. Amelia's cupboards were not bare, but she and Hoot had little in abundance. Molly had a husband who owned part of the land he farmed. Two men to plow and harvest and hunt for food if it came to that. She had to stay, hard bed and all.

"*Aunt 'Melia?*"

Chest deep, Amelia sighed. "Go home," she said. "That's what you gon' do. A woman with a child don't leave home over nothing like that."

Amelia let Molly sit and weep as she quickly set out the rest of her cuttings, the joy of planting gone, the fancy arrangements forgotten.

• • •

Joh came home from the hog pen to find Molly asleep at the kitchen table, head on folded arms. Her book lay open in front of her. The stove was cold. The skillet from breakfast sat unwashed. Plates, frosted with grease, waited in cold dishwater. He shook Molly until she woke.

"This what you been doing?"

She raised her head and looked around as if she expected to wake in a different place. Gradually, her features settled. "I went to Aunt 'Melia's," Molly mumbled.

"An left the house like this? An come back an ain't fix supper?"

"I come back in time," she said defensively, rising awkwardly, her body still adjusting to the weight and ride of the baby. "I was just tired, I guess, from the walk."

"Ain't too tired to put your eyes in that book."

"What my book got to do with anything?" Molly snapped. "You hungry, I'll get you something. Gon' wash."

Joh came in from the pump to find leftover hominy and ham warming in the skillet, but the breakfast dishes were still in the pan. Molly sat at the table, her fingers skimming over pages.

"You ain't wash that frying pan," Joh said.

Molly shrugged. "Bacon grease is bacon grease."

From the backdoor, Joh reached her in three strides. His fist hit her book like a hard-swung bat, knocking it to the floor, shattering the rotten thread of the binding.

"What's wrong with you!" Molly screamed.

She threw herself down, stooping and squatting, gathering the strewn leaves. Joh raised his foot.

He stomped near Molly's fingers, near her face, until she crouched on her haunches; only her bewildered gaze followed Joh. Dirt and hog shit from the tread of his boot smeared the pages, imprinted a chapter deep. He ground his heel until layers of pages ripped.

"Now!" Joh yelled as he stood over Molly. "Tend to something!"

. . .

Namon arrived not long after Joh stalked back to the fields. He came upon Molly as she stood by the stove staring down at her belly with an expression too fierce to be love.

"How come you looking at it that way?" he asked.

"What way?" Molly asked. "I ain't looking at it no kinda way." She made up her face like she made up the beds. Folded and tucked. Neat around the edges.

"You ain't so dumb after all, is you?"

"Hominy and ham all there is for supper," Molly said.

"Dish it up then." Namon approached the table. Her book lay there, pieced together, even the shit-covered pages. "Book don't look so precious today," he said, flicking it with one finger.

"Leave it 'lone, please."

Namon withdrew his hand. "What got hold to it?"

"Joh."

"What for?"

"Hateful!" Molly teared as she asked in a quieter voice, "What it hurt y'all if I read my book and go to school?"

Namon gripped the back of a chair. He only knew that all of her talk of going to school caused a desperate anger to well in him. It was a filthy feeling, like when a pounding rain caused the outhouse to flood and run over, but he could not help it.

"That ain't your place." He sat at the table, waiting for Molly to bring his plate.

Instead of spooning grits and ham onto a plate, Molly stared at Namon. He stared back. Between them was the same feeling that had risen in Adock's store. The tension felt like the moment just before the cocks were released.

"It moved," Molly said. "I was looking at it that way cause it moved."

. . .

For two days and nights, Molly and Joh performed the obligations of marriage—he brought in stove wood, Molly cooked his breakfast—but little else passed between them. On the third night, Joh dropped heavily onto his side of the bed. He shucked off his shirt. His back was stamped with a spreading bruise, less apparent because of his dark skin, but painful. Stiffly, he bent to unlace his boots. Molly turned her miserable face to his injured back.

The boy into whose truck she'd climbed was not this boy. That Joh had been a charming thing, a slim dark boy with a sly, easy smile. She likened him to something beautifully wild slipping through the woods. Molly had meant to go only close enough to take a look. One day, she left her books beneath a covering of flowers. Then another day, then another, never imagining she would not make it back.

Joh worked the ties on his boots. "Namon say he gon' get a secondhand tractor if we make a good crop. He do, he won't need me so much." One boot hit the floor with a thud. "We could leave here."

Molly rose onto her elbow. "Go where?"

"Virginia. Newport News. I might could get on at the shipyard."

"A big colored hospital's there. Whitaker Memorial."

"I know," Joh said.

He put out the light and crawled into bed. Molly lay back against her pillow. Neither slept.

After a while, Joh asked, "You feeling all right?"

Molly answered, "I'm feeling all right."

· · ·

Amelia brought baby clothes, cut and stitched by her own hands, diapers with sharp shiny pins, and a cradle mended and varnished. When she left, Molly pushed everything beneath her bed, out of sight. She felt the anticipation and fear of an expectant mother only for Namon's crop.

For this, she put her book away. Like Namon, she examined the soil and watched the weather. Without being asked or told, she worked the fields, squatting, bending, weeding on the days when squares nubbed the young stems and when those squares split into buttery flowers. Molly gathered the fallen blossoms in each of their short-lived stages, purple tipped, then pink and red, and saved them like first teeth, like locks of hair.

Early in the season, when the first trembling, sunlit-green stand of cotton appeared, Namon set Joh and Molly to thinning out the plants. The task was simple. Where the seed bunched together, the new plants were to be dug out of the earth and resettled ten inches apart. Namon trusted Joh, but he kept close watch on Molly, finally leaving his own rows for hers. "Not so rough!" he ordered as he knelt beside her in a furrow.

Namon snatched the dented and rusted spade from Molly's hand, but with seedlings he was tender. He dug a circle around a clump of plants, mindful of roots, and untangled them like a finger smoothing a wild brow. Molly noticed his hands—scarred from plow lines and wire punctures— coarse hands moving cautiously, not only, she suspected, because there was money at stake.

"You love this work."

Absorbed, so unguarded, Namon grunted, "Yeah."

Molly touched the miniature, hand-shaped leaf of a cotton seedling. She took a delicate stem between thumb and forefinger.

"I could rip it up," she said, "the way Joh done my book."

She saw Namon's dismay before his face sealed in anger. Namon stood, but Molly held his gaze.

"I feel like that about school."

"Just do like I say," he ordered. He moved many rows away from her.

Molly knelt in the dirt, stretching beyond her growing belly, ignoring the low ache in her back. She worked the plants just as Namon had shown her, cautious with the fragile roots, each plant, in her mind, a separate page.

• • •

Over the months of summer, Molly followed the men, chopping weeds that came up faster than cotton, always alert for weevils. One day, Joh ordered Molly home when he found her pacing the rows shaking poison from a thinly woven croker sack onto the leaves. White dust enclosed her.

Joh pulled her to the edge of the field. "Don't you care *nothing* 'bout this baby?"

"Weevils eat the cotton, we can't leave," she said firmly.

Molly had taken to heart words that Joh wanted to take back. In the time it took for bruises to fade—blood reabsorbed into blood—Joh had forgiven Namon. Not many days after Namon kicked Joh, he came confiding the dream of a secondhand tractor. "You good with machine things," Namon said. "When it break, you'll fix it." *Sorry*—the only way Namon knew to say it.

Joh found himself trapped between the hard hopes of Namon and Molly. He pretended that he could serve them both. He did nothing to discourage Namon, who planned an easier and more prosperous future with two men and a tractor. And Joh did not caution Molly, who, in her ninth month, September, when cotton lint burst the bolls, looped a sack around her chest and headed to the fields.

· · ·

The ginnery, like most vital things, was located at a crossroads. It was not modern—a mule-driven holdover from the last century—but the only gin that Namon and other small farmers could afford. It sat directly across from the firehouse and cater-cornered to the large general store where people bought gasoline and groceries, but traded news and gossip for free. On the other side of the road was the ball field. Some Saturdays white men played, and some Saturdays colored men played. Colored or white, the women cooked. They sold pulled pork barbecue, fried fish with white bread, white potatoes fried with onions, and grape or orange Nehi. Small children scrambled underfoot while the women wiped sweat and fishy grease from their faces, too busy to hear the calls of the umpire or enjoy the play.

But there were no games during cotton harvest. The playing field was overrun with wagons and trucks and trailers pulled by Rumley and Model D John Deere tractors, as the local farmers waited to have their upland cotton ginned. The wait was many things: long and thirsty if a man had used up his credit at the store; tense with a season's work piled in one place; worrisome with each man comparing quantity, texture, color, praying for a good grade, a high price.

Namon knew he had quality cotton. He had begun with high-caliber, short-staple cottonseed and picked only the ready bolls. He'd cautioned and badgered and eyed Joh and Molly to make sure they did the same. Once picking was done, Namon minded the cotton personally, sleeping but a little, taking care that the seed did not overdry, trusting Joh to check the lint only a handful of times. Now, as Namon waited in line, he tried not to think how little any of that mattered. The quality of his cotton was determined as much by the vigilance of the ginner as it was by anything Namon had done while his crop was in the ground. The ginner's job was to take utmost care with how the cottonseed was pulled through the saws, grates, and brushes. If he allowed the machine to jam or even looked away as the saws drew the cotton though the grate, knots could form in the fiber. A year of work could be greatly diminished or even lost.

Namon arrived to find farmers already waiting. Wagons and tractors rolled forward slowly until, a couple of hours before sundown, Namon stood on the slatted floor of the ginnery, his cotton mounded around his feet. Around him, the dark faces of women who moted cotton were softened by the gauzy haze of floating lint. Their talk of children, in-laws, and men revolved slowly in the humid evening air. In soft, ashy voices, they called to the barefoot colored boys who hung around the gin, running errands for pennies, and offered them nickels or paper money damp with bosom sweat to fetch Coca-Colas and peanut butter crackers. The marriageable women aimed flirtatious looks at Namon. But one woman, older, with fingers that picked trash from the fiber faster and more deftly than the rest, did not aim to seduce. Her gaze traveled pointedly to the ginner who mounted the stairs.

Roy Gilliam crossed the gin house floor and stood in front of the cotton gin machine like a concert pianist. He nudged a mound of cotton with his boot. With a quick check of the belts and wheels, he glanced around for the farmer.

Namon stepped out of the shadow of a low-hanging, slanting beam. He kept his face expressionless; Roy Gilliam did the same, but they recognized each other. Their eyes, like glittering grindstones, gave them away.

Almost casually Gilliam asked, "You by yourself?"

"Yes, sir," Namon said.

"Adock ain't sent you?"

"No, sir."

Lifting the cotton, measuring by feel, loading the machine, Gilliam said, "I thought he'd sent you."

"No, sir," Namon repeated, each *sir* feeling like a lit cigarette stubbed on his skin.

Gilliam kept close watch on his hands, filling the machine with dirty seed cotton. His tone was no different than if he said, *Sure is hot today.* "I thought you was his boy. The way you cleaned his floor, I thought you was his boy. Ain't you?"

Gilliam spoke loudly, but the moters pretended not to hear. An impatient cotton farmer, come inside to escape the mosquitoes and wait his turn, cocked his head to listen.

Namon glanced at the woman on the floor. Her fingers moved quickly and surely through the cotton lint. She did not look at him, but she did not have to. *Yes*, she would say. *Put a roof over your head. Put food on your table.* Put a tractor in your field. Put money away in case Joh's new baby takes sick.

Namon knew the words and posture that would get his cotton ginned to perfection. Grade A. Top price. He lowered his gaze to Roy Gilliam's collarbone. In the humblest voice possible for a man of Namon's size and ambition, he said, "*Yas, sir.*" The words tore from his throat like a ribbon of flesh.

Gilliam inhaled. He nodded. "I knew you was," he said. "I knew you was."

He fed and adjusted the machine. The teeth grabbed the first bolls. Seeds rolled down the grate.

Though he saw the parts move, Namon was oblivious to the din of the saws and the rattle of the housing and gears. The approving nod from the woman was incomprehensible. Only shame reached him; humiliation so dense, it felt as if he'd crawled inside a cotton bale.

But as he watched, clean lint fell over the brushes; he forced out his hand. Namon clutched one fistful of seed-free, grade A cotton before Roy Gilliam said, "Got to feed the mules."

He sent the owner's son, a boy of sixteen or seventeen, to gin Namon's cotton. Downstairs, Roy Gilliam smoked a cigarette as he watched the mules—hungry, dumb, obedient—churn in the track, and the gin chewed Namon Pember's cotton.

. . .

Hardly able to sleep for her own excitement and the baby stretching and curling within her, Molly woke instantly at the sound of the knocking truck motor. She shook Joh.

"Namon's back!" she said, throwing off the sheet and maneuvering her legs over the side of the bed.

Joh pressed his face into the pillow. "In the morning," he mumbled.

"This can't wait 'til morning." Molly grabbed her dress from a hanger behind the door. "Joh! Get up!"

She stood by the window tugging on her dress. Nothing outdoors moved as excitedly. Grass and leaf-laden branches swayed. Some small vulnerable animal crept into a weed clump near the shed. Only Molly and sleepless whippoorwills disturbed the night. She scanned the long trails of moonlight until she found Namon's shadow. He sat motionless on the tailgate. He did not honk the horn or bellow for Joh to help carry cottonseed to the shed. He did not stomp through the house, rousting Molly out of bed to cook hot food on the night he'd sold his best cotton crop. Namon sat straight and still like the grief stricken sit at funerals, as if minding heartbeat, breath, and thought, anything that could race away and burst from him as screams. Molly sat that way one time, the day she understood she was pregnant.

Just over her shoulder, Joh heaved a months-old sigh. He stood in shorts and long-toed bare feet, thin chest and arms as wiry as his hair. Slowly, Molly took her hands from the buttons of her dress and turned to better see him. His face softened, caved like the center of a cake. They saw the same thing: There would be no shipyard job in Newport News, no training at Whitaker; he would not be blamed.

"There ain't gon' be no tractor," he said. "We ain't leaving."

In a voice like skin splitting, Molly asked, "Why didn't you let me alone? That first day? I *told* you—"

Joh, a stick-and-stuffed scarecrow limned by the moonlight, shrugged his shoulders. "I thought you'd let go of the notion."

• • •

Namon softly spoke, "Go inside, you know what's good for you."

Molly ignored him. She heaved onto the tailgate.

They sat together in the churl of unseen frogs, the sound lingering, vacant. Separately, their gazes found, again and again, the moon-flooded field of withering stalks.

After a long while, Namon lifted his hand, trembling, and rested it on Molly's belly.

Sometime before daybreak, Molly pressed her hands upon his.

FARRADIYYA

Reem Kassis

I was barely twelve years old when Baba fell ill. We had been in Rameh for about a year with asbestos sheets and corrugated metal replacing our stone home in Farradiyya. The Christian and Druze inhabitants of our new village were friendly to us when we arrived, offering food and clothing, but they remained in their homes higher on the mountain, and we continued to live in our makeshift shelters at the bottom. It was the olive harvest, so Baba found work picking some groves for a family in Rameh, sorting the black olives from the green, separating some for pickling, others for cracking, and the rest for pressing. In exchange, the family gave him a portion of that harvest's bounty.

I remember he came home one evening with a tin of olives and another of oil. It was the first time I saw a smile on his face since we left Farradiyya. He even brought us boys back bars of halaweh candy, the way he used to before we left. We sat down to eat—a bulgur and lentil mujadara with yogurt Mama had soured from goat milk the neighbor had given her in exchange for bread—and on the table was a small plate of the black olives. Baba ripped a piece of markook bread and scooped the mujadara into his mouth.

He followed it with a shiny black olive. I saw his jaw move, then his lips expelled the pit into his fist. He quickly put in another olive, and another, continuing to chew and discard pits until he stood up and spit the contents of his mouth into his plate.

"These aren't like the olives of Farradiyya," he said, loud enough for Cousin Rabiya to hear through the one wall we shared and our neighbor Walid to hear through the next. Ali giggled nervously and finally spit into his plate too. Our timid mama shook her head but kept silent. Baba always said any weakness in my bones came from her.

"When are we going back to Farradiyya?" I asked. I was anxious to get back to school. Mama flinched before Baba even raised his hand to strike me in the face. Afterward, he turned and went into the second room. We watched him through the yellow curtain as he sat on the pallet and let his head drop into his hands.

• • •

I had been doing my numbers and Mama had been boiling cardamom coffee when the knock at the door came on that fall day in 1948. A man in military uniform handed my father a paper saying the orders had to be fulfilled within twenty-four hours. Baba glared back at the man. "Leave my house now," he said. "You will never belong here." His voice was strong, but his weak leg was quivering. The man repeated the orders, then turned on his heel and walked down the street to our neighbor's home.

"*Kheir inshallah*," Mama said when Baba closed the door. Those two words were her favored refrain, as though professing Allah's ability to do good could keep us out of harm.

Thus far, it had. Baba stood upright, but his shoulders were hunched. "We have twenty-four hours to leave and go north."

"North to where?" Mama said.

"Anywhere. Lebanon. Another village. We just have to leave our houses, doors open. Any house found locked will be demolished."

"What about our things? The olive harvest? The boys?" Her voice was trembling now, her eyes moist.

"We pack what we can, the rest we leave for when we come back. You can carry Ibrahim on your back, the walk is too long for a two-year-old. The older boys will have to walk."

My father started coughing a year after we arrived in Rameh. We lived in two gray rooms separated by a floral yellow curtain. The rugged hills of the Galilee were carpeted with dry greenery, and the dandelion weeds were sprouting under olive trees. His breath stuttered in his lungs before he pronounced it, his barking cough floating through our house like the leaves floating down from the trees.

"Naji, *Allah yirda aleik ya ibni*," Mama said, again beseeching God to bless me. Whatever God was cruel enough to kick us until we fell down, then kick us some more. "We need food and medicine." She was never direct. Maybe she was told to never speak openly to men, maybe she trusted God too much. Who knows. But I think she was weak, just like Baba said.

I left our neighborhood with my rucksack in the morning. It held my math book and a handkerchief wrapping my *zuwadeh*: a piece of taboon bread; a hunk of salty white cheese; a pickled eggplant, bitter and dark. I passed some boys on their way to school and remembered when I was in school in Farradiyya and how my father boasted to the men at the masjid. "Naji has a way with numbers," he said. "Just watch, he'll be running his own business one day."

I looked for work in the village center plowing land, taking the trash out for butchers, sweeping barbershop floors. On my first day at the Dabbah butcher shop, I tossed the fat and scrap meat trimmings into gray plastic buckets outside. Stray cats feasted until I scattered them with a wooden thistle broom. When I collected my coins for the day, I returned home and put them in our mother's palm. "Bikafee?" she asked, wanting to know if the money was enough to buy the medicine for Baba and some lentils and flour for the week. I counted the liras. A 50-mil coin, two 10-mil coins, and one 5-mil coin. I did the math. "We have enough," I said. "Maybe we can even buy some eggs."

. . .

After the general's orders came in November of 1948, the day went by in a flurry of visitors—neighbors, cousins, friends—my parents didn't even bother closing the front door. I wanted to ask what was happening, but their faces, the seriousness of their tones, said this wasn't the time for childish questions.

Finally, Baba told us we were all leaving our homes until the Arab armies drove out the invaders, and we could not take anything with us. All hands were needed to carry the essentials. The relatives joining us brought different supplies with them: Uncle Bshara, pallets wrapped in cloth; the neighbor Walid, tins of cheese and sacks of flour; Cousin Rabiya, her Singer sewing machine, cradled in her arms like a newborn for the entire ten-kilometer walk we ended up taking from Farradiyya to Rameh. I nodded respectfully at him, but the questions in my mind fell over themselves like the flock of fleeing refugees we were to become. I only dared mutter one in the end. "Do you know how long we'll be gone?" Baba stared back for a long instant, then bent his head and walked away.

That evening, with no one paying attention to me, I stole Baba's pocketknife and disappeared into the bedroom. I tore a sheet into thin strips, using two of them to tie my math book tightly around my chest. This way Baba won't know that I have taken the book with me, I thought, and I can keep up with my work until we come back. I quickly buttoned my shirt up and went to the kitchen. It was noisy and full of cigarette smoke. Everybody already knew we were being sent out.

· · ·

Dawood's house sat up on a hill in Rameh with a giant palm tree towering over its gate. When he answered the door that morning, I told him I could help with the housework, whatever he needed. A pale boy stood quietly behind him. His name was Rizek, I later found out. He was eight years old.

Dawood pointed to the math book in my rucksack. "What is that?"

I handed it over and told him that it was just a book from when I used to go to school.

"You're good at math?" He smiled. "I tell you what, habeebi. I'm making arak today in the room next door. Come help me with measuring things out. My eyes are not what they used to be."

I hesitated. Our Muslim religion said never to go near alcohol, and this man was asking me to help him distill his own. I didn't have a choice. We needed the money, and the other villagers were becoming more hesitant to hire these days. Their own futures were also uncertain in this war. I promised Allah I wouldn't touch it. I was sure He would understand after what He'd put us through. I pointed in the boy's direction. "What about him?"

"Rizek? He'll join us. Never too early to learn."

Dawood took a large metal key from the wall, and I followed him outside to the storeroom. He opened a blue-and-white door. Rizek and I stood against the wall as Dawood set up his tools. In the cool dark room, I helped measure juice, weigh aniseed, and mix it all with the twice-distilled spirto.

"I have five liters of this alcohol," I said to Rizek. "I need one hundred grams of aniseed per liter. How much will you give me?"

Rizek was quick, handing me a five-hundred-gram bag of aniseed to soak in warmed alcohol, and his pale complexion brightened up every time he answered correctly.

"Why aren't you in school anymore?" he asked.

I wasn't sure how much to tell him, but in truth, I wasn't sure how much I was comfortable admitting to myself. My father still said we would return, but at night, when the angry demons came to my head, I often wondered if we would ever go back.

After school, we were joined by Rizek's two older brothers and a stern-looking woman. "Lunch is ready," she said as she peered through the door. "Who's this?"

"Ah, Salma, this is Naji from Farradiyya," Dawood replied. "He's helping me with some work."

"He'll join us for lunch then," she said. I often think of the aubergines she fed me that day. The rich meat and pine nut stuffing was a delicacy we couldn't afford at home. In my entire life, I had never tasted such a thing. All these years later, I can still feel the soft flesh melting in my mouth as sharply as the shame.

• • •

We left Farradiyya at daybreak, doors unlocked, keys in our hands with an unspoken promise to return. We marched through the rolling hills of the Galilee, until the sun was overhead. We were at the foot of a mountain; green with specks of yellow, it looked like it was blanketed with sesame za'atar, and I could see houses scattered on the slope in the distance. Around us were wild weeds, olive trees, and piles of corrugated metal. Squatting on rocks, we ate arayes labaneh and made sage tea to warm us from the chilly November air.

Feeling a bout of courage from having carried a heavy water tank on my back like the rest of the men, I approached Baba. "Help me gather the metal sheets," he said, and with the other men I started pounding them together to build temporary shelters for the families.

The weeks devoured the days, and all the families quickly grew accustomed to the humble shelters we inhabited and the surrounding land that I often wondered what made one village our true home and not the other. Where did our sense of rootedness come from? Was it the land that had housed and fed our family for generations? Or was it our family that had given meaning and value to the land? Nobody would have answered my questions if I asked, so when they stirred, I pushed them aside the way I did my stray hairs, long now, not groomed in the six months since we left Farradiyya.

. . .

It was a windy December morning when I saw a carefully dressed schoolboy with straight-cut bangs laughing with his friends. He wore brown wool trousers and must have been Ali's age, no more than eight or nine at the time. The schoolboy was carefree, even the top of his leather satchel was open and flapping on his back. I will ask Cousin Rabiya to sew me the same brown wool trousers with her Singer machine, I thought. When a paper flew out of the boy's satchel and landed at my feet, I picked it up. Neat handwriting with numbers perfectly aligned on graph paper. At first, I started toward him, but he hadn't noticed the stray paper . . . or me. I crumbled the paper with my hands and slid it into my pocket. I spent the day at the Dabbah butcher shop again, tossing fat and scrap meat into gray plastic pails outside and chasing stray cats with the thistle broom.

. . .

I quickly got bored with Baba's illness. He was covered in more and more blankets, wrinkled and threadbare like the man they were supposed to warm, and yet he complained of cold even as April's sun became less shy.

"The new blanket is ready," Cousin Rabiya said when I came home after working in the fields. She handed me a brown woolen blanket, and I covered my father. Mama trailed the short distance from his pallet to the clotheslines outside where she dipped cloths in a cool water bucket before putting them on his forehead. Ali and Ibrahim collected sage and za'atar from the bushes near the olive groves, and Mama boiled them to make Baba tea.

I counted the days and months the way I counted the coins.

Eighteen months since we left Farradiyya.

Baba started coughing eleven months ago.

Three 50-mil coins and seven 10-mil coins from making arak.

One 50-mil coin from cleaning meat and scattering cats.

I was on the floor next to Baba's pallet after dinner, counting. It was just the two of us in the second room when he put his hand over mine. "It's under the table." He strained to speak. "The metal box. Get it for me."

I set it on his mattress and inched closer to him on the floor, tucking my knees beneath my chin.

"Open it," he said.

He slid his hand inside, resting it for a few seconds, then took out his pocketknife and a photograph. He looked at the picture in his hand and smiled. "You and your brothers." He wheezed. "Our last summer in Farradiyya." He held it out to me. Taped to the back was the key to our home. He squeezed my hand when I took it, then closed his eyes.

Mama was illiterate, so it must have been Baba's handwriting on the bottom of the picture, *Naji, Ali, and Ibrahim*, and on the back, *Farradiyya, August 1948*. Us boys under an olive tree. Behind, a clothesline. Ali is grinning mischievously, a bar of halaweh tightly clasped to his chest. Baba always brought back three bars of this sweet tahini concoction with his weekend pay, and Ali saved his halaweh to barter with and tease us once we devoured ours. I can still hear the sound of the camera shutter as Baba snapped that picture. We had been flying a kite through our olive groves before stopping for a rest in the shade of one of the tree's soaring branches. We popped halaweh into our mouths, like disappearing strands of sugar, and with our father's pocketknife carved our names into the tree's trunk.

"Summer is almost over," Baba said. "Stand still for a minute. You will soon be taller than this tree."

Rizek no longer asked me questions about my past, or my future, as if I were destined to always exist in a vacuum, with a past too painful to bring up and a future too uncertain to discuss.

I helped Rizek and his brothers with their math homework, and they helped me, even for a few afternoons a week, escape back to a normal childhood again.

"I stole our father's cigarettes," Rizek laughed one day.

"Give them here," one of the older boys threatened.

"I'm bartering them for apples," Rizek said, his eyes challenging a boy double his size.

"I swear we'll tie you to the palm tree like we did last summer if you don't share," the other one threatened.

He ran off, and I chased him until we had negotiated for our apples. Seven. We each hid one in a pocket and went back with four. We split them evenly with the older brothers. We chased his mother's goats in the fields, fed them the seeds and skin leftover from making arak, and watched them bang their heads against the wire pen. We laughed until our sides hurt. When the sun got hot, we sat under their grapevine picking husrum, which hadn't ripened to sweet black grapes yet, and dipped the sour fruit in salt.

I thought of my own brothers then. "Did you bring us any halaweh?" Ali often asked. I always lied and told him that I didn't make enough money. I wanted to hit him, to scream. Did he not feel the same sadness and emptiness I did, the kind that nestled its ache into the bones? How could he think of candy now? But men can't ask such questions, or have such feelings, so I chased them away just like Rizek and I chased the goats hours before.

. . .

Over the following months, as spring's sun gave way to an angrier summer one, Baba's condition worsened. Most days I preferred to go to work alone. But on some mornings, I walked with Uncle Bshara and Walid to the village center.

"Shu, sayer zalameh, Naji!" they always said, proclaiming I was a man. But I got tired walking the whole way with lifted shoulders, especially if the rucksack was heavy with tools.

"The girls in this town are pretty," Uncle Bshara commented on these walks. "See, they even look you in the eye and smile."

Walid, the neighbor with a wife and two young children, scolded him. "That's not what you want in a wife. You need a good Farradiyya girl. She'll make your dinner and wash your feet after work, and then she still won't look you in the eye!"

Bshara laughed. "Have the boring life you want." I laughed along with them.

My mother was a good Farradiyya girl, I thought to myself. A proud one too. I remember coming back from Dawood's house one day and handing her a bundle wrapped in a brown-and-blue-checkered handkerchief. "*Shu had?*" she asked.

"Fatayer za'atar," I said. "Rizek's mother was baking today, so I wrapped five for us at home."

"Naji." She shook her head disapprovingly, never speaking directly.

"What? She told me to eat as much as I wanted. I couldn't eat it all then, but it's as much as I wanted."

. . .

I had been working for Dawood's family for almost ten months when Dawood came up behind me. His smiling eyes were bent down at the corners.

I sensed something strange, almost fatherly, from this man. Baba was kind, proud, but life had made him rough on the edges, a little bitter and closed in on himself. I am certain he loved us, but emotions were reserved for the weak in his eyes. I remember coming home from school one day, crying because a classmate had pushed me to the ground in front of my friends, when I felt a vibrating pain as his hand whipped across my face. So swift he'd been, I hadn't even noticed it coming, only heard the crack of his skin against mine.

"Men don't cry! Next time he pushes you, teach him a lesson." He had glared at me. "Don't run home like a girl."

I hated myself for crying in front of my father, and I hated him. I couldn't imagine Dawood, ruddy cheeked and jolly, like he was in on a joke nobody else understood, slapping his Rizek like that.

"I've found you some work," he said.

"Not making arak?"

"Not in Rameh," he clarified. "The war is making it hard on everyone. You need more than what this village can offer to support your family."

I felt tired. Weren't we going back soon, I wondered. Wasn't Baba going to get better with the medicine I kept working and shelling out coins for? It was fleeting, but the thought came anyway. Wouldn't it be easier if he died?

"It's a Jewish contractor," Dawood said. "I know him from my days in the Palestine Police Force under the British Mandate."

Yitzhak was how he introduced himself when we met. A short, thin man with a pointed nose and a large mustache, he had three wrinkles creasing his forehead, like ridges hiding murky waters.

"But he's from them, how can I work for him?"

"Habeebi, it's decent work you will be doing, and you need to buy medicine for your father. Your family needs food too, and oil. Winter is near."

The digging, moving, and piling work Yitzhak gave me was harsh, but it kept me strong, stopped my mind from wandering back to those looming questions.

• • •

Less than two years after the war had moved us from the lush mountains of Farradiyya to the rocky valleys and olive groves of Rameh, I returned to hear Mama wailing. "It's Baba," Ali said as he greeted me at the door. He shuffled uneasily from one leg to another, tugging at his shirt. "The doctor told her to keep him comfortable, nothing else she can do now."

I had always dreaded this moment, knowing my father was the only remaining root I had in this world. People rarely called me Naji. I was Naji, ibn Hassan, my father's son, defined and introduced by his name. I walked over to my mother, sitting on his mattress, and not knowing what to say, lay my head on her shoulder. She sighed, her chest heaving, her eyes red from hours of crying.

"Maybe Doctor Hani is wrong," I tried, "inshallah Baba will get better again."

She attempted a smile, but her face, leathered by sadness, wasn't supple enough to oblige. "Habeebi, your father died the day we left Farradiyya."

He lived for two more nights before his heart gave out. The neighbors and townspeople flooded our two-room house in Rameh for three days. The women sat on straw mats inside, the men on plastic chairs stretching out to the alleyways. The air was crisp. Uncle Bshara poured bitter cardamom coffee from a dallah into cups and passed it around. When he reached my chair, he held the tray out to me. "*Tfadal*," he said, offering me a cup. For a moment I thought he must have confused me for one of the adult mourners. Children were never served coffee. I hesitated, but he caught my eyes before I could move them. "For me?" I asked. He nodded. "Go on, take one," he said.

The following week, I went to see Yitzhak again. I told him that my father passed away and I needed to find more stable work.

"You're in luck, my boy," he said. "The government wants to build a kibbutz nearby. We need to clear the land now. It will be hard physical labor. Harder than what you've been doing."

I had expected a fight, and prepared an argument. Instead, I stared back, silent.

I assured him that I could work.

"Meet me here at 6 a.m. tomorrow," he said as he walked me to the door.

I went back home that evening and told Mama I had found work that would sustain us throughout the summer months. "I start tomorrow."

She blessed me, and there was a hint of a smile on her lips. "*Allah yirda aleik ya ibni*," she said as she stroked my hair. "I'll pack your lunch from tonight." The four of us sat down on a straw mat, gathering round some bread, labaneh, and olives. When we finished, she found a small blanket to wrap what little food we had left for my zuwadeh the next day.

• • •

The mosquitoes were relentless that night, and I suffered from the heat, waking up, falling asleep, and waking up again in fitful bouts. At dawn, I got up. In a clay pitcher was some water, still cool in spite of the summer night's sweltering heat. I leaned my head back and streamed some into my mouth, using a few stray drops to freshen my face.

I dressed and quietly left our home, marching to my meeting point with Yitzhak. He was already there waiting next to a small truck. He greeted me in his language. "*Boker tov*," he said. I nodded quietly in response. He ushered me into the truck, and I climbed into the passenger seat. In the back, I saw shovels, saws, rakes, buckets, and sheets of plastic. A large ax stood among the resting tools. The drive was short; it felt like ten minutes, but maybe it was thirty. Yitzhak was silent, and the time was marked with my thoughts, not the minutes.

When we arrived, the sun had fully risen, but a gentle breeze caressed my face as I stepped out of the car. Maybe my nerves were misplaced; it wouldn't be as strenuous as I had feared after all.

"I need you to clear this site," Yitzhak told me, pointing to a landscape filled with rubble and weeds. Thistles sprouted out between them, standing tall, refusing to surrender. A few olive and fig trees framed the border of the plot, branches bent as if mourning the loss of what they once guarded. Whoever he'd hired for the first clearing had done a shoddy job, leaving behind clusters of debris and some ragged stumps of carelessly torn-down olive trees.

We unloaded the tools from the back of the truck. "Can you find your way back to Rameh when you're done?" he asked. I nodded, fearing I would lose my job if I asked for a ride back. Now I wished I had paid more attention on the way up. Rameh looked like every other village in the Galilee, squat stone houses, clustered on rolling hills of dancing olive trees. Would I recognize it?

"Right, just walk down the mountain here." He pointed. "When you get to the Orthodox church, make a right and follow the road. You'll see the village from there." He handed me a few coins and told me to go see him at the end of the week for the rest of my pay. He got back into his truck and drove down the mountain, becoming smaller and smaller, until he was nothing but a black dot like the millions of pebbles strewn among the trees.

The digging wasn't too strenuous, the stone wreckage in manageable pieces, and I started piling things to one side. The thistle was more difficult to manage, but I kept at it, pulling as much as I could. The hardest were the stumps with their roots, like arthritic fingers clawing into the ground, refusing to let go in spite of the pain. Moss sprouted from the cracks on the olive tree stumps, their countless rings telling the story of a generation reduced to fragments. I started to dig, moving the dirt away from the tree roots. I lifted the shovel and struck the ground, up and down, and up and, with all my force, down again, beads of sweat trickling down my temples and my back. I must have spent some time getting to the roots because by the time I looked up, the sun was directly overhead.

I crouched on the ground and unwrapped the zuwadeh Mama had packed: bread, olives, and a tomato. With my head hunched between my knees, gazing at nothing but the pebbles between my feet, I took a bite. I couldn't chew fast enough.

My eyes surveyed the field as I took a sip of water from my pouch. The same unease I had felt on arrival washed over me again. The rise and fall of the hills, the smell on the breeze of dry dirt fragranced with za'atar bushes was so familiar.

I walked the edge of the land, brushing my hands against clusters of stones, once the foundation of someone's home. I wondered if the dreams born in this place, the lives this house had sheltered, were as shattered as these rocks. Nothing remained. There were no standing houses, only broken stones where houses once stood; no markers other than the dip of the valley giving a glimpse to the summits of other hills; nothing to confirm my suspicions.

I dropped to my knees and clawed at the ground, a sense of urgency swelling through my fingers. I don't know what I was looking for, but I burrowed until my nails were black and my sweat turned the dirt to mud. How the ax found its way to my hand I don't remember, but with all my force, I swung at the stumps in the ground like a madman. I struck once, twice, and again until my body trembled with exhaustion and my knees buckled. With the bulk of my weight on a tree stump, I pushed myself up.

And that was when I saw it.

Naji, Ali, Ibrahim. Carved into one of the stumps I had spent the day digging up were our names, from two summers ago.

I sat back down and stared at what was left of the olive tree, fingering our names until the sun moved and a light breeze stirred. I took one last look around and then, head bent, started down the mountain. I touched the coins in my pocket. I counted enough to buy two bars of halaweh.

WORK

DéLana R. A. Dameron

You had a friendship bracelet business in elementary school, so you knew what work was. You convinced your father to take you to Michaels craft store to buy the embroidery string, the safety pins, the bobbins to wrap the string around, the clear plastic box to organize it all.

You could knot the string into intricate designs: the tornado, the V, rows of diamond-bodied fish, hearts, and rainbows. You watched your father build an invoice sheet for his computer business and so you did too. Classmates/customers could custom design their friendship bracelets with the colors, and wait a few days and you would hand deliver the fresh wrist adornments during recess or lunch, and they paid the $0.75–$2.00 depending on what design they chose.

Eventually, you had enough business to have one or two people knotting the embroidery string into bracelets for you, and so all you had to do was take the orders, give the orders, take the money, and deliver the product. Some weeks you made $12–$15, and after you paid your employees, you still had something like $5 or $6 left over—enough to buy a Capri-Sun + Crunchy Cheetos for snacks instead of the no-name-brand juice and cheese crackers. After you made your premium snack allotment, you decided to save the rest. You put some of your earnings in your seashell jewelry box you inherited after your Aunt Olive died, and once almost had $100 tucked away in there. You didn't quite know what you wanted to do with all of that money, but you were proud that you had it anyhow.

Your uncle Junior stayed with y'all on account of Tommy, Weesie's foster boy, sleeping in Junior's bed now, was eating up Junior's sausage patties and salmon cakes and grits. Drinking Junior's ginger Chek soda. Your mama Rhina couldn't let Junior stay in the house too long either because the Learning Funhouse Daycare was an in-house childcare operation and the Department of Social Services loved to do unannounced visits, and if it was evidenced that Junior was staying there with the six children—cousins mostly—Rhina could lose her license and they all could lose the house. Because you heard your parents argue about the cost of rent and why Rhina needed to max out her six slots allotted for children instead of a more comfortable four.

Though the house was crowded, and on most days since he got back from jail he slept on the floor of your room, Uncle Junior was nice enough to you, especially after his second child was born and no one had enough to scrounge for bail so he had to stay in jail and y'all all prayed he'd be out early on good behavior.

You watched his baby girl Nella for him because you loved them both. You taught her how to drink out of a straw, and eat real food. She had a hard time learning to say your whole name so she started calling you Mika and it stuck. You were there when she first learned to walk, unassisted by her toy vacuum cleaner.

Once Weesie's money ran out for canteen, and then, too, collect calls, you thought about how lonely Uncle Junior must have been in that jail cell, all alone and no one from the outside seeing about him. So, you wrote him once or twice. You gave him snippets of house gossip you had—you heard Tommy was making friends with the NewCastle Ganstas, and he had stopped working at Hardee's. Y'all all knew that because your father, called Major, had stopped by Hardee's three times on three different occasions when he said he was working and he wasn't there. And yet, he had in his room the nicest stereo with a five-CD disc changer (you left out in your letter the part that you saw it in his room the night Tommy asked you to lay in bed with him, and you did, fully clothed, but that's how you saw it).

When your $100 went missing though, you knew it was Uncle Junior but couldn't prove it. No one but you knew you had it, and so everyone's first question was always, How did you get $100? What you need that kind of money for, Mika?

Major felt sorry for you in the way that he does and said he would help you replace it, so maybe don't make much of a fuss of it to everyone. It was hard to believe that Uncle Junior would go so far as to take from the only person who thought to still care about him in some way when he had been locked up, and hard for you to believe that he didn't understand that you used your nice stationery and Thurgood Marshall stamps so he could have a piece of home with him on the inside.

So you made up your $100 deficit by babysitting on the weekends. You kept Malik and Ayanna from 10 a.m. until their parents came to get them at 6 p.m. You walked the tots through breakfast, lunch, snack just like you watched Rhina do during the week when you were home on summer or school breaks, sad that you couldn't go to summer camp like your classmates or sleepaway camp like on *Bug Juice*—the reality show about a sleepaway summer camp on the Disney Channel. Malik's and Ayanna's moms paid you $25 for the full day and then Rhina and Major asked for $5 each kid to replace the chicken nuggets, instant grits, and animal crackers and milk you used up. It was good, easy money.

Mr. Eliot, your sister Sasha's program director at the Boys & Girls Club, had been asking if you were looking for summer work one day when you accompanied her to the after-school program and noticed that you weren't restless like the other kids. Your focus on your social studies and English homework was "commendable," he said, raising his left eyebrow. You liked Mr. Eliot because he was tall like Major, but *he* had finished college and talked to you about Black history and Black literature and slavery in a way that Major never did and, of course, like none of your white teachers—not even the ones you liked.

He asked you how old you were, and you said fourteen, and he asked if you ever worked before? You said yes. For your father's computer business, which was technically true though you never got compensated. Whenever Major was out of the house, customers called with their computer problems. Once Jack Jones called to say his WordPerfect program was frozen and so you walked him through the process of finding and pressing CTRL + ALT + DELETE at the same time. You waited on the phone with him listening to him breathing and calling out the commands while the computer restarted and auto-recovery had returned to him the flyer for the used Honda Civic he was trying to sell. Jack thanked you profusely and reported your good services to Major and soon enough you were his software troubleshooter.

Another time Ms. White, who did your father's taxes, called to say her *Encyclopedia Britannica* program disc was swallowed by the computer and you had told her to get a safety pin or paper clip and unfold the little piece of metal until it was one long stick. You didn't ask why she didn't have a paper clip—doesn't everyone have them?—but when she said she didn't have one you thought quickly on your feet and asked if she had a cookie tin with sewing supplies? She laughed and asked how did you know? *Everyone has one*, you said. You told her to get the longest sewing needle and use that. To go to the front of the CPU unit and stick the needle in the tiny hole just beneath where the CD goes and push hard. Ms. White squealed when the computer tower relinquished the disc. You were now the Major Communications and Services Software and Hardware troubleshooter, unofficially. Though, one of Major's customers was so impressed that a little Black girl knew so much about computers and spoke so *articulately* about how to fix problems, you were featured on the local news segment about your knowledge, so that verified your title.

When you tell Mr. Eliot this, and of course about your friendship bracelet business and babysitting services, he first asks if you might keep his own son one Saturday or two? Then he asks for your résumé, says he might be able to help you find a *real* job—he lifted his eyebrow again—to make some *real* money.

The little paper clip man in Microsoft Word helped enough for you to draft a document that looked like the templates titled "Résumé." When you printed it and colored in the heart next to your name because you didn't have a color printer, you were proud, even when Mr. Eliot smiled and pointed to it and said its nice and to keep an eye out for a call from Tonya Young at Youth Workforce Development.

Sasha had seen you hand Mr. Eliot a piece of paper but didn't know about the arrangement. He was still smiling when he folded the hard-won résumé that you stayed up half the night for into a small square and slipped it into his gym shorts pocket—the same pocket that had his whistles and keys and lanyard sticking out. Determined to not be defeated by his lack of care about the document he asked you to prepare, you straightened your back when Sasha inquired and told her that Mr. Eliot had asked you for a résumé and would help you get a real job this summer.

You didn't figure into what it would mean for everyone else's life for you to have a real job, Monday through Friday for six weeks over the summer, but here you were. When you told your father, he sighed. Major now had to accommodate an early morning drop-off and afternoon pickup during the summer when even he thought he had a reprieve. You tell him the Department of Health and Environmental Control building was just across the parking lot from the State Archives building where you and Vanessa had gone to accept the regional and state awards for eighth grade advanced history research papers. Vanessa's mom felt bad for you when you said you might not be able to attend to accept the award for best paper in the whole state of South Carolina because you didn't have anyone to take you and stay all day, even though it was a Saturday. There was a football game that day at the university and on those days, Major had to post up in a small four-by-four-feet room to ensure that the broadcast went off without a hitch.

You never asked Rhina to take you anywhere, and that weekend was her biweekly hair salon appointment and it was time for her relaxer and she could not, would not, miss it. So it was you and Vanessa, and Vanessa's mom. Major sent you with $5 for lunch, but Vanessa's mom bought the $8 sandwich and Coke and said congrats after you accepted the award.

The first few days of your real work were *real* boring. There is no other way for you to describe it when Major asks how it went. By Wednesday, you begged Sasha to let you take her Discman so at least you could listen to music while your supervisor shrugged and pretended to drum up real work for you to do. You were stationed in the water control division where residents just outside of Columbia, SC, who had well-water sources had to bring in samples of water to make sure all of the allowable amounts of chemicals weren't above the undrinkable amounts. You couldn't imagine there were people who didn't live with the same type of water you had—wasn't it, what, 1999 now?—but there still were, and a whole operation went along to make sure people's water was safe to drink.

You had many hours of idle moments waiting for someone to come in with a mason jar or Sprite bottle of cloudy water. You were instructed to put on latex gloves to handle the sample—a new pair each time—so as not to jeopardize the integrity of the test.

You put whatever container they brought the sample in into a gallon-sized ziplock bag and waited for them to fill out the required intake paperwork. Everyone in that department was white, and it amazed you how many folks who may or may not have had safe drinking water reminded you of your grandparents Weesie or Teeta or any number of their friends.

When the older Black man who looked like he could have been Deacon Jackson's father shuffled to your desk, you brought out your "Yes Sirs" and "No Sirs," and even when you saw him struggling to negotiate the small text on the page, you first handed him a magnifying glass like what Teeta would have used for reading his Bible, but when the gentleman studied it and held it up to his face, close like a monocle, you shook your head, picked up the pen, and asked his name and address, how long had he been living at the residence with a well, etc., until the paperwork was filled out. You asked him to sign and he simply marked an X, and despite protocol, you found an empty bottle to transfer his sample from the 409 cleaning solution bottle he brought it in into one that would be accepted for processing.

The gentleman kissed your gloved hand and held it a touch too long while he thanked you for your help. You had saved him from embarrassment, he said. You were much nicer than anyone in here had ever been to him after all these years. He said it loud enough for your supervisor to look up. The man that looked like he could have been Teeta, if he had lived, smiled at you and tipped his hat on his way out.

You went home your first week of work feeling like maybe you made a difference, and despite the long lulls and the long hour you had for lunch staring at a television with court shows, you wondered why it was Major came home each day, looking worn down.

He tells you because he doesn't have a "nice cushion-y office job" like you.

The next week found you folded over a countertop with a mountain of labels and a barrel of empty test bottles. Your supervisor explained that because this was a work-to-learn environment for summer interns, every week would look different. This week: affixing labels on ten thousand bottles for the number of known well-water users within a two-hour radius of Columbia. He chuckled when he said this should keep you busy, and you were so thankful you snuck out of the house Sasha's Mariah Carey CD and, even though you didn't care for it, her Tom Petty CD, and the Cranberries. You made do with what you had at your ready.

Because your grandfather, your grandmothers, all at one point worked as cleaning people in big office buildings, and many times you accompanied them, you smile at the janitor who mops the floor of the hallway outside your office every day after lunch. When Teeta had retired from working as the mental health hospital mortuary lab assistant, and because he and Weesie still needed some money, he started cleaning a network of dialysis centers along Two Notch Road. You did anything Teeta did, even waited in an empty dialysis room pushing the reclining chairs back and upright, back and upright, back and upright, because what else was there for you to do? His shift started before the center closed, and you saw how the white nurses didn't look at him, not even the patients. Once there was a white nurse who saw Teeta walk in, you carrying a broom behind him, and the dustpan, and out of his back pocket like a tail or wedding dress train were the clear trash bags that he replaced each receptacle with. The nurse rolled her eyes, even though Teeta said *Good Evening*, and she balled up whatever paper was next to her and looked at the other white nurse who never even turned in your direction, and threw the ball of paper right at you both. It came and it came toward you like a bullet, and then it hit the floor. The nurse who didn't throw the paper said something about "missing the trash" and they both shrugged and went back to whatever it was they were not doing. It took enough of these aggressions to teach you to acknowledge the invisible people.

When the janitor mopped his way by your bottle-label-assembly line for the third time and scrubbed real hard, you looked up, nodded, and smiled like you were taught. He motioned for you to remove your headphones. You do. He asks what you are listening to, and that day you snuck out Major's *The Best of the Spinners* and *The Best of the O'Jays* CDs. He called you "Young Gun" when he heard what you were listening to, and hadn't yet asked your name. One time, you heard your supervisor say he wished Tony didn't use so much water when he mopped the floors during the height of water-sample-intake time, so you knew his name. You smiled when he said Young Gun, and maybe you shrugged your shoulders, but you were careful to only walk on the area of the hallway he hadn't mopped yet when you walked to the bathroom, and looked back at him so he could see your conscientiousness, and he was looking and you smiled again, and slinked into the bathroom.

The next day Tony mopped by again, of course. You don't have to look at the clock to know it was 2:15 p.m. On time. This time your supervisor had snuck out for a cigarette break so you were alone in the intake room and Tony stuck his head in, asked you what you were up to. You tell him summer work, trying to "make a dollar out of fifteen cents"—you say this knowing he will be impressed with your reference, and he goes, "Tell me, sister, can you spare a dime?" And does a little jig while raising his voice. Just like the O'Jays. You laugh, think of your father. They both have goatees, though Tony's is grayer. He has a stomach that rolls over his belt, and a vest that is a touch too small, and you can't help but think of Winnie the Pooh when you see Tony. Wonder if he rests his arm on his belly after a good meal. But who are you to judge? You still can't order clothes from Delia's or the junior's section of Belk, not since Teeta died and everyone kept buying you chocolate and your favorite roast beef and cheddar junior sandwich from Hardee's. Anyways, Tony is in the room with you, and you had a moment, and finally he asks you your name and you tell him, and you hear him start to say he has something, but then he stops. He probably was going to say daughter. He stops and then pulls out of his back pocket his cloth CD case, one that was almost exactly what you hoped to buy with your first paycheck.

Tony plops down the CD case on the table on top of the water bottle labels, and tells you to peek inside. You look at him while you're opening it, and if your mother saw you she might have popped you in the mouth for the ways your eyes curved up instead of focusing on the thing you were doing. You rub your hands along the canvas case, admire it first. It's probably a twenty-CD holder. You ask him if he has any Michael Jackson, because that's probably what Major would say he liked to listen to, and he laughs when you open the CD case and Tony is presenting you with: Dead Prez *Let's Get Free*, Miles Davis *Sketches of Spain* and *New York Girl*, Missy Elliott *Supa Dupa Fly* (you knew this because of the afternoons you watched *TRL* and *106 & Park*), Notorious BIG *Ready to Die*, and Charlie Parker *Ornithology*.

From sitting at Weesie's and Teeta's sides during spades while you were learning and not playing, you know how to not give up anything you don't want to by expressions on your face.

You keep your face as stoic as possible now to not give up your hand that you have no idea who these artists are—except Missy Elliot and maybe Notorious BIG, but Uncle Junior was definitely a West Coast music head so you know at least that if you knew Tupac, you did not know Biggie's music.

Tony leans in close on the table and at first you wonder why he smells familiar, and then you realize it's the secondhand smoke caught in his clothes, covered by Old Spice. He says you can borrow his collection to keep you company while you're at work, and if you had a CD-W on your computer at home (you did, you showed off knowing that you knew what he was saying) you could take it home to copy the CDs and bring them back tomorrow.

You had to think about how to ask Major for blank CDs and also how to copy CDs without showing him that you had these CDs from Tony to copy because then he'd want to know how you got them, and how do you say a Black man at work gave them to you? He did show you how to download Napster though and how to choose more stable MP3 files and even though you had to clog up the phone line overnight while you waited for two songs to download, you were starting to gather some of the songs from the Mariah Carey albums you didn't have yet.

You remember this fact and decide to just ask him for an advance on your paycheck so that you can buy CDs to burn your Napster songs so you can have more music at work, and of course a CD case for you to carry them in so as not to scratch. You knew exactly which one you wanted.

Major tells you actually he was planning on taking you to the credit union to open up your own savings account. Because you were getting a check from a real job you could also get a checking account but it would also have his name on it because you are a minor, but you could get checks, and your own stack of deposit and withdrawal slips with an account number that was especially yours. Because you now worked real hours for your real job, Major met you outside the moss-covered DHEC building Thursday during your lunch hour. It shouldn't take more than an hour to set it up, he tells you, then says that it would be ready for you to deposit and cash the check tomorrow. You didn't remember telling him that you got paid that day, but he said because DHEC was a state agency and he too worked for a state agency the pay periods were the same. You shrugged. On the way to the credit union Major tries to tell you about managing money and says that he would cut you a deal: For every dollar you put into your savings, he would put in a dollar so that your money could double by the end of the summer. You would more than replace the $100 that went missing and that you tried to make up by babysitting, and you could have real money sitting in a real bank account that Uncle Junior could not touch.

You like the idea of that and agree to the challenge. Friday comes and Major picks you up again during lunch to deposit the check in the bank. He encourages you to take out $20 for next week's lunch, and you look at him. He smiles, says, *You're making real money now, Mika.* You fill out the withdrawal slip for $40, and when Major asks what's that for, you say to cover any yard sale or flea market shopping you would be doing with Weesie, and also to purchase a sweet snack from the vending machine, which was two doors down from Tony's office. You don't mention Tony.

Major drops you back off to work, and you hear the slop-slopping of the mop coming down the hall. Because your supervisor is in the room, you sneak off this time, say you need to use the bathroom. You don't know why you feel like you can't talk to your colleague—how you heard Major call the people who go into the same office with him—out in the open, but you tiptoe down the unmopped side of the hallway toward the bathroom, and Tony stops and watches you walk toward him, smiling.

You preempt the conversation and say afternoon, say you didn't have any leftover CDs and could you hold his CDs for the weekend and copy and bring them back on Monday? Tony says sure thing, Young Gun, enjoy them this weekend. You motion back to the office and scurry back to affix labels on the water-sample bottles.

Weesie has no idea where you disappeared to when you asked her to go to Walmart to buy some school supplies and she looked for you in all of the aisles and you were already at the front, checked out, and waiting with a plastic bag. You asked the clerk to double bag the CD case and the blank CDs because you'll need to figure out how to bring them into the house without anyone asking. You haven't thought this all the way through or else you would have bought some pens, or a new notebook. You would have left yourself some actual money for lunch next week, but the two purchases took up the majority of the money you took out, and now you have to get to next Friday (Major promised to take you every week to help you manage your money better) with $9.87 and the sandwich from the cafeteria costs $7 after tax. You knew Weesie would take you to Walmart without questions, but the computer you needed was at home so now you had to tell Weesie that you forgot you had to babysit Malik this weekend and actually you needed to go home tonight. You'd come back next week. Weesie looks absolutely disappointed because she had wanted to go out into the country to the special flea market and didn't want to drive out that way by herself, but you tell her you can go next week and you tell her you have a job now so you can help with gas money. Weesie drives you home.

Of course, you forget on Monday you were moved to a different department all together.

Monday went by and you now have two CD cases in your little purse, with your Discman, and you were ready to see Tony to give him his CDs back, and you smiled because it rained that day and you wanted to walk up to Tony and say, "It's my window // I can't stand the rain."

After you buy the Captain's Wafers Cream Cheese & Chives Crackers because they were only $0.50 in the vending machine for lunch, you return to your computer desk.

Not only were you on a new floor, but they didn't have AOL so you couldn't even go online. Eventually, you gave up the lyric'd music and went for Miles Davis's *Sketches of Spain* that Tony had given you. You liked this because it was music that Major didn't listen to, so you felt more educated, more . . . refined. You had jazz now. Real Jazz.

It didn't occur to you yet that Tony wouldn't be in the hallway at 2 p.m. because he'd be mopping the third floor, probably looking for you. You didn't think about that when you went out to the restroom thinking you'd hear the squeegee of the mop against the tile hallway.

The rest of the week went on like this: Major driving you to work, not giving you lunch money, you typing the same three words into small boxes, trying to learn the words to the new music you had but no one to talk to about it, and so on. Thursday morning, Major made mention he would take you to the bank during lunch so you could get money out to go with Weesie to the flea market for the weekend. You wait outside for Major to drive up, and of course he is late.

You told your supervisor you'd be back by 2 p.m., and it was 1:25 p.m., which meant if Major did show up you really only had time to go to the bank and then come right back. No convincing him to stop by Hardee's. Another cheese cracker lunch.

On the way to the credit union, Major instructs you on how to look for the withdrawal slips, and the whole process. While you are at the counter filling out the appropriate paperwork, Major asks you how much you think you might need for the weekend trip? You tell him you promised Weesie some gas money, so $10, plus $20 for you for the week. Major reminds you: Lunch money? You nod your head, annoyed that he'd stopped giving you money for lunch, and say, OK $50, and start to write the number five down, and Major stops you by putting his hand on the withdrawal slip. You look up at him wondering what's wrong, and begin to say the numbers out loud to prove you could do that simple math in your head. He tells you last week you deposited $309 (he assured you that you'd get what money they took away back next April), and only took out $40. If you take out $50 this week, you'll have $219. The credit union requires a $30 minimum to maintain the account, so that leaves about $190. It's actually $189, you say. Major nods. He looks up at the teller, at the folks piling into the credit union during their lunch hour, and then off into space in the way that he does so often when he's trying to say something that it annoys you to no end. You break into the stare and say *yeh, so what?* And he turns to you and says, what if he paid you back $250 next week when his paycheck comes? You know, like an interest loan?

What do you say?

He spills into your silence to explain that he had to help Weesie with her insurance payments, and a neighbor had come by with a plate of greens, fried chicken, and cornbread and asked to borrow some money so her lights would stay on, and just this Monday the oil light on the car *and* the check engine light came on, and he looked up and just like that he just needed this little bit to make it to next week.

What do you say?

He said so then, you'd withdraw $239, and it'll be like you didn't have to take out any money for yourself this weekend, because you'll get that back plus more. He looked up to the ceiling lights and started whispering numbers, suggesting he was doing the math in his head.

Just like that, your account is empty again. Slowly, you write $239 and sign your name and you and Major walk slowly to the teller window. She smiles at you, not smiling. Major laugh-talks in the way he does when he's nervous trying to explain you have a "big purchase" this week. Major pats you on the shoulder. You ignore him and dig around in the candy dish looking for a Cream Soda Dum-Dum. Any small joy. The bank teller doesn't know who to hand the money to, and so Major reaches out his hand, counts to $50, and hands you the bills, then puts the rest in his pocket. He push-taps you toward the door and you drag your feet behind him back to the car. Before he turns on NPR, he reminds you next week you'll have it back, with interest, he promises. Did you want him to hold on to your $50 until you got home so you knew it would be safe? You shake your head.

It took you longer than you thought it would to get back to the DHEC building. Now that you're already late, what good is fussing to be *only* ten minutes late versus any other time digit?

When you get on the elevator you press the third-floor button. As the elevator climbs, you smell the cleaning solution wafting through the elevator shaft, and you'd almost sprint into the hallway if you didn't know that the floor would be wet. But you knew that Tony always kept one side unmopped until one side dried, so you looked for where the WET FLOOR sign was not and sprinted toward the body bent over the mop handle. He didn't hear you call his name when you got out of the elevator because he had his headphones in. Just as he was about to lift the mop into the bucket you run up between his mop and the bucket and wave your hands. Tony's smile is so big, he moves to take off his headphones and says he thought you had left him, Young Gun. You shake your head no, no. You shake your head no.

He says he has something for you, and reaches into his vest pocket. He said he kept it here because he thought that maybe eventually he'd run into you. It's a little notebook, like what you get at BI-LO in the stationery section or a gas station. He says he saw you writing in a notebook once on lunch break, and figured with your new music maybe one day you'd write songs, that he thinks you're going to be famous, a big big deal.

And you don't know why, but you felt your ears go hot, and your chest tighten like you were about to cry.

Tony asks you what's wrong, Young Gun? And you just shake your head. And move in to hug him, and you feel him tense up, then relax, then pat your back and say it's OK it's OK why are you crying, Young Gun? It's OK. He starts reaching for reasons you might cry: Is this about the CDs? Something happen to them? It's OK, Young Gun, they can be replaced, it's OK. You hug him tighter, and run your fingers along the spirals of the notebooks. You tell him it's all gone. So many folks only just take take take take from you. He asks takes what?

You say *everything*.

WITHOUT A BIG ONE

JP Infante

1.

You thought about jumping.

It's a cold winter night and you sit next to Queeny on your fire escape. The cars on the freeway come and go like waves. The lights from the George Washington Bridge reflect off the Hudson River like the shine in glassy eyes, and the river is a giant bathtub without a ship or boat to save anyone who might be drowning.

Your babysitter, Nilda, says suicide is like killing someone, and if you were to survive jumping off the fire escape, the police would arrest you for attempted murder. If you do try killing yourself, you plan to live through it because suicide only works if you survive. Nilda laughed when you told her the attempt is meant to get people's attention. She laughed because it's true.

You feel the cold wind. Look at the buildings across the river in New Jersey. They are far apart with too much space in between. There's no space between you and Queeny because you both need the warmth.

They used to call you Minene, and before that, Chungo, even though your birth certificate says another name. Your stepfather, who's been away at school for three months, calls you son. Son, get me the TV controller. Son, listen to your mother. Son, stop talking about your heart.

Your stepfather can draw you and your extra-small heart. Queeny asleep at your feet. He can draw anything and anybody. He knows everything about sports, anime, video games, comic books, and toys. He's the strongest man you've met and the only man who has ever kissed you. He has never lied. When he turned himself in to school you felt like crying, but didn't, because you've never seen him cry.

Mary gave birth to you. She calls you Minene or Ray and sometimes your stepfather's name by mistake. Mary doesn't hear it when you call her mom. She calls you Raymond when Queeny plays with her shoes or does poo in the house. Mary doesn't love Queeny like your stepfather. Mary is younger than all of your friends' mothers. Mary looks young like your babysitter, but you know Nilda's younger because she's happier than your mother.

Sometimes you sleep with Mary in the bedroom. You like rubbing her hair on your nose. Sometimes the smell of shampoo and cigarettes makes you sleepy. Sometimes the mix keeps you up at night. You usually sleep on the sofa bed in the living room because of your bladder disease. Recently it's been hard to hold your piss at night.

Your new doctor says Konnichiwa all the time. He said kids who drink soda wet the bed and Mary believed him. You don't trust this doctor because when you asked if he was Chinese, he pointed to a red circle at the center of a white rectangle and said, Japanese. Then he smiled at Mary.

One night you fell asleep with Mary in the bedroom and her snoring woke you around midnight. The TV showed old men talking about bladder disease. The next morning at the kitchen table, you told Mary about bladder disease. She was shuffling mail, knife in hand. She stopped, looked at the bowl in front of you, and said, Mentiroso before cutting open a red envelope in one try. She usually doesn't speak Spanish so you didn't understand her. The way Mary pronounced that word made her a stranger.

That morning you realize the Chinese doctor was flirting with her. You make a mental note to tell your stepfather when he calls from school. He's only called a couple of times since he left because the apartment phone is always being cut off and there are never minutes on Mary's pre-paid cell phone.

Your babysitter, Nilda, calls you Ray Ray. She loves Queeny. Nilda is taller than Mary and has a fat ass. Whenever you hug her, you touch it and she doesn't say anything. Nilda is in love with you. You don't tell her you know because she has a boyfriend. Every time Nilda sees you she laughs, but not at you, it's just she's embarrassed of being in love with someone your age. At night in bed you imagine kissing Nilda and licking her lips.

Nilda is smart and Nilda is beautiful and Nilda reads you stories with curse words and words you don't understand. She says you're mature. She says you should draw your own drawings instead of tracing. One day, Nilda told her friend with the huge boobs you'll be a heartbreaker. Her friend asked, Would you be my boyfriend? It took a while before you answered because you didn't want to hurt Nilda's feelings. You blurted out, It depends, and Nilda's friend laughed. Nilda barely giggled because she was jealous. That day you knew you had to make it up to her. So when Nilda asked for a drink you put ice in her ginger ale. And when you gave her the soda you saw her face through the glass and Nilda looked like she was made out of gold.

Nilda reminds you of your homeroom teacher Mrs. Vicioso because she doesn't paternize. *Paternize* is a word Nilda taught you. When she caught you tracing your stepfather's sketches Mrs. Vicioso said, You can do better.

Your stepfather did a sketch of Big Ralph, the supermarket owner from New Jersey who is always eating. Anytime Ralph tells you something he ends it with, Know what I mean, Jellybean? Ralph is scary because he's bigger than that gorilla you saw in the zoo. His breathing sounds like he just climbed up the stairs even if he's been sitting in a chair. Sometimes while standing he nods off. It looks like he's gonna fall on his ass and never get up.

Nilda called Ralph a Glue-Ton once. She says the word comes from the Latinos in Greece and it means "to swallow." Nilda says Latino is a language that's dead because it killed itself or someone killed it. You're not sure how Latinos made it to Greece, but Mrs. Vicioso says they live all over the world because of Spain. You know the word means more than "to swallow." It has to do with someone who can't get enough of something, but you can't remember what Nilda said.

Ralph used to bring shopping bags full of food from his supermarket before your stepfather left for school. The fridge has been empty since then, and you haven't seen

Ralph. You have seen Nilda's secret friend, Gregorio. You almost forget about him because Nilda said not to tell anyone he comes around. You don't like Gregorio because when he visited he only paid attention to Nilda. You went to trace your stepfather's drawings and fell asleep on the sofa.

2.

Today you wake up to the smell of piss and alcohol. Not the type the Chinese-Japanese wannabe doctor rubbed on you, but the one Mary smells like. Did you wet the bed? Feel your underwear. Take them off. The faded Superman looks normal. Dry. Put your clothes on for school. Mary is not awake to make you shower.

Today is different. You won't walk the long way through boring Riverside Drive or climb up a mountain hill to Fort Washington Avenue. Today you'll take the shortcut with your best friend Frankie even though your stepfather told you not to take the short way without him.

Frankie calls you Ray Ray like the rest of your classmates. When the two of you walk to school he talks nastier than a cockroach-filled radio. You two always take the long way because the shortcut takes you under the George Washington Bridge through a pathway of broken glass and needles. Where zombies live. Frankie says zombies smoke crack. He knows all this because he has two older brothers. One is away at college, like your stepfather, and the other is in jail for having weed.

Frankie decides to wait after school to take the shortcut. After school you meet Frankie and follow him through Fort Washington Park. He ignores the other kids on the monkey bars and swings. You notice two empty swings, but Frankie doesn't stop. Ask yourself if you're scared. Are you scared? The thought of taking the shortcut without your stepfather makes you wanna pee. You pass the dog pen and wonder what Queeny's doing. Some dogs bark, others sniff around, and the rest run in circles.

Frankie sits on a bench that faces New Jersey when you reach the back entrance of the park. He starts talking about two airplanes crashing into the George Washington Bridge and ends up talking about his brother calling from Rikers.

"Is he scared of jail?" you ask.

"Nope. It's only the skinny guys who get raped."

"Are you scared of taking the shortcut?"

Frankie doesn't answer. He kicks a diaper down the stairs.

You remember your house phone might be back on so you stand and exit the park. You rush down the stairs that lead to the freeway. Shattered glass crunches like cornflakes with each step. You almost slip on frozen garbage. You make it to the sidewalk next to the freeway and see a large brown box under the scaffolding between the George Washington Bridge and the buildings on Riverside Drive.

"There's a shoe coming out the box over there," says Frankie.

Pick up a plastic bottle. Throw it. The bottle bounces off and rolls down the cracked pavement. The shoe doesn't move.

"Shit, Ray Ray, he's dead," says Frankie.

Frankie and you collect whatever bottles and rocks aren't smeared with shit. Wait. 1. 2 . . . 3. Attack! Bottles shatter and rocks dent the box. Stop. The laughing ends and the hum of speeding vehicles on the freeway and the bridge returns. The box stands still.

Walk on the sidewalk by the freeway. There's a path that diverges into the street that leads to your building on Riverside Drive. The cars pass fast and close to this narrow path so you walk under the scaffolds where the zombies live. The scaffolds are part of an abandoned construction next to the bridge. There are broken handrails, burnt benches, and dirt with cracked pavement. A zombie folds a garbage bag big enough for two bodies. He smiles at you.

"That crackhead keeps looking at us," says Frankie. The two of you turn around before walking any closer to the zombie with the giant garbage bag. You walk back the long way home. When you reach the stairs that lead to Fort Washington Park you notice there's no shoe coming out the brown box.

"He's not there cause he's alive," says Frankie.

"Let's see what's inside."

Pick up a bottle. Frankie is behind you. Glance at the stairs that lead to Fort Washington Park and the dog pen and your school and everything that's safe. Touch the cold cardboard. Listen. Meowing. Look through a hole while holding your nose. No cats. Turn around and a few feet away a zombie in a ripped black sweater has a rock in his hand. You freeze. Frankie runs up the stairs. The zombie throws the rock. You duck.

Frankie shouts from the top of the stairs. "He's got a knife!"

Worry. Hold the dirty glass bottle with both hands. The zombie walks like he's on a tightrope about to fall. The closer he gets the more it smells like piss and the more you want to pee. You hear someone calling your name. Look up the stairs. Frankie's gone. Look over your shoulder. Feel the cold wind from the passing vehicles. Imagine your stepfather is watching, waiting to yell at you for taking the shortcut without him. Throw the bottle. It bounces off the zombie's chest. Run up the stairs and take the long way home.

A breeze of shit and piss blows out of the apartment when you push open the door. Mary whips Queeny with your stepfather's belt. Queeny runs to you whimpering with a trail of blood behind her. Every seven months she bleeds. Mary's eyes are swollen like she just woke up or finished crying. She isn't wearing any makeup. The darkness under her eyes looks like shadows. As Queeny trembles between your legs, you realize how ugly Mary's become.

"This dog is gone," yells Mary. "We're getting rid of it today."

Nausea. Hold your nose. All this could be easily cleaned: the drops of blood, the pieces of shoes, the chewed corners on the sofa, the rubbles of shit, and the puddles of piss.

"Just clean it," you say.

Mary throws a shoe at you.

You duck and shout, "I hate you."

After hours of crying and threats of running away, you find yourself on Pinehurst Avenue close to where Olivia, a friend of your stepfather, lives. Queeny is on a leash ahead of you and Mary.

"Rich people live around here," says Mary. "They'll adopt her."

Drop the leash. Hope Olivia finds her. Follow Mary. Don't look back. Queeny follows you, dragging her metal leash over the concrete. So you end up in Fort Washington Park and leave Queeny in the dog pen where she forgets about you and chases after the other dogs.

That night Mary asks if you want to sleep with her.

You say, "I hate you," and lick your lips, tasting the salt from tears and boogers.

"We can't afford that dog. She was starving," says Mary, slamming the bedroom door.

3.

Three days have passed and you haven't killed yourself. Your stepfather hasn't called. Frankie hasn't been to school since the day you attacked the zombie. Mrs. Vicioso says he's sick. You've asked the dog owners in Fort Washington Park about Queeny, but no one has seen a reddish brown dog with hazel eyes that looks like a bulldog but is really a mutt.

This morning Mary woke you up for school by caressing your face because she knows you're mad about Queeny. She caressed your face at the hospital after almost drowning in the bathtub. You saved her that day by pulling her head out the water and holding on tight to her hair.

After school you find Nilda sweeping the kitchen. Pass her and go to the living room. Sit on the sofa. Wait for her to say something. She says something. Ignore her. She drags the broom into the living room and stands under the lamp like an angel-witch with a glow over her head.

"I'm sorry about Queeny," she says.

"Queeny's dead."

"You're wrong, Ray. They adopt dogs like Queeny."

"Don't paternize me."

"What?"

"Don't paternize me."

"You mean patronize. Do you think I'm patronizing you?"

"Depends."

You go and sit at the kitchen table and look out the window. Think about jumping out. Nilda throws words at you while cooking spaghetti because it's the only food left.

"Stroke," yells Nilda.

"It's like to strike, but only harder like a punch."

Stirring the pot, Nilda says, "Nope, it's a gentle touch like petting a cat."

"Didn't you say it was a heart attack?"

"Nope," she says with her back to you. "It's a soft touch. Next word . . . Independent."

"Being single and happy—"

There's a knock on the door. Think about your step-father. Think about Queeny. Think about Nilda's secret friend, Gregorio. Nilda checks her cell. She turns a knob on the stove and walks out the kitchen. Think about jumping out the window and breaking one leg.

"Come on, baby, she ain't gonna say shit," says the man in the hallway.

"I can't. It's my job," says Nilda.

"Come on, love."

"Only for a few minutes."

The door closes. Locks click. A man in a Yankee baseball hat extends his hand. Stare at it. He wears a leather jacket, jeans, and black boots. He's younger than your stepfather.

"Hi, Mr. Rodriguez," says the man.

"This is my friend, Nino," says Nilda.

"Yes, her boyfriend," says the man.

Your chest feels funny. Think about your heart murmur. Cavity. Nilda says anything can have a cavity, not only teeth.

"Daydreaming, Mr. Rodriguez?" asks the man with his hand out.

"Stop calling him that," says Nilda. "He's not in the mood."

Her friend, Nino, says he's seen you around. He says most stray dogs are adopted. Ignore him. Walk out of the kitchen with your plate.

You hear loud whispering in the kitchen.

"Are you seriously thinking of going?" asks Nino.

"I'm going," says Nilda. "It has nothing to do with Greg."

"What is it with you and this Greg guy?"

"Some of my friends are going to be male."

"I ain't bring Gregorio up. Why travel so far?"

"Because I want to," says Nilda in five hard whispers.

Dishes slam in the sink.

Wake up after falling asleep on the sofa. Water runs in the bathtub. Nino sits on the other end. A picture book and a jackknife rest on his lap.

"Mr. Rodriguez," says Nino fixing his belt. "You think keeping a secret is important if it could get someone in trouble?"

Rub your eyes. Don't say anything.

"Would you get me in trouble, Mr. Rodriguez?"

You don't understand. Stay shut. He's a stranger.

"Have you ever gone under the bridge?" asks Nino.

"No."

"You sure you haven't gone under the scaffolds?"

"Yea . . . But with my stepfather. I can't go alone."

"If you snitch, Mr. Rodriguez—"

"Why you call me that?"

"Respect," says Nino. "Nilda says you hate being patronized . . . I'll get to the point . . . You ain't tell Nilda you saw me under the scaffolds because you ain't a snitch. If Nilda found out you saw me she'll think I was doing something wrong. And if I tell your mom I saw you throwing bottles at bums you'll get in trouble. But I ain't a snitch."

Nod because you almost understand. He thinks you saw him taking the shortcut under the bridge.

"You kept a secret. I trust you, Mr. Rodriguez."

Nino flips through the pages of *Where the Wild Things Are*. "Lonely boy surrounded by monsters. Sounds like *Beasts of No Nation.*"

Nino doesn't look like someone who likes books. His hat is now to the back. He's like those guys with red eyes who lean with one foot against the wall and sit on milk crates by the corner. Guys like Frankie's drug-dealing brother.

"His mom sends him to bed without supper," says Nino.

"That book is for little kids," you tell him. "You know about heart murmurs?"

"Heart problem?" says Nino, scratching the few hairs on his chin.

"I have one. Mary says I was born with an extra-small heart."

"Who's Mary?"

"My mother."

"You look healthy. Nilda said you wanna run away."

"Sometimes."

"Me too," says Nino, "but I wanna run back to my parent's place."

"Why?"

"I got kicked out for selling . . . for . . . taking the shortcut."

"I haven't talked to my stepfather in mad long," you say.

"Reading helps you not think about people you miss. You gotta read a lot to be with a girl like Nilda."

Don't believe that Nino reads. He's not like Nilda.

"Imagine you had a girlfriend with a new friend named Gregorio," says Nino. "Now imagine this girlfriend mentions this new friend lent her a boring book called *School Days* by Patrick-something. And your girlfriend says it's better than the book that you like, *Beasts of No Nation*."

"She thinks that other *School* book is better than the *Beast* book?" you ask and try not to think about Nilda's secret friend.

"Yup, that's what Nilda thinks. She's never finished *Beasts of No Nation* cause it's too violent. I read it and loved it and I don't even like reading. I never finished *School Days* because it's boring. I wonder why she likes that boring book, *School Days*, so much."

"Because it's not violent?"

"No, no, wrong, Mr. Rodriguez. Remember this Gregorio friend told her about the *School Days* book." He starts cleaning his nails with the jackknife. "How would you feel if you finally read a book to impress your girl and she doesn't even read the book you read?"

"Jealous because she likes Gregorio's book better."

"Shit, you're smart . . . Has Nilda talked to you about Gregorio?"

"Nope," you say, rubbing your chest because your heart hurts when you lie but would hurt even more if you snitch. "Is Nilda your girlfriend or your friend?"

"My girlfriend," he mumbles.

"Are you scared that Gregorio is bigger than you?"

Nino laughs. "I'm never scared. He might be taller but not bigger—"

Nilda comes out of the bathroom with her hair messed up. She asks for clean blankets. Nino puts one finger over his lips. You tell her they're dirty. Go to the bedroom. Nilda makes the bed over with the same dirty sheet even though Mary had already made the bed that morning. When she's done you fall on the bed. Underneath one of the pillows is a moist spot that smells like Clorox. Fall asleep.

Fall with Mary. She holds your hand tight. There's a bridge in the sky above. The wind feels like a cold shower. Steam comes out of Mary's mouth because of the cold outside or something deep inside. The fall isn't so bad and it feels like a roller-coaster ride. As you plummet notice two objects falling below. The two objects grow closer until you drop past them. Look up. See your stepfather and Queeny floating in the air. Both bodies disappear. You can't find Mary. Try flying. Feels like you're swimming. You're drowning. Swim.

Wake up and smell Queeny. The lamp reflects on the TV screen, where the only clean spot is your handprint in a thick layer of dust. The hamper teems with dirty clothes and a puddle of jeans around it. Shades cover the two fire escape windows. Stretch your legs. It's not Queeny you smell but your own piss. Mary will go mad when she finds out.

Nilda could dry the bed with a blow-dryer. Ever since Nilda surprised Mary with a visit she fixes everything. Nilda was dressed in black slacks and a gray shirt. She wore makeup, her hair was blow-dried, and an ID hung around her neck. Nilda wrote in a black notebook and asked about you dialing 911 and saving Mary's life when she almost drowned in the bathtub. At first Mary told you not to tell Nilda anything because she was going to try to take you away. But Nilda helped Mary get food stamps and a sofa bed and babysits whenever Mary goes out.

If Nilda doesn't dry the bed Mary will go mad. Your jeans stick to your legs. You almost shower, but change jeans instead. The living room is dim with the kitchen light. Nilda's gone. Mary snores on the sofa like always. She probably forgot parent-teacher conference is tomorrow. Scratch your tear ducts. The crust goes in your nails. The floor creaks. Bite your nails. Run away because she went crazy the last time you wet the bed. Put your coat on. Look at Mary dreaming before you leave. Grab her by the wrist and touch your face with her hand. Her watch says 11:30 p.m. There's a hole in between her nostrils. She coughs and gasps for air. Press on her heart like the ambulance man. She coughs. She doesn't open her eyes like when you pulled her out the bathtub.

Mary says, "Chris?" but doesn't wake up.

It's nighttime but Riverside Drive is not scary. It's not like morning when there are no parked cars. The yellow in the apartment windows tells you who's awake. Sometimes you can see the shadows of families on walls and ceilings. You cross the empty streets in the dark cold. The winds are angry on Pinehurst Avenue. Stop coughing. You can't. Keep coughing.

Boogers run down your stuffy nose. Wish you had a hole between your nostrils like Mary.

Surprise! Ralph is in front of Olivia's building. The fat guy from New Jersey who used to bring food to your house, but disappeared when your stepfather left to school, sits on the stoop with shopping bags. He is nodding off like a zombie. But Ralph is too fat to be a zombie. If Ralph sees you he'll snitch and tell your stepfather. Run back home.

Run up your building's stairs. Hope your stepfather hasn't called.

Mary blocks the door to the apartment. "Where have you been?"

"Nowhere."

"Want me to tell Chris you ran away because you wet the bed?"

The cuticles on your middle finger bother you. Bite them off. It burns. "I saw Ralph taking food to Olivia's building."

"What?" asks Mary. "Big Ralph?"

"Yeah."

"Let's go," she says.

When you and Mary get to Pinehurst Avenue she tells you to stay across the street from Olivia's building. She leaves you her cell phone and tells you to call the cops if anything happens. Mary enters Olivia's building. Wish Ralph was taking food to your house. Think about how the light posts glow the color of pee. Look at the moon. It doesn't look like it's made out of cheese.

Mary runs out of Olivia's building with two shopping bags. "Let's go," she says. "Let me get the phone."

Keep up with Mary as she talks on the cell.

"Answering machine, Ralph? You fat piece of shit. If I find you in the Heights buying from that cutthroat, Olivia, I'm gonna make Chris cut your balls off when he comes out. I could've gotten you what you needed like Chris used to but you go behind my back to Olivia . . ."

"Why you mad at Ralph?"

"He's a drug addict," she says. "I don't want you around junkies."

The next morning you wake up alone in the bedroom. Mary didn't wake you up for school but she never does. You hear a man in the living room. Think about your stepfather.

Nino is on the sofa, talking on his cell. ". . . I won't throw it in your face. I'm doing the boy a favor, not you . . . Studying abroad ain't about studying. People travel to fuck." Nino sees you, puts one finger on his lips and hangs up.

"Is Mary in the hospital?"

"No, your mom's running errands and Nilda's at work."

"I'm late for school."

"You won't miss nothing. It's half day today. Don't tell Nilda I let you stay home . . . Hungry? I ordered Chinese for breakfast."

"It's half a day because it's parent-teacher conference today."

"I know," he says. "Nilda and your mom won't be back until later so I'm gonna take you."

Around dusk you and Nino take the shortcut to school. One of the zombies yells from under the scaffolds, "Arturo!"

Nino throws a hand in the air and says, "Dry."

When you reach the foot of the stairs that lead to Fort Washington Park, you ask Nino, "Why does Nilda help my family?"

"It's her job. Plus, you remind her of her cousin Juan."

"Does Juan have a dog?"

"Nope."

"Did Juan get left back?"

"I don't know. Maybe. Community college is like being left back."

"Was Juan born with a heart murmur?"

"I'm not sure, Mr. Rodriguez."

"Did Juan's mother try to suicide herself?"

"Juan's mother died from taking drugs," says Nino, cleaning his nails with the jackknife.

The moon is out when you reach an empty Fort Washington Park. No runaway kids on the playground or runaway dogs in the dog pen. The swings are so still they look frozen. You can see right through the monkey bars. There's no line for the big slide. Nino and you sit on a bench by the water fountain because you're early. There are no stars, just an airplane's red light in the sky.

"Nilda said she's going to Spain."

"I know." Nino opens his eyes wide like they need air.

"You sell drugs?"

"I know people in jail for selling drugs," says Nino.

"That bum called you Arturo. You got different names for different people?"

"Yup and different secrets," says Nino. "Mr. Rodriguez, if you knew Nilda had another boyfriend would you tell me?"

"Depends."

When you enter the school Nino leaves to talk to Mrs. Vicioso and drops you off in the gym where there are no adults. There are big kids throwing basketballs at smaller kids and boys and girls under the bleachers. A girl in a pink coat chokes a girl in a blue coat. A boy runs up to you, screams, and then runs away leaving a sneaker behind. Two boys howl at the ceiling lights.

You sit on the bleachers ignoring the kissing sounds below you and watching everyone's parents drop them off. Frankie enters the gym with his father. His father looks old and stupid because he doesn't know English. Frankie is a liar who abandoned you. Your stepfather would kill Frankie's father in a fight. Frankie's father doesn't care about Frankie because he leaves him behind with all these crazy kids in the gym. Frankie runs across the gym and the closer he gets the more he looks like his father.

"I spoke to my brother," says Frankie. "He's not in Rikers. He's in the S.H.O.C.K. program. Like a boot-camp jail. He saw your father. There's this drill sergeant with a tattoo on his arm of a Black baby hanging on a rope that makes them do push-ups—"

"He ain't my father. He's my stepfather and he's in college."

"It's not a real college like my other brother is in. They just let them take a test for a diploma."

"Stop lying."

You punch Frankie in the face. He walks backward, crying like a little bitch. Frankie covers his nose with blood dripping between his fingers. He might bleed to death. A crowd forms around the two of you. Run to the backdoor exit. Hurry!

Run across the street to an empty Fort Washington Park. The police will arrest you. Think about drowning in the Hudson River. Run downstairs to the freeway. Pause at the foot of the stairs. On the other side of the eight lanes of freeway is another park and after that is the Hudson River. Think before crossing. Feel the wind of the cars speeding by like they're racing.

Someone grabs your arm. Scream.

"Give me money."

"I don't got nothing."

The zombie puts you in a headlock and presses a cold metal on your throat. He searches your pockets. "I'll rip your heart out."

"I was born with a heart murmur."

Close your eyes. Pray to your stepfather. The zombie flies off you. Nino slams the zombie on the ground. He jumps on the zombie, chokes him with one hand, and holds his jackknife with the other.

"Don't stab the zombie, Nino."

Nino looks at you. He looks at the zombie before letting him go.

While on your way home Nino's cell rings.

"Yes, he was in the park," he says. "His mother will call you."

Nino doesn't ask why you punched Frankie.

"Let's make a deal, Mr. Rodriguez. If you don't let Nilda leave to Spain I promise not to tell anyone about tonight. Deal?"

"OK, but tell me . . . Is my stepfather in jail for selling drugs?"

"Yeah, Raymond," says Nino and pats your head. "I'm sorry."

Believe Nino. Your stepfather is in jail. You don't want to snitch on Nilda but you'd rather be a snitch than hide something from Nino. So you tell him about Gregorio.

"Mr. Rodriguez, you don't gotta pretend you know Nilda's friend. I won't tell anyone about tonight regardless."

Don't tell Nino anything else about Gregorio because it hurts his feelings. He doesn't believe you because he doesn't want to believe.

The next morning Mary's snoring wakes you in the bedroom. It's Saturday but you don't feel like watching cartoons. On one window the shade is halfway down so you see the dust the sun brings. On the other window the shade is fully drawn so there's no dust. It's better to keep the blinds down because the dust makes you sneeze.

Mary's cell phone vibrates on the floor.

"Hello?"

"Will you accept the collect call from Christian Ruiz?" asks a robotic voice.

"Yes."

"Hello," says a raspy voice.

It sounds like your stepfather is crying. Stay shut. Listen.

"I'm sorry I haven't called," he says. "I didn't want to—"

"Nilda says men cry . . . You know Queeny is gone?"

"I heard. Is Nilda that Children Services woman?"

"Yeah. She helped Mary get a job but Mary got sick and lost it."

Your stepfather coughs. "If she's sleeping give her a kiss."

Rub your nose against Mary's and smell cigarettes. Love the smell. Remember how she used to laugh with a cigarette in her mouth, one eye squinting because of the smoke. Touch her lips. The dryness feels like torn plastic. Lick your mother's lips.

"Are you drawing?" he asks.

"Yeah, tracing yours."

"You can't trace my drawings or take the shortcut."

"Are you in jail for selling drugs?"

He clears his throat. "Son, I told you I'm in school."

And even though Frankie, Nino, and the voice inside you all say that your stepfather is in jail, you decide to believe your stepfather.

PANAGBENGA

Daphne Palasi Andreades

Mama told you not to suck on the bead, but you don't know what else to do in the room with the chalkboard. The bead is shaped like a dolphin and is gold. You trace its ridges with your tongue. You're perched on a tiny green chair by the cubby that holds your lunch box and coat. Cinderella is on your lunch box, but her milky face is smushed. Letters snake across the room like the dirt paths of your old home. The Philippines. Some days you wake to dreams where you are running through them again, those dirt trails in the mountains, running, until Mama is shaking you awake saying, Seya, Seya, wake up, anak!

Your eyes follow the letters, their little illustrations. Alligator. Beach ball. Car. Auntie Paz taught you these letters this summer, on days when she and you and your baby brother, Javier, would walk to the park. There, you marveled at the eggs the neighborhood boys had hurled to the ground. How the eggs sizzled in the heat atop the asphalt haloed by cracked shells. That was the summer the entire city lost electricity, and for three whole nights the sky was as black as it was in your old home, but with less stars.

Other kids shuffle through the door. Note that a few resemble Americanos from TV, blond and shiny and perfect. One boy wears a ballerina skirt, and one girl cannot stop wailing. Her cries ring through the room. You chew, faster, on your bead. You are not the only one here.

Alrighty, class, says the old woman in the front, whose eyes you'd been avoiding. The maestra. Her hair is the color of ash at the bottom of the votive candles in church, where you and Mama would light one for her dead mother. The maestra's glasses are crooked and remind you of the whale poster you and Auntie Paz hung next to the bed you and Javi share.

A girl sits next to you. She stomps one foot. Her sneakers flash. She smiles, revealing tightfisted eyes and a gap between her front teeth.

You blink.

What's your name? she asks. Her voice reminds you of a cartoon character's. You stare at her marshmallow skin.

Name? Hell-oooo, she says. Your name?

Seya, you think. Instead, you whisper, Casey.

• • •

The walls were stripped bare of their few decorations—namely, the cheap reproduction of the Last Supper and the oversized wooden fork and spoon that flanked the kitchen entrance. The cupboards were emptied of charred pots, the one frying pan. Mama swept the concrete floors over and over. A brand new comforter, your best clothes, and a bleached pair of sneakers were among the items arranged into three large suitcases labeled MICHELLE KINDIPAN, your mother's name, and NEW YORK, NY, your destination.

The rest of the items—the mismatching mugs, the TV whose screen was the width and height of a sheet of paper—were given away. You watched as your house grew emptier each week and, while it was happening, promised Mama you'd keep an eye on Javi. You and Javi escaped to play outside with your neighbor and best friend, Boy.

You and Boy rolled the marbles in the dirt and held them up to the sun where those hard little balls were especially glassy and green. The marbles were one of the many gifts sent over from Boy's mama in Saudi. Javi squatted next to you. He couldn't understand the rules and, instead, plucked pebbles from the ground and collected them in his pockets. The three of you tossed a ball, slightly deflated but still fine, climbed into the back of a rusty pickup truck, and harassed a flock of chickens together. Each time you caught a bird, you cradled it tight in your arms until the creature burst from your grip, wings spreading like an angel's.

Seya! Your mother called from the doorway, her face flushed from packing, scrubbing, cooking, preparing. Play with Javi and make sure he keeps his hat on, it's chilly today! Go with Boy to collect more potatoes. Anya met?! Why did you just drop them all over the table? Can't you see I'm chopping cabbage here? Our farewell party is tonight, don't you remember? Go help Lola Belén collect the laundry. She's old, do you want her back to break? Hai, dios mio! Just stay out of the way.

And so you raced Boy up the third-highest mountain in the municipality. You ran past the gardens chiseled into the side of the mountain, past the plants growing in perfect rows, the cabbage heads blossoming in the sun as you climbed higher and higher. You moved so that bamboo shoots wouldn't jab your ankles. Your feet beat into the soil that ascended to where the clouds veiled everything in mist.

Boy! you called. Boy! Stop running so fast!

Javier toddled behind you, pebbles bouncing from his pockets. You stopped and grabbed his arm. Boy's shaggy head bobbled ahead of you.

Come on, Javi! Let's get him!

You were close enough to see the patches sewn onto the seat of Boy's pants, his hoodie whose sleeves stopped beneath his wrists. You catapulted yourself onto Boy to stop him. Latched onto him. Javier bumped into the both of you and his weight and your joy were too much to bear. The three of you collapsed in a heap.

Panting, you untangled yourself and scanned beyond the cliff at what you could see below you: farmers bent over, their hands digging into the flesh of the green earth, their bodies like dots scattered across spiraling trails. Fertilizer—ripe, pungent manure—filled your nostrils. But you didn't crinkle your nose at the scent. You knew the manure housed bean sprouts, carrots, cauliflower. Your heart pumped.

The three of you pressed your palms into the soft, damp ground.

Do you have to go, Seya? Boy said.

You shrugged. You laid your palm into the handprint Boy had made. Pressed deeper.

· · ·

When your aunts, uncles, and neighbors kissed you good-bye the morning you, Mama, and Javi were to leave—that is, before boarding the bus that would take you to Manila, where you'd see skyscrapers for the first time, and before getting on the airplane where your home zoomed into some-thing unrecognizable, and you weren't sure what was earth and what was sky—you breathed in your family's scent. When their arms encircled you, you inhaled the ash that had settled onto their coats and woolly hats after the last bonfire, their hands that had tilled the dirt and sifted through grains of rice. They had nothing else to give you.

Do not forget us, Seya, they said. Do not forget your family here.

When Boy said goodbye, you clung to him.

Your best friend fiddled with a gap in his sweater where a button should have been.

Seya, your mother said. It's time. The van that was to take you to Baguio was loaded with your suitcases and boxes. The driver, bored, smoked a cigarette.

I don't want to go, you said to your mother.

Seya, she said.

I don't want to go!

Goodbye, goodbye, goodbye, everyone said. You screamed, No no no no no! Your mother picked you up, carried you to the van.

• • •

In this new place—which you learn is called Elmhurst, Queens—there are no chickens. No dirt trails, no mountains to climb. No carrots and potatoes to dig up. No packs of stray dogs you must avoid. Instead, there are squirrels. There are rats and cooing, gray birds that swoop and peck the sweet bread, the one Mama bought you at the Chinese bakery, right out of your hand. There are sidewalks speckled with black, hardened gobs of gum, a man who tailors shoes and sells his old electronics beneath the overpass. There are no tricycles to take you from home to the marketplace with Mama. No Lola Belén. No aunties. No uncles. No Boy.

Just Mama, Javi, you—and Auntie Paz, Mama's sister, who greets you at the airport.

Is this Seya? My little niece? she says.

She turns to Javier, cups his face in her hands. Hello, guapo! Her skirt swooshes around you as she embraces you and Javi. Her pregnant belly smacks your face. Her bracelets— Bangles, anak, Auntie Paz says when she catches you marveling at them in the taxi—clink together in your ears. She could be a movie star. You instantly fall in love with her.

You and Javi exit the airport and stand shivering in the February night air. Ice covers the ground and people hurry left and right. You have never seen so many people before. Auntie Paz hands you a puffy purple coat and one with an astronaut on the back to Javier. She tears off the tags with a yank.

You had never needed a coat so thick. You had never known the cold.

Your new home is also Auntie Paz's home, which is above a nail salon. Canvases whose surfaces are swirled with paint are propped against the wall.

I cleared out my art studio for you guys, says Auntie Paz.

The room, which still smells sharply of turpentine, holds two beds. The bathroom, to your surprise, contains a toilet that flushes without you having to throw in a bucket of water.

It is your Auntie Paz who watches you every night when Mama begins her new job at St. Paul's Hospital. When Mama gets home, she describes her night as you eat your breakfast of scrambled eggs. A sixteen-year-old girl, Mama says. Pregnant. Her own father too—Dios mio. She says,

This old woman who broke her hip? Her family dumped her in the hospital. Didn't visit once and squabbled over her will. Other days, Mama is too exhausted to speak. Her head droops in slumber at the kitchen table.

When you ask if you will see Papa, who has been in the States for two years, Mama snorts, says in English, Your Papa? He's who knows where.

You wonder if Who Knows Where is a place with dolphins that screech when you wave at them like the ones in the aquarium Auntie Paz took you and Javi to see. You are obsessed with dolphins.

But when will he be back? you ask Mama, who continues to iron her scrubs with the emblem of the American hospital stamped above her heart.

Seya, she says. Please.

With a kiss on your head, Mama leaves you with Auntie Paz. We're lucky your Auntie's on maternity leave, she says, pulling her coat on. And *I'm* lucky they have this sort of thing in the States.

So Auntie Paz plays Snakes and Ladders with you and Javi, cooks sinigang na baboy, whose salty vinegar scent fills the apartment. Other nights she makes mac and cheese from a box. But always, without fail, are her art supplies, which are never far. Paints of every color and consistency, brushes whose soft bristles you like to smooth across your face, beads, clay, and a special box of pastels for you. Maize, Strawberry, Cerulean, Tangerine, Auntie Paz reads when she picks up each crayon. You test out these colors with tiny strokes. The pastel called "Forest" is the one you like the most because it reminds you of crops ready to harvest. Beside you, Javier lines up his collection of miniature toy race cars bumper to bumper. Mama purchased them for him at Dollar Tree after he'd cried and cried for them.

Auntie Paz helps you write your name on the small canvas. She places her fingers over yours. Together you write

SEYA

in the sky, by the sun.

• • •

The weather grows warmer, rainier, and one day, you wake up to fog covering everything outside your window. You think you have been transported home. You haven't. You shed your puffy coat and take note of the green stalks that rise from the ground, though not at all in the graceful way you are used to seeing plants bloom. Here, weeds spring from pavement cracks and parched dandelions stretch toward the sun. When you squat and touch the grass growing from a little square plot at the park, strewn with candy wrappers, it prickles your skin.

For your fifth birthday, Mama buys peonies, roses, and carnations dyed cerulean from the minimart. She arranges them in vases scavenged from the clearance section of HomeGoods. She places dahlias by the doorway, which perfume the entrance and mask the ammonia stench wafting from the nail salon. She puts roses on the windowsill and carnations and lilies at the kitchen table.

We missed the Panagbenga Festival, anak, but we can still celebrate with our own flowers. And it's my Seya's birthday!

Mama says, When I was pregnant with you, I almost didn't make it to the hospital.

Crowds of people were there to see the parade. I thought about naming you Sampaguita, after the flowers blocking the road. That would've been a mouthful, ha, Seya?

You think that she looks truly happy as she trims the stalks, clasps and unclasps the flowers to let them fall in place.

Panagbenga, she says. The season of blooming.

You stick your nose into the center of a daffodil. It is the color tangerine. You practice pronouncing this word, which buzzes on your tongue: Tan-gerrr-ine.

When Auntie Paz arrives and sees all the flowers, she says, Oh!

She calls to your mother. Michelle—Is everything OK?

Your mother nods, waves her hand absently in the air as if to say, Yes, yes. Dips her head into a bouquet.

Seya, Auntie Paz says. Umaika itoy, mon. Come here.

You go to her. She reaches into the pocket beneath her swollen belly and removes a bracelet with turquoise beads and a lone dolphin charm. Pins it around your wrist. It is the prettiest thing you own.

I brought you something else, she says.

At the table, you spy a cake. It is decorated with plastic figurines from Cinderella: the magic pumpkin carriage, the fairy godmother, the glass slipper, and of course, Cinderella herself decked in her signature powder-blue ball gown.

Javi! Javi! you scream. Look what Auntie Paz got me!

Mama frowns when you push aside her sticky rice wrapped in banana leaves. You had never tasted ice cream before. You were used to milk poured over shredded coconut, red beans, and gelatin cubes all mixed with crushed ice. Instead of these textures, the ice cream is smooth and will taste vaguely of strawberry.

Paz, Mama says. Really. You didn't have to.

I love it! you say.

The bubblegum-colored icing reads, HAPPY BIRTHDAY, SEYA! You pluck the plastic Cinderella from the cake and squeeze your eyes shut to make a wish. When you open your eyes, Auntie Paz asks what you wished for.

• • •

You're working on your latest drawing of a dolphin in an airplane, while lying on your stomach. It is your twelfth dolphin drawing of the week. You paste beads onto the spot where the dolphin's eyes would be, your fingers tacky with glue. Auntie Paz towels off your little brother and changes him into pajamas.

Nag linis! she says, burrowing her nose into his hair. All clean.

As you color, you sing the chorus of something you heard on the R train, until Auntie Paz asks you to recite your alphabet. A, B, C, D.

Good, she says. Now how do you spell Seya?

The front door slams.

Michelle? Auntie Paz calls. What's your mom doing home so early?

Your bedroom door opens. It isn't Mama, but a man who stands in the doorway.

Your butterfly lamp rotates, projecting monarchs and the delicate, cutout patterns of their wings onto the walls, your bed, and the man's beige jacket.

Auntie Paz shoves you and Javi behind her. The man stands there, watching. You do not know him.

Alonso, Auntie Paz says. Michelle told you not to come back here.

Paz! says the man. Ay sus, that baby is coming any day now. But what happened to that lalaki who—what is it the Amelikanos say? The lalaki who "knocked you up"? That Mexicano?

Get—Auntie Paz says each word very slowly—Out.

Alonso, you think. You peer at the man's face. You realize, with a rush, that it is your Papa. He is back from Who Knows Where! But he looks different than the photo you found when you were playing with Mama's makeup one day. The photo lay in her underwear drawer and was torn into four parts. You placed the raggedy edges together, like a puzzle, and saw Mama and Papa standing outside a simbaan, Mama dressed in white. Papa's arm was around her waist and his chin was tilted upward, proud. You hid the photo in your jewelry box.

But Papa's hair is longer in person, and his eyes are tired.

He looks at you. Is that my Seya?

You want to go to him. Tell him about your birthday party, show him your dolphin masterpieces, and pull up Javi's pant leg to reveal the stitch he received after he slipped on ice and tumbled down the slide.

Papa?

My mahal, he says. Oh, my mahal. My love. Seya, Javier. My Seya and Javier. He says your names the way rain falls during monsoon season, so heavy and sudden that you must shut the windows. You struggle against Auntie Paz's grip to go to him. Thrash your body away from her. This is the first time, though certainly not the last, where you do not want her to touch you. But she holds on.

I can spell now, you say, hoping that this will keep him. S, E, Y, A. Seya.

Papa bellows, Caterina Seya Kindipan! as you try, again, to escape Auntie Paz's hold. He begins to laugh. As he does, a butterfly shadow rests on his tongue, flits to his cheek. Javier starts to cry.

Won't she need an American name, eh, Paz?

You need to leave, Alonso. Or I'll call the fucking police.

I mean, she's an Amelikana now, isn't she?

No, you say. I'm not! You want him to stay, to see your dolphin drawings.

But aren't we all, mahal? Papa says. Like it or not. He takes one step into the room.

Auntie Paz squeezes you and Javi behind her. GET OUT, she screams.

He says, Everything changes in the Land of Milk and Honey, my Seya. He gazes at you one last time and leaves.

. . .

The following week, Auntie Paz gives you a new one—a new name. Teaches you how to spell it while Mama works her night shift. By then, the lock to the front door has been changed. She teaches you how to spell this new name while Javi rides his plastic bike around the kitchen table. You trace the curve of the C, the peak of the A:

CASEY

. . .

Auntie Paz takes you to your first day of kindergarten. When Mama returns from her shift that morning, she lies on the couch, watches as you eat your Cinnamon Crunch cereal before you go.

Listen to your maestra, ha, anak, she says. You nod.

You wear a coat that touches your knees and scratches your neck. It flattens the muffin-shaped sleeves of your dress. But you don't care. Instead, you and Javi run past the trees, scattering the brittle leaves as you go. You and your brother halt. Wrap your arms around a tree trunk. Auntie Paz snaps a photo. Javi says, I want to come too. Holds your hand.

You say, No, Javi, you have to play Power Rangers and wait for me at home, OK? You let him carry your lunch box instead. Standing outside the entrance to your school, Javi and Auntie Paz wave Goodbye!

Two nights ago you heard Auntie Paz crying in the bathroom. Her skirt sagged, and you found her bangles strewn on the sofa and in the sink. Her stomach had shrunk, and Mama stayed home from the hospital for three days to watch you and Javi. And when you asked Auntie Paz, Where is the baby? she opened her arms and held you. You are my baby, Seya, she said. You are my baby.

• • •

The girl sitting next to you kicks her feet under the desk. Her sneakers flash like lightning. I'm Giselle, she says. She points to your bracelet. Can I borrow that? I promise I'll give it back.

You do not know what she is saying. You put your hand over your bracelet.

Welcome to K-106, the maestra says. My name is Mrs. Manzini.

Man-zeee-ni. You'd never heard a name like that before. Let's all sit around the rug and say our names!

My name is David. Ali. Chase. Annika. Theodore. Joseph. Lila. Dante. Giselle. Matthew. Rosany. Casey.

You discover that the whole day is a series of "Let's."

Let's all go to the mat and read a book. Let's remember to be gentle with the book. Let's all count to twenty. Let's leave Dante alone—he needs a minute. Let's not forget to use kind words in class—Do you think "dummy" is a kind word? Let's all hold hands with our partner and walk to the bathroom. Voices off, K-106. Let's all eat our lunches.

You are ravenous. You unpack your rice and adobo when everyone else pulls out sandwiches and bagels. During Coloring Time, you pick Forest, your favorite color, and when the girl with the cartoon voice sees, she says, Ew, that's a *boy's* color.

You hear "Boy" and look around, alert. Is Boy here too?

But he isn't. So you exchange "Forest" for "Eggplant," even though you don't fully understand what she's saying, that suplada, that mean little girl, and you hate Eggplant because it reminds you of bruises. When the class counts to twenty, you count to ten in English and the rest in Ilocano. When you hear you are wrong, you move your mouth and try to mimic everyone else's actions: the way they smile, the way they run, walk, laugh, sneeze. No one wants to sit next to you or hold hands with you down the hall. You walk with Mrs. Manzini instead.

Where are you from, Casey? she asks.

You don't know what to say. You point to your dolphin bracelet.

The only thing you do right is "Casey."

You and the other kids choose sleeping bags to nap on the floor. You rush to pick the one with dolphins. If you fall asleep, you wonder, would you wake up somewhere you recognized by heart?

After your nap, Mrs. Manzini says another "Let's." By now, your hair clips slide and jab a spot behind your ear. The stockings Mama made you wear itch. You are hungry because someone pinched their nose at your lunch and said, Eeyuck! And everyone laughed until you said, Ano? Gaga sika! Stupid, you're stupid. You spend the rest of the day silent. By now, home feels far away.

Let's draw pictures, everybody, the maestra says.

And so, you pick up the colored pencils, long and thin. You are tired, so tired, but you draw anyway in broad, sweeping strokes like Auntie Paz taught you.

You steady yourself. You fill the page.

You draw Javier on the bike he wanted. You draw Auntie Paz with a smile, a real one. You draw everyone in a big house. You draw fields around you, and Papa back from Who Knows Where. You draw yourself as Cinderella, without the drooping stockings. You draw a bagel for lunch.

On another sheet of paper, you draw mountains. You do not know how to draw crisp air, men atop water buffalo farming the land, the sari-sari store where Mama bought you little chocolates. But you draw the mountains and the sky as you remember them. You draw Boy. You write Seya at the bottom.

MAGIC CITY RELIC

Jennine Capó Crucet

The day before Noche Buena, I decided I'd waited long enough and set off to Tío Fito's apartment to find my dad. I'd been back in Miami for three days at that point, and Papi had only called once—the day I got in from Rawlings, to make sure my flight landed and that I'd been on it. He didn't ask how my first semester went, or make plans to see me so he could ask me this in person over a meal or something. I figured he'd call again, and when he didn't—and when Noche Buena, the most family infested of holidays, crept up on me faster than it ever did when I was a kid—I decided to just be pissed off. I thought, *What is the most Latina thing I could do right now?* (I thought about my choices in these terms since being home, after my sister Leidys said, when I described the new coral paint job on our apartment complex as "sufficiently tropical," that I should "quit acting so white"), and decided that it was this: jacking my mom's keys and yelling that I was borrowing the car as the front door slammed behind me, driving to my dad's brother's apartment, demanding whoever was there to tell me where my dad lived now, then driving to *that* place, and then yelling as many fuck-as-adjective expressions at Papi as I could generate, all the while still standing in the street in chancletas. It would be a lot like the fights I'd seen him have with my mom, and therefore definitely *not* white.

I got to Fito's apartment half dreading my dad's car would be in the visitor's spot, but it wasn't, which meant I would get a practice run at yelling at someone in addition to the lame sassing of the rearview mirror I'd done at red lights on the drive there. Two of Fito's sons, cousins a little older than me, stood talking and smoking in front of the apartment's sliding glass doors, which led out to a railing-surrounded patch of concrete just off the complex's parking lot. I parked and walked up to the railing into the open arms of my cousins, who were, as they put it, *chilliando* (not a word, but I kept that to myself, since identifying something as "not a word" is a Leidys-certified white thing to do). We hugged and they held their cigarettes way out from our kiss-on-the-cheek greeting. I stood still for a second, the railing pressed against my hip bone as my hand worked the gate's latch, and waited for them to say welcome home or something, but the blank faces looking at me from behind swirls of cigarette smoke just said, So . . . what's up, Lizet?

—I just got back from New York, I said, knowing they'd think I meant the city and not upstate.

—What, you went on vacation? the older one said. I only knew him as Pato and I realized I wasn't positive on his or his brother's real names, even though we counted each other as cousins. The other one was called Fito like his dad.

—No, college, bro. I was away at *college*. I just got back from, like, three months away. *Hello?*

—No shit, Fito said. All the way in New York? That's fucking crazy, whoa!

—Wooooooow, Pato said, less impressed. He put his cigarette back in his mouth and held it there, turning his head to the parking lot.

—I thought we didn't see you cuz of your dad! Fito said. Or, I mean, you know, your mom?

He wrinkled his eyebrows and looked at his cigarette like it had the answer to this delicate etiquette issue: how to address my parents' separation, the one that allowed my revised financial aid package to be enough to make Rawlings a real option.

—My dad didn't mention I was away at college? I said.

The tip of Pato's cigarette flared orange.

—No! Fito said. I mean, yeah, he did, but I figured you were *around*, like at Miami-Dade or, like, FIU.

I was about to tell him about Rawlings—the rankings, the profile in *Newsweek*, how freaking hard it was to get into and stay in that school—before thinking about Leidys. The fourth or fifth time she accused me of acting white was when I told her about how I'd gone with my mom to pick up Dante, Leidys's ten-month-old son, from daycare, and that the girl ranked number nine in my graduating high school class was working there as a teacher's helper and was five months pregnant with her boyfriend-turned-fiancé's kid. I handed my nephew over to Leidys after carrying him in from the car and eventually (and without really thinking about it) said that seeing that girl there was depressing. I think my exact words were, *It just really bummed me out.* I thought that was delicate enough, considering that Leidys was nineteen and still trying to convince her ex-boyfriend (and Dante's dad) Rolando to, at the very least, show up on weekends and hang out with his kid.

—What the fuck is *bum you out*? You sound *so freaking white*, she said, Dante squealing between us. Stop thinking your shit don't stink and freaking help me.

I almost made some reference to shit stinking and diaper changing, but she gestured to the bags of groceries still waiting outside the apartment door, which she'd picked up on her way back from her job at the salon, and started cooing in broken Spanish to my nephew as she swept him into the room we were sharing since I got there.

I'd hurt her feelings without realizing it, which, based on my social interactions during my last three months at mostly white Rawlings, felt to me more *white* than anything else I'd done since being back. That, and my weird reaction to the Ariel Hernandez protests happening two blocks down from our building, which I felt were getting seriously out of hand but which every other Cuban around me in Little Havana thought were a totally acceptable way of behaving. My inability to get as upset as my mom about the possible deportation of some Cuban kid who floated over during my Thanksgiving break, his omnipresent face on our TV screen pretty much ruining my first time home, made me think that Rawlings had changed me in a way that I worried was, for the first time, bad.

I decided to explain Rawlings to my cousins in the way I'd first thought about it, which was not accurate, but was enough to get me past them and into the apartment.

—The college I'm at is more like UM than FIU, in that it's freaking expensive, but the football team is shitty, and I got this stupid scholarship that covers a lot of it, so, yeah, that's why I'm there.

Fito nodded and smiled. Pato pulled the cigarette out of his mouth, tossed it over my head into the parking lot behind me, grabbed the sliding glass door's handle, and said, You wanna beer?

Inside sat Tío Fito—Fito the Elder—eyes glassy and with a bottle of Becks (la llave, we all called it, because of the little drawing of a key on the label) snuggled between his legs. He was watching a Marlins game, which confused the hell out of me until Little Fito explained it was a tape of the 1997 World Series.

—Two years later and he still don't believe we won it, Little Fito said. Pato laughed and went to the fridge to get bottles for everyone.

Tío Fito stood up, placing the bottle on the tile by his spot on the couch, and staggered over to me for a hug. He was shirtless and—aside from the preponderance of gray chest hair, the broken little veins sprawling over his cheeks, and the deep lines on his forehead that spelled out the eleven years he had on Papi—looked pretty much like. an alcohol-drenched version of my dad, down to the goatee and the heavy eyelashes.

—Meri Cree Ma! he slurred.

He'd come over from Cuba later than my dad, and his English was never as good as it would've been had the Mariel boatlift dropped him off somewhere farther north of Miami, or if he'd come over as a kid, like my dad.

—Merry Christmas, Tío. Where's Papi?

He backed away from our hug and fell back into the couch, into the spot where the cushions held his shape. He breathed in sharply, then pressed his hand to his belly and burped.

—Yo, this dude is so drunk, I said with a fake laugh. Pato muttered from the kitchen, Shut the fuck up.

—Eh? Tío said. Tu papi? No here.

He shook his head and flapped his arm around to indicate the living room and kitchen of the apartment. Pato yelled in my direction, You forget how to speak Spanish in New York?

—No, I mean, where does he *live*?

—You don't know where he *lives*? I heard Pato say into the fridge.

—OK, that's messed up, Lizet, Fito my cousin said from behind me.

I whirled around to him and yelled, He never *told* me.

Pato yelled from the fridge, You ever *ask*?

I hissed, *Of course*, and believed it for all of two seconds. Because, as I turned back to Big Fito, whose face, in the glow of the TV screen, looked brighter and younger than it should, I scanned the last three months—only two sad phone conversations, the botched Thanksgiving reunion that the traffic surrounding Ariel's arrival crowded around as we talked on my mom's buildings steps—for the moment where I actually said the words, Papi, can I have your address? I couldn't find it, and that's when I started to worry that maybe *he* was mad at *me* for not asking.

—He's still in Hialeah, Tío said in Spanish. He kept his eyes on the screen while picking up his bottle and said, In the apartments by your old house, what are they called? Hialeah Gardens Villas, him and that Dominican guy from his job, like roommates.

The idea of my dad having a roommate almost made me laugh: All this time, the stories we could've told each other, maybe helped each other out. Then I thought about mine: lacrosse star Jillian, now back in Cherry Hill, New Jersey ("The good part," she'd been sure to tell me), celebrating not Noche Buena, but just regular storybook Christmas, sledding and drinking boozy eggnog and reading Dickens around a fire and hunting geese or whatever white people did on Christmas. If his roommate was the Dominican guy I'd met a few times, a tile guy—my dad's age, maybe in the US a year or two, claiming to look hard for a wife but only meeting hoochies—that Papi met while doing drywall at a jobsite a couple months before him and my mom split up, then our experiences of having roommates probably didn't have much in common. His guy seemed totally normal.

—Apartamento dos, Tío said.

—No, Papi, it's doce, Pato yelled at him. He stepped across the tiny living room and tipped a bottle in my direction. Apartment twelve. Papi's bad with numbers.

—Why do—, I said. *You* know where he lives?

—Yeah? Pato said. He pulled the bottle away. You wanna say something about it? You wanna bitch about it like your mom?

Little Fito stepped between us and yelled, Yo, chill, man! It's, like, almost Christmas and shit!

He put his hand flat on Pato's chest.

The most Latina thing I could have done then, I think, was smack him and tell him there was more coming if he wanted to talk about my mom. But his squinting eyes, the cocked head, the white knuckles choking the neck of the beer bottle, the muscles flashing around his jaw—all of it said, Get out. And I felt suddenly very cold and scared of him. Had he always been quick to get mad like that? Was me noticing it for the first time right then a sign that I'd already been gone too long? Had they always been so loud and aggressive in the house, or did I, without even realizing it, somehow grow used to nice, mostly quiet white girls like Jillian, who showed you she hated you by folding her laundry extra sharply and clearing her throat while she did it?

—Oye! Old Fito yelled. He shushed us and pointed at the TV.

I looked at Pato, then at Little Fito, and said, Number 12, in the Villas?

—Yeah, Little Fito said, letting his hand drop. He took the beer his brother had offered me. I took a step back toward the sliding glass door. Tell him we said wassup, he said, opening the door for me.

—Or don't, Pato said.

He stared at me a second too long and then turned around, disappearing down the apartment's hallway, his words—in an annoying, high-pitched girl voice, in an accent that I know Leidys would have a word for—trailing behind him: *Yo, this dude is so drunk!*

Out by the railing, Little Fito said, Pato's a dick. Forget him.

He kissed me on the cheek and opened the gate for me— the bitter beer on his breath wafting across my face. I wanted to ask Little Fito what I was missing, but to need him to tell me was worse than anything. Asking questions would only show Little Fito that his brother was right about me.

—Merry Christmas, he said, the gate still open. Hope things get better with Tío.

I said, Me too. I clicked the gate shut behind me and hurried to my mom's car, only getting it when I turned the key in the ignition, the car baking me inside even in December: He didn't mean Tío Fito. He meant *his* tío. My dad. He meant that what came next for me could be worse than just a drunk uncle. By the time I pulled out of the spot and passed their apartment, no one waited outside, new cigarettes in hand, to wave goodbye. The glass door was shut, and through it, I saw the glow from the TV, the green of the baseball diamond on its screen washing over my uncle, making him look like a memory of someone—like a ghost I only barely recognized—as I drove away.

COLD

Naima Coster

The cold is a thing any woman can grow accustomed to. Lacey May learned how in precisely three days, which was quicker than anyone who knew her would have ever expected.

It was a Wednesday, newly November, and she was raking the leaves in the front yard, when it occurred to her to check the gas tank. Her knuckles were red and sore from the few minutes she had been outside, and it wouldn't be long before the nights started to dip toward the thirties. The tank was shaped like a tiny submarine, and it stood in the shadow of the house. She pulled up the metal lid and saw the needle on the gauge pointing down to 15 percent. Lacey ran inside, still holding the rake, and she dropped the heat down as low as she could stand.

She passed the rest of the day in her good coat, the one Robbie bought her the winter she was pregnant with their first. It was big on her now, but she was more or less fine with it on. She kept the kettle boiling because the steam felt good rising on her face while she stood at the stove, and if she drank cup after cup of coffee, she could keep her hands warm too. By noon, she was shaking from all the caffeine, her fingernails tinged with blue. She wanted Robbie to call so she could tell him about the tank and ask how long 15 percent would last, but he didn't. She called the agency instead to ask again if they'd found anything for her yet.

"It's kinda hard when you haven't worked in ten years. And all you've ever done is fry fries." The receptionist spoke slowly, as if she didn't expect Lacey to understand.

"I've been raising my girls," Lacey said.

"I mean real work, out of the house. Employment."

"I'm pretty sure I could answer the phone."

"You don't have any qualifications."

Lacey wanted to hang up on her, or to insult her again, but the receptionist didn't seem interested in a fight. Besides, she shouldn't risk ticking off the woman who could decide whether to move her folder down to the bottom of the pile. So Lacey mentioned how she had earned decent grades in high school, was quick in the kitchen, better behind the wheel than most.

"You can write that down if you want," she said, and the receptionist was quiet for a long while. Finally, she said she would add a note to Lacey's file and give her a call if anything opened up. Lacey thanked the woman for her time and got off the phone.

Later on, when she heard the school bus turn up the road, Lacey climbed into the crawl space and hauled down the old duffel bag filled with the children's winter clothes. She waited at the door for them, her arms loaded down with woolen things that smelled of dust and damp, from months spent shut up in the dark. The girls blazed in, chattering, their cheeks windblown, and Lacey handed them each an extra sweater and a pair of mittens, a scarf for Margarita.

"It's winter in our house!" she said, and the girls caught on quickly. They dropped their schoolbags and swathed themselves in the new layers, made a big noise stomping around the living room. Soon they were all explorers, sliding across a stretch of ice in Alaska. Somehow, Lacey became a sled, and the girls scrambled on top of her, and although she couldn't move, it made them laugh. Diane pretended to be a dog, one of those racing wolf dogs, so she got down on all fours and howled, which made the real dog Jenkins dart behind the couch to hide.

They kept on their sweaters and scarves while they cooked grilled cheese, the yellow squares gobbled up by their hands faster than Lacey could set them in the pan. They were pleased when they were all allowed to lie down in bed with Lacey, and she didn't make them crawl out from under the blankets to wash their greasy fingers or their unbrushed teeth. Jenkins dozed beneath them on the floor, as if he couldn't feel the cold at all, and the girls watched their breath puff overhead.

"That's oxygen," Lacey said. "It's what we breathe. You spell it O-X-Y—"

Her oldest, Noelle, liked to look at picture books about the ocean and outer space. In the summer, she tended to the tomato plants in the yard and caught dragonflies and burned their wings off under her magnifying glass. She could be a scientist one day, if she started her extra learning now. Lacey was spelling for her.

Noelle looked a lot older than almost ten, the little swipes of purple under her eyes a reminder that no matter how fine they all seemed, the girls missed their daddy. She repeated after Lacey, a blanket tucked under her chin, and her face serious, as if she knew how much every letter was worth.

"G-E-N." Diane and Margarita gave a little round of applause when their sister got it right.

The next morning the girls went off to school, all of them with pink noses and runny eyes. Lacey saw them down the hill, and she was jealous of their little Black heads disappearing into the bus. They were off to somewhere the thermostat was set much higher than fifty-five.

She took a shower to beat the cold, and it was the most pleasure she had felt since Robbie went away. Had water always been this warm? The stream of it so steady and mighty and good? Her hands set to work on every inch of her—her elbows, her neck, the insides of her thighs—and the heat seemed to sink in deep, underneath the top layer of skin—what was it called? The epidermis?—she had learned the name in high school. It was only these last few weeks, since the nurse moved in next door, that Lacey started remembering she hadn't been half bad at biology. She had seen the nurse driving down the road to third shift at the hospital and thought, *I could have been you.* Sure, the nurse was fat and had no husband and left her boy with a babysitter overnight and didn't bother with the leaves in the yard, but it was probably seventy, seventy-five degrees over in her bungalow, and wasn't that worth something?

After the shower, Lacey felt the sin of her wet hair. It made the cold worse, a new chill dripping on her neck and shoulders, so she wrapped her head in towels. How much gas was she using now? How many percents did it take to heat the house every day? She wondered whether to go out and check the tank again, but she decided against it. She couldn't have been using that much, not when it was only fifteen degrees warmer inside than out.

Lacey opened all the curtains to let in the sunshine, thinking some light might warm the place. Half an hour later, she went around drawing them all closed because maybe she was letting in a draft. She had lived in the house for four years, ever since Robbie's promotion at the shop, and still she didn't know how it all worked. When she took off her robe to get dressed, she had a sudden, terrible thought: How did the water get heated? Did that use up the gas too?

She didn't want to call her sister-in-law but she did. There was nothing else to do.

"I'm worried it might be bad for the girls. All this cold. And the next check doesn't come for another two weeks."

"Why don't you sell your food stamps?"

"Cause we got to eat, Annette."

"Well, the cold never killed nobody. When we were kids, it was always cold in our house. And I turned out just fine. And we can't blame the cold for Robbie—"

"It's not his fault, Annette. I've told you. He's got—" Lacey searched for the words, tried to remember the doctor's exact phrase. "A chemical unbalanced."

"I told you to get a job. I said it a year ago when he started disappearing."

"I thought he was getting better."

"And I told him not to buy that house, that one day the mortgage would get him. Nothing in this life is free, least of all houses. You played dumb for too long, Lacey May."

"Why don't you come by and see how cold it is for yourself? All we need is a little loan."

"No ma'am," Annette said. "Robbie already cleaned me out, remember?"

Lacey started to cry. Her sister-in-law tried to calm her but it was no use.

"How'd you burn through the last check so quick anyway? It's only the middle of the month."

When Lacey didn't say anything, Annette made sense of her silence and cursed.

"You're as shit-rotten as he is," she said. "You don't love those little girls half as much as they deserve."

Lacey put herself to bed, her hair leaking all over the pillows. The dog followed her into the room, whimpering, and settled on the floor by her side. She drew three blankets up over herself and started talking out loud. It was like she was praying, only she was talking to Robbie.

Why'd you buy me this house if it was going to be so cold? Why'd you buy me this house if you was going to leave me alone?

It had been good for a long time. All through Noelle and Diane being babies, and the first years of Margarita's life, they had lived in town. They had less, but it was fine. Then they bought this little house, blue with white shutters, at the top of the hill on a patch of cleared land. There were only two other houses out in these woods. The first had been empty for a year, after the last family moved closer to town, and the other belonged now to that nurse and her kid. Before, their neighbors had been the Kings, an old couple that took afternoon coffee out on the porch. They died within a few weeks of each other, both in the spring, in their sleep, which Lacey thought was the best kind of ending you could ever expect from life.

Their house was drafty and small, all wood except for the concrete porch that wrapped all around, which Robbie had built himself. There were swings out back for the girls, a plastic slide Diane and Noelle had outgrown but that Margarita still liked to climb.

When he was all right, they would go out to the back porch and drink beers after the girls had gone to sleep. If they drank too much, he would fuck her right there on the porch, Lacey down on all fours, the concrete scraping her knees. *This is freedom*, he would say. *I can fuck my wife under a sky full of stars, if I want.* There was no one around, not in this dark, these twenty miles from town, and he could slap her rump and pull her hair, and she could bite down hard on his finger, and Lacey wanted it all, how he handled her, how it could feel like they owned not just the house, but the whole hill, and the woods, their own skin, one another.

Those were the only times he was rough—he'd never hit her, or the girls, not even after he got real bad. He would get mean and he would cry and he would scream, but he never raised his hand. Only if she asked him, only if they were out on the porch, and it was just a part of their way, as good a feeling as his nimble cock poking at the inside parts that made her sing.

It wasn't that he had stopped loving her, no, and he hadn't stopped loving the girls. The unbalance in his brain came first, then the drugs. And once he had the drugs, his brain needed more, and he started doing things and disappearing so he could have more. It was like being sick. She hadn't made it all up to defend him—the lawyer had shown her papers, a diagnosis, to prove it was true. But when she told Annette, all Annette had said was "You're planning on telling that to a judge?"

Lacey was all out of tears in a while, and she was shivering under those blankets, as cold as if she weren't inside a house at all. She got up and found the coin jar under the sink. She had been filling it back up ever since Robbie left. It was mostly pennies. She gave Jenkins a pat goodbye and carried the jar out to the car. She drove downhill along the service road to the store. Inside she found a clerk and asked for Hank, and she waited for him by the coin machine, trading in all her pennies for a flimsy receipt that explained she had earned nine dollars. Hank surfaced from one of the aisles in blue jeans and a pretty yellow workers' vest. His hair was long and combed over so it hung down one side of his face. He waved her out the sliding doors and into the parking lot, where he kissed her behind the ear and lit a cigarette to hear her out. He didn't offer her one.

She explained about the 15 percent, and how she still had stamps for food, and she had paid the mortgage, and she had been careful and budgeted for everything, everything except the gas. It hadn't gotten cold yet since Robbie went away. She didn't know.

"God, Lacey, you're as pretty as you ever were. Do you know that? Your teeth are fit to eat."

Lacey had hardly felt beautiful at all these days; her eyes were red from too little sleep, and she hadn't been able to afford her good shampoo in weeks. But she did still have her smile, at least. She looked at Hank and turned it on.

"You ever think about selling that house?"

"Robbie wouldn't like that. It's the only thing we got to pass down to the girls."

"Well, you're not going to be able to pass down anything if they freeze to death."

"Can you bring me on to work or not?"

Robbie finally tapped a cigarette out of the pack and handed it to her. She bent over the lighter in his hands, and when she straightened up, she saw he was staring at her. She blew the smoke out in his direction. They had been teenagers together, all three of them, her and Hank and Robbie, when they were all in high school and working at the Hot Wing. Hank had a face full of acne then but it had cleared now to nothing but scars, dark shadows along his cheeks. He didn't look half bad anymore, with his braces off, his hair washed clean. He had always wanted her, she knew, and she had liked having him get things off a high shelf for her, or rush over with a washcloth if she burned herself on the oil. But Robbie was the one who had won her. They had all stayed friends for a while, until the girls came and they moved out of town, and forgot all about Hank until they came in to do their shopping with the girls, and he would nod at them, and they would ask after his mother, and he would look down at his walkie-talkie and wait for someone to call for him, to request a manager in an aisle on the other end of the store.

"You know I got a place?"

Hank sucked on the tip of his cigarette and let it dance between his lips.

"I've got a yard and everything. You and your girls would fill it right up."

"You would do that for us? You've got an extra room?"

"I've got a pullout in the basement."

"It would be tight, all four of us on the couch, but it's better than letting the girls freeze—"

Hank laughed and shook his head.

"Lacey May, you never could take a hint."

Lacey tilted her head and looked at him confused.

"Let's put it this way—if you stayed with me, it wouldn't cost you nothing, but it wouldn't be free neither."

The wind blew hard and kicked up the smell of gasoline from the pump at the edge of the lot. Lacey noticed she hardly felt the cold, her skin slowly getting used to the chill, but she pulled her coat around her anyway.

"How would I explain that to the girls?" she said. "They think their father's on the coast, working a fishing job."

Hank shrugged. "I'm a man, not a saint, Lacey."

She stared at the white button on his vest: TEAM LEADER. Until now she had never believed the stories she had heard about him. The rumor was that he was so lonesome he had started taking the high school girls who stocked the aisles out to the back lot during his breaks. He gave them overtime and the shifts they wanted if they let him fondle their tits for a while. It wasn't the worst thing she'd ever known a man to do, but she wouldn't have pinned it on a man like Hank.

"I think I'll go inside and get a few things for the girls," Lacey said. She stepped around him and walked toward the store.

"You were always too proud, Lacey May."

When she didn't turn around, Hank called after her again.

"You made the wrong choice!"

This time Lacey hollered back.

"I told you it's not his fault! It's his brain!"

With her nine dollars, Lacey bought a tin of coffee, another block of cheese, a magazine about TV stars and their weddings, and a fistful of bubblegum lollipops for the girls. She drove back with the heat on low, but still she felt like she was suffocating, so she rolled down all the windows. It was as if she missed the cold. She let the frosty air whip around her, even if she might regret it later, even if she'd have to fight the temptation later on to go sit in the car and let the engine run.

When the girls clattered in after school, Lacey gave them each a lollipop, and Diane, who had prematurely lost three baby molars to cavities, looked at her mother, as if to see if she were sure. Lacey nodded at her and said, "That's right, sweetheart. Go ahead, let it rot your teeth."

She asked the girls to tell her what they had learned in school while she made their sandwiches and mixed choco-late powder into hot milk. Diane and Margarita huddled under a blanket on the floor, Jenkins weaseling his way underneath. Noelle sliced up the cheese into perfect thin squares.

"You could perform surgery with those hands," Lacey said. "Gifted hands!" She knew she'd heard the phrase some-where but she couldn't remember exactly where. Noelle didn't seem to be touched by the compliment and didn't look up from the cutting board as she pushed the knife through the brick of cheese.

"How come Daddy doesn't come back on the week-ends? We've been to the beach—it's not that long a drive."

Lacey gave her a little tap on the nose. "Cause that's when they catch the biggest fish—something about the tide. When he calls, I'll have him explain it."

They ate on the couch, the plates on their laps, their hands over their blankets, Jenkins's fur starting to knot into the fibers of the wool.

"Is it still winter in our house?" Margarita asked, and Lacey kissed the top of her head.

"Yes, ma'am. Isn't it fun?" She turned on the TV.

They watched a cop show, and the girls didn't mention their father. They didn't notice Lacey look away when the officers caught up to the burglar. They wrestled him down onto the shoulder of the highway. They knocked his head against the grass.

The phone rang, and Lacey leapt up. It was Robbie! He'd finally gotten the money she put in his commissary, and he was placing a call. It would all be worth it—heat or no heat, the girls would hear their father's voice, they'd remember they had a father, and that he hadn't wanted to leave.

The phone was painfully cold to her ear and Lacey waited for the operator's voice to come through, for her chance to press a button and choose to accept a call from a county inmate.

"Miss Ventura," said a bland voice. It was the receptionist from yesterday.

"Yes, this is Mrs. Ventura."

She waited to hear they'd found her a job, maybe in a laundromat, selling those tiny bottles of detergent to people who had forgotten theirs, or maybe even a doctor's office where she could put away supplies, label the samples of pee, point people to the bathroom. She would smile and give directions like "Yes, ma'am, make a left at the end of the hall." She had a good manner—her boss at the Hot Wing had told her so—and she had her smile. Most of all, she wasn't stupid. There was plenty she could learn to do.

"Mrs. Ventura, the check you gave us with your application bounced. We can't process any of the paperwork until you write us a new one—and refund us the thirty dollars we got charged for your bad check."

"I had the money when I first wrote the check. Why'd you wait so long to cash it?"

Lacey didn't hear the receptionist's answer because Margarita had started to cry.

"Mommy, I'm so cold. Why is it so cold?" she said.

"Cause Daddy's fishing," Noelle said, shaking her head. "Cause he left us. Didn't he left us? He doesn't want us anymore."

Lacey dropped the phone and slapped her child. When Noelle started shouting, Diane joined in, saying they shouldn't fight, so Lacey slapped her too, and Margarita for good measure, and sent them all to their room. When she picked up the phone, the receptionist wasn't on the line. She could hear Margarita in the bedroom, still crying about the cold. They would be warmer if they all gathered in her bed—she knew that—but she let them cry softly into the dark. She had been stuck with the cold for two days and they were carrying on as if the heat weren't on at all. When the girls were quiet, whether because they fell asleep or gave up on crying, she stood and turned the temperature up five degrees.

She hadn't wanted to send the last of the government check to Robbie, but he needed all kinds of things: new underwear and cups of instant soup because the meals they served inside were rotten. He was clean and seeing a doctor who gave him pills that helped, so she did the math and then deposited the money. He had promised to save some of the money to call.

In the night she went to check on the girls. She stuck their little feet underneath the blankets, sealed the covers around their skinny bodies like cocoons. It was easier for them. They weren't around all day. They only sensed his absence in the few hours before bed—Lacey never got away from it.

Diane woke with a fever. She was eating her cereal too slowly, and when Lacey touched her hand to the girl's forehead, her skin was burning up.

Noelle put her hand on her hip and stood up from the table. "You did this," she said. "This is all your fault."

And Margarita chimed in, "When's Daddy coming? When Daddy's here, it never gets so cold."

"It's sixty degrees in here!" Lacey screamed. "That's the temperature right now in California!" She had made up the fact, but it sounded true. What did they know? When they were home, they were under blankets, and sixty degrees wasn't bad for such short whiles—it took hours for the cold to snake into your bones. It had started to happen to her. She had risen with a pain in her knee, a stiff back, as if, in two days, the cold had managed to make her old. She started yelling at the children that they were spoiled, that they were off to school where it was warm while she had to stay behind.

"Well it's Friday now!" Noelle shouted. "What's going to happen on the weekend?"

And while Noelle yelled at her, and Margarita started moaning about her daddy and a tingling in her fingers and toes, Diane vomited on the kitchen floor. Jenkins started to lap it up, and Lacey kicked him hard.

The girls nearly missed the bus, and Lacey had to chase it down in her slippers and her robe. The only girl who kissed her goodbye was sick little Diane, her face crimson, her hair sticking to her face with sweat. She had to have the heat on by the time the girls came back. She was determined.

On her walk up the hill, Lacey couldn't understand how tired she felt. Ever since they took Robbie away, her days were emptier, as if he had been the one she stayed at home to raise. Part of it was autumn—there was nothing to do in the yard, no vegetables to water or uproot, no grass to cut. The house was clean, the girls gone. There was hardly any cooking to do without Robbie's paycheck—no chickens to roast, or turnips, no beef to bread and fry. She couldn't spend a day making sandwiches, slathering government mayonnaise on bread, waiting for the cheese to get slippery and hot. And there was no more of the sweet waiting—for him to call between fixing up cars to see how her day was, or to apologize for the scene he'd made last night and say he didn't remember, no more running to meet him at the door, his clothes thick with the smell of paint thinner, sweat, and other men.

Lacey went to the shed for her rake and shears, then she walked across a quarter acre of woods to knock on the door of the fat, unmarried nurse. Lacey read the name on the mailbox—*Amelia Green*. She started rehearsing the lines in her head. *If you'd be so kind, Miss Amelia.*

It was a while before the door opened, and Amelia stood in a checkered pajama set, fleshy and tall, her hair in a big wet knot on top of her head. Lacey could feel the heat streaming out the open door, and it seemed to overtake the cold outside to touch her fingertips, her frozen nose, and her lips, which she hadn't realized were cracked. She was embarrassed, but she smiled her smile anyway.

"I wanted to see if I could help clear up your yard."

Amelia Green stared at her as if she had no teeth at all.

"You know, prune back the bushes and pull up the weeds, rake the leaves. I could wash your car too. The front steps." The gutters could use a cleaning, as well, or she could sweep up the leaves covering the porch. If Miss Amelia had a ladder, she could even clear the roof.

She realized then she should have changed out of her robe and slippers. She could have put on her good blue blouse. Her boots. She could have dressed herself like a woman who worked.

Amelia Green clucked her tongue.

"Why would I pay you to clean up this yard when it's gonna be covered up in ice in a few weeks?"

Lacey wondered whether to tell her about Robbie, whether this nurse, whose lights were always on, whose house was warm, who had a babysitter drive up through the woods to watch her boy while she went to the hospital to draw blood or clear bedpans or take temperatures or whatever it was she did, could ever understand what it was to have a husband, to love him with your bones.

"My propane is down to 15 percent. Probably 10 now."

"That'll last you till Monday when the truck comes around. You need their number?"

Lacey explained her middle girl had a fever; her youngest was only six. They were making out all right with Robbie gone—it was just the heat.

"What I'm trying to say is, I ain't got it, and I don't know what else to do."

Amelia crossed her arms. "You see, the rest of us, we work. We don't depend on the government or no husband."

"Maybe you could just lend me a few gallons out of your tank to hold us over."

"If you expect me to pity you, I don't. You're not the only one who married some son of a bitch who can't take care of his own kids—"

"It's not his fault. He's got a chemical unbalance—"

"They all do," Amelia said, and she went to close the door.

Lacey pushed her hand against the frame.

"My babies are freezing."

"This is real life, sweetheart. Find a way—that's what women do."

"You fat cunt."

The nurse slammed the door.

Lacey stomped through the woods, smashing down fallen branches and the still-green grass under her slippers. When she got near the house, she could hear her phone ringing. She ran to make it in time.

"Robbie?"

It was the school nurse. Diane had vomited again on the bus, and she needed to go home. Could Lacey come and pick her up? On the long drive to the school, Lacey found herself shaking. When she went to the office and gave her name, they sent her straight to the principal's office.

Margarita was the one who had spilled the beans. When her teacher asked her why she kept putting her head down on her desk, she said she hadn't slept right because it was winter in her house. And since Diane threw up on the bus, it wasn't hard to put two and two together.

"I'm working on a solution," Lacey said.

The principal shook her head and asked what was going on—wasn't her husband a mechanic at the body shop off Haw? Lacey hadn't realized that they didn't know. Shouldn't there have been a letter that got sent from the court or the jail to the school? Wasn't there something the government had done to spare her this moment?

"My husband got high and stole a cop car. Not one of the black-and-white sheriff's ones, a regular one. It just belonged to a cop. It was parked in front of a bar downtown. He didn't know."

The principal said she was sorry, but she couldn't look the other way. Lacey said she knew she wasn't the only one to ever have to lower the heat, one November or another, but the principal didn't back down.

"I'm sorry, Mrs. Ventura, but after Monday, I'll have to make a call. You've got the weekend."

Lacey went around to the classrooms and got all her girls. They drove home in silence, past the houses all in a row, then out of town to where it was all fields and forgotten barns, the railroad tracks where they had to stop and wait for a train to pass.

"Woo-woo!" sang Margarita and it made Diane smile weakly, her cheeks pink.

Back at home, she boiled cans of broth for the girls, peeled and dropped in potatoes, a tin of shredded chicken. And then she made grilled cheeses too and chocolate milk and they carried it all into Lacey's bed, where she piled blankets on top of the girls and then crawled in herself.

"If one of us is going to be sick, we might as well all be sick together," she said, and she kissed her girls on the nose. It was still light out, hardly past midday.

"Aren't you going to turn up the heat? You heard what the principal said."

Noelle still wasn't looking at her, her ears flushed bright, and Lacey wondered whether she was catching a fever too, or if she was just ashamed. Maybe her friends at school knew now how they had been living.

"Hush," Lacey said. "I'm going to tell y'all a story."

The girls squeezed in closer to their mother, even Noelle, although she probably only wanted to get warm.

"Once upon a time, there was a princess, and she lived in a castle deep in a forest. And she lived there with her sisters, but there was no one else around cause all the men were at war. It was a kingdom with no old people, you see, so there was no one to show them what to do while the men were gone. How to fill the moat, how to feed the horses, how to keep the torches lit, and the dungeons clean—"

"What's a moat?" Diane asked, sucking on a Tylenol and making a face. Lacey told her to swallow it.

"So they saddled up the horses, and they went riding, far and far, over valleys and streams to a kingdom they had heard of where all the men went to war and never came back. The princesses in this kingdom showed them how to do all the things they were afraid of—how to clean the stables and grow wheat, how to cast spells, and burn the dead—"

"How to fill the moat?"

"Mmhm—and when they knew everything they needed to know, they went riding back to their kingdom, all day, and all night, and when they got there, they weren't afraid anymore. They were all ready to rule, but they didn't have to after all, cause while they were gone, the princes had all come home. They had won the war."

Diane asked whether they had a party, and Lacey explained they hadn't just held parties but weddings. One wedding every day, one for each princess and her prince.

"And they feasted and they drank and they ate chocolate cake, and when the moon came up, they would go out on boats and talk about how it felt like there never was any war at all."

Noelle rolled her eyes. "Short war," she said.

"I like that story!" Margarita shouted. Lacey told her to lower her voice.

"I hate it. It's stupid," Noelle said, and she crossed her arms. "They ride their horses all that way to another kingdom and they learn all those things, and it doesn't even matter. They never even get a chance to rule."

Lacey wanted to explain that at least they knew how, and you should never give up a prince if the prince really loves you, but Noelle plugged up her ears, and Margarita shouted that she wanted to be a princess, and Diane stood solemnly and asked for someone to go with her to the bathroom because she had to throw up.

After the girls nodded off, Lacey slipped out from under the blankets to clean up the bowls and the mugs they had left on the floor. She shut off the light and went out to the back porch with one of the leftover lollipops from the supermarket. She sucked it down to the white stick, cracking the hard candy between her front teeth. She counted the days on her fingers since she had sent Robbie the money—five—and he still hadn't called. *Goddamn you, Robbie*, she thought. Goddamn.

She went back inside, and she didn't feel a difference anymore between inside and out. Maybe it wouldn't matter for her anymore, whether the heat was high or low or off. She wouldn't be able to shake off the chill for a while—it was under her skin now. But the girls.

Lacey found her old address book in a drawer, and she went flipping through the pages until she found him there, alphabetized by last name. *Sommer, Hank.* She carried the address book and the phone out to the living room. She muted the TV and dialed, waited for the ringing to stop.

"I knew you'd change your mind," he said, and Lacey smiled. With her free hand, she turned up the thermostat a full ten degrees.

STRAIGHT DOLLARS OR LOOSE CHANGE

LaToya Watkins

I been sitting here, waiting for them to lead you in. Fifteen minutes feel like fifty. I distract myself by counting the number of water stains on the ceiling. Then I figure how many women in the room. How many men? Children? The brother and sister that were carrying on during the bus ride up here are now begging their momma for money. Banging on the glass of the vending machine again and again. They stop when one of the guards finally stomps over and motions for them to sit. Stay. Some folks pacing now. Others holding up the wall. We all waiting. Waiting for the sound of locks to spring open.

I study the women in the room with fresh makeup and fresh dollars. I have neither. There was no time to stop at Phillips 66 this morning, not after Mr. Bodee took sick. So I wait for you with two crumpled bills in one pocket and a folded-up piece of paper in the other. The sea of orange jumpsuits will soon roll in like some riptide. I stare at the big metal door you will walk through, and hope I can find the words this time before they're swept away. My eyes go back to the vending machine, to the rows of salted chips in C6 and the rows of Reese's in B4. You always had a thing for peanut butter. That's about the one thing that hasn't changed in all this.

There's no line at the candy machine when the men file in. They all serious until they scan the room and see their families. Then their faces light up. Finally, I see you. You being led in my direction by a guard who looks like he's still in high school, his face dotted with pus pimples.

You start talking fast before you sit down. We got two and a half hours.

"Hey, sis," you say as you start drumming on the table between us. "How you been?"

I study you long and hard. This visit has to last. You only thirty, and already balding at the top. Your eyes like hard rust on an old penny. Before all this, they were brown.

"How's Grandma?" you say. "She still giving you a hard time?"

Grandma has never been here to see you. Not once in the eleven years you been in Lamesa. Neither has Momma, for that matter. I open my mouth, but the words are swept away. I want to tell you that Grandma put a lock on the refrigerator door last week. She was always like some sentry on watch when it came to food. At three hundred pounds she can stand to miss a meal or two. The thought of a padlocked icebox makes me bust out laughing, especially since I know she hid the key in the bottom of her shoe. She should have put a lock on Uncle Elroy's door. Kept him away from you. I think about Elroy now and my stomach knots up.

"She fine, Calvin," I say. "I know how to stay out her way."

You nod. Smile. Look away. Your eyes dart around the room. A long line has formed at the vending machine. One by one they feed fresh dollars and loose change into the slot. You shift in your seat before turning back to me.

"How are things out there, G? What's going on?"

You the only one who calls me G. On his good days, Mr. Bodee calls me Gem. Short for Gemini. He tells me that I'm a jewel. I start to tell you about Mr. Bodee ending up in the hospital and my being up all night waiting for his family to come in from Dallas. I've only known Mr. Bodee for about a year, but already he feel like family.

"Remember the man I work for?" I say. "Had to rush him to the ER late last night."

Calvin laughs out loud. "What you do to that old man, G?"

I want to tell you that I button his shirt and cook his potatoes, and that we read together. But the words leave me again. Before I know it, someone else catches your eye. You follow a tall skinny gal walking toward the long wall for a telephone visit. She is carrying her bra in her hand and all the men are staring at her. Women too. Her breasts look like they'll bring her to the floor. I have nothing to speak of, so I can get by with a boy's T-shirt most of the time.

"Look at her," you say.

I saw her pacing before, but I look again. She sits down in front of bulletproof glass and picks up the receiver. The man opposite her touches the scratched glass and she follows suit. It's as close to a contact visit as they will get.

Their raised hands remind me of Momma, waving at me. I saw her from the bus this morning. First time in years. I don't know whether I should share the news everybody been whispering about since Uncle Elroy and your trial became the gossip of the day. Momma's not your favorite subject. But then I decide to just come out and say it.

"I saw Momma from the bus on my way up," I say.

You look back without a word.

I don't tell you the rest. That it was at least 110 degrees in the shade and she had on a purple turtleneck sweater and denim shorts. I was embarrassed for her at first. Then Mr. Bodee's words came into my head and I tried to remember who Momma was before the track marks and before the state took us. All I can come up with is how she smelled like Blue Magic pomade whenever she hugged me. Mr. Bodee says that's a start. He was a sixth grade teacher for thirty-seven years before he started forgetting stuff, like how to button his shirt and find his way home. But he still knows a lot.

Your penny eyes grow harder. Still, you say nothing. I take advantage of the silence and say one last thing.

"She waved at me. She knew who I was and waved at me."

You are disgusted. You roll your penny eyes. "Yeah," you say. "She call you out by name?" You don't wait for me to answer. You shift in your seat and breathe in deep. I bite my lip and wish I could call the words back. But it's too late. We sit stone-faced.

We are saved by the children laughing at the next table, reading with their father. It is the sister and brother from before. I wonder if they're teaching their father how to read the way Mr. Bodee is teaching me. Me and Mr. B. use picture books too. The little girl is doing the reading. She helps me find the words to tell you.

"Calvin, I can't come Saturdays no more," I say fast. "At least for a while."

"Why? You sick or something?"

"No. Not sick." I pull the folded-up paper from my pocket and push it toward you.

"What's this?"

"I'm starting classes at community college. Saturdays. My free day."

You look at the paper. Then you stare at me with your hard penny eyes as if you are trying to place my face. I'm your only family.

"Good for you, G," is all you say before you look away from me. There's another long line at the vending machine.

"You bring change with you?"

I shake my head. I think about Archie, the white guy who opens up Phillips 66 on Saturday mornings. He was probably waiting at the register with my ninety-nine-cent bean burrito and five crisp dollar bills, the way he does every Saturday. But I missed him this morning.

I stretch out my leg and stuff my hands deep into the pocket of my secondhand jeans. I fish around until I find the dollar I've been searching for and pull the crumpled thing out. You look down at the dollar and frown.

"Awh, Gemini. What I tell you about them raggedy dollars? You know that machine be tripping. You better hope it works or you owe me two next week."

It's as if you didn't hear one word I said about college. I try to remind you, but you cut me off.

"Yeah, whatever. Just remember for next time. Straight dollars or loose change. And get some money together to put on my books for commissary."

"Sure, next week," I say as I nod my head. Then I get up and make my way to the end of the line. I can feel you stare hard at me, like Mr. Bodee do sometimes. I look your way and see you drop your pennies to the floor like so much loose change.

LA HIJA DE CHANGÓ

Ivelisse Rodriguez

Every day there is the exaggerated slurping of my mother drinking her coffee. She occupies a small table by the wall that is overrun with knickknacks, sticky placemats, and unopened mail centered on the table where napkins should be.

"Morning, Mom," I say as I bend down to kiss her cheek.

"I heard you on the phone last night," she says. She slouches there in a navy sweat suit, frizzy bangs, and a careless ponytail as if my father just left last week and not nine years ago.

"Mmm hmmm," I say slowly.

The kitchen is cramped; two people fit uncomfortably here.

"I'm sorry, Mom. Boy trouble, the usual," I say in an overly peppy voice.

She shakes her head at me. "It's not fine, Xaviera. Not fine at all. You're too much like your father."

The refrigerator is crowded with memories and magnets. Tacky fruit magnets hold up pictures of me in elementary school, me in Puerto Rico with my grandmother the last time I saw her, and a picture of me and my parents when I was younger.

I turn away from her. It's not an insult like she thinks.

. . .

"You three are really going?" Steve asks with a mouthful of broccoli. "What if she chops your titties off?" The rest of the kids around the lunch table bust out laughing.

"Shut up, Steve. What do you know about Santería?" I say.

That's the problem with these Whitney School kids, all this education and you'd think they'd be less apt to make stupid-ass comments. Me and Melo are the only ones from Spanish Harlem here, and as much as they sweat us for being from there, it doesn't stop them from lapsing into their privilege. And hanging around them so much, me and Melo sometimes participate. Melo more than me because she enjoys all this rich shit, but every day I have to go back home and smack myself back into reality.

My new boyfriend, Anthony, makes fun of me. Hey, little princess, you want some tea? Is your chauffeur waiting for you? He goes to public school and is just some guy from around the way. And sometimes I fear that he might look at me in my black sweater, with "The Whitney School" scripted in pink over my heart, and think that I'll walk down these streets one day and see him as something else, or as nothing at all. Like the ones before him.

Ever since I've been at the Whitney School, I've had nothing but dating problems. Back in junior high school, all a boy had to be was cute and dress nice. Now, I'm looking for a boy who's smart, likes the things I do, and is going to go to college someday. But I don't go out with any guys from the Whitney School. Most of them are white, and the few Black guys here just seem corny. It's enough that I've made friends and that I play on the lacrosse team. I'm starting my third year, but at first, it was hard here. Me and Melo didn't even bother trying to make friends with anybody; we figured they would just be stuck up. But Tania and a couple of other girls who were in our classes were nice to us a few weeks into our first semester here.

Tania, who is a Park Avenue girl all the way, is making the trek uptown with us today to the botánica. Even though she's Puerto Rican, I know she's never been to East Harlem before, and I'm sure that she'll sit here tomorrow during fifth-period lunch and regale them with stories of the big bad ghetto. But she wanted to come when she heard we were going, in fact insisted. She says she has problems too.

I've known Melo since we were in the third grade, and even then, boys would turn away from their marbles to sit by her during recess. But now, some boy, Chris, a transfer student, won't give her the time of day, so she's bugging out, hence her sojourn with me to the botánica. But to me and the majority of the world, Melo is through and through exquisite. She doesn't realize that she is one of those girls who 99 percent of the time will never be alone. And Tania, no matter what, is vivacious; her laughter can be heard across the school cafeteria. In the end, if she doesn't have a boy, she has herself.

And me? I come from a long line of spinsters. On looks, sure we could get a man, but there must be something in our hearts that sends out signals. Like a snake ready to strike. So I have boyfriend after boyfriend. Anybody else would have been branded with a big "S" on her school uniform, but my strength emanates and they don't. They find weaker ones to brand.

On this long line I want to be a shining star, different from my mother. I want that pounding of the heart that I'm sure somebody promised me when I was young. Some neighbor, male or female; family friend; doctor or nurse—not knowing my family's charred history—must have pulled up my pigtails and looked at my open face and said right into my ear: "Someday some man is going to be lucky." And I took that to mean that I would be lucky too. Symbiosis.

· · ·

Tania keeps giggling at everything she reads. We try to ignore her even though we have matching uniforms on and it's obvious to anyone that we're together. We should have brought her tomorrow, Friday, when we can wear what we want to school. The moment we've been waiting for, or rather dreading, arrives. She calls me and Melo over to her from across the store. She hasn't taken into account, either, that the store is the size of my living room.

"Oh, my God. Xaviera! Melo! Come look at this. It says that to get a man, you have to go to the mountains. Take ALL your clothes off. Mix some menstrual blood with rat feces and smear it on yourself!"

The customer at the counter makes a point of rolling her eyes at us. We navigate our way toward Tania trying not to break the ceramic statues of Jesus and Santa Barbara that seem to follow our every move. We reach Tania and try to remain serious, but as always she infects us. Lizard tongues for love. Lettuce and hair to get rid of your enemies. Milk and honey to solve your money problems. We giggle and gasp with her until Doña Serrano, the woman behind the counter, finally comes over.

Women dressed like her are the kind we make fun of in the halls of the Whitney School. Bright-blue leggings and an oversized yellow T-shirt with a company's logo barely legible. "Alex's Autos. Springfield, MA." And I wonder how many arms poked out of that shirt to travel here, to a botánica in the middle of Spanish Harlem. 116th and Lexington.

"Te puedo ayudar?" she asks.

I understand her, but I edge Tania toward the front, just in case. Even though Tania is from the wrong side of the tracks—Me and Melo's code for the rich kids at the Whitney School—she probably speaks Spanish better than all the people who live in East Harlem.

In the meantime, I try to get my courage up. Think about how I first met Anthony. It was four months ago at the Puerto Rican Day Parade festival. Melo pointed him out, saying, "That's the one. That's the one you usually like." I laughed, but his look was familiar. Curly black hair, wearing the latest gear. We kept looking at him and his boys until he finally noticed. He brought me an alcapurria and a coke. Anthony was the first boy from my neighborhood who told me he wanted to go to college since I've been at the Whitney School, so, naturally, I swooned.

I pray that this woman speaks English. I step up and say, "Love spells," even though I know it's probably not right to call them that.

She looks us over and smiles. She reminds me of my grandmother. And not in some superficial way where all old people look alike. But she really does look like her. Caramel skin that is still taut but makes you feel like it's wrong. That it would be far more attractive and true to this person's nature if it were crinkled and creased. And she has the same short white afro.

"What kind of spell are you looking for? Do you want him to love you more? Less? Do you want to use him and then throw him away? Do you just want his attention . . . ?" she asks.

"Well, I want my boyfriend to stay with me and fall in love," I say.

"But you're la hija de Changó," she fires at me. Then pointing to Melo. "Yemaya." Then Tania. "Oshún. You three must make all the boys melt."

That's what she called me. La hija de Changó. My grandmother first, now her. I don't know much about Santería—my mother's keeping her knowledge on the hush hush—but I hope that this woman is for real and will show us something.

. . .

"So, you're all alive, I see. And you, Park Avenue Princess, I see you didn't get robbed," Steve says the next day at lunch.

"Steve, one day I'm going to bring your white ass home with me and drop you in the middle of East Harlem with no cab money to get out," I say.

Steve speaks and sprays. He always talks with his mouth full. "Latino boys love me, which is more than I can say for you and Melo. So, I'm sure I can find a way out." He swipes at the ketchup running down his chin. "Anyway, back to Tania, how was it?"

I wait for Tania to sell us out and talk about how nasty she thought our neighborhood was, but she surprises me.

"It was fine, Steve." She shrugs her shoulder. "It was just a normal New York neighborhood. Nothing scary about it."

Melo smiles at me. Tania sees the neighborhood the way me and Melo have always seen it. Tall stone buildings, worn sidewalks, and intermittent graffiti that is just regular to us.

"Well, what did you get? How does it work?" Steve asks.

Tania looks at me, and I speak up. After all, my grandmother and my father knew all about Santería. "First, the woman, Doña Serrano, told us we were daughters of certain orishas. Meaning we have the characteristics of these gods, and they protect us too. My orisha is Changó. He's a warrior and kind of a player."

"Uh-huh," Steve says, rolling his eyes.

"You asked, Steve. Then she told us to buy candles and pray to our saints. So we did. But I also bought a book about the history of the religion."

"OK, but do you think it will work?" he asks.

"Well, when you fall in love with me, Steve, you can let me know," Tania says, and the rest of us start laughing.

"OK, that's when we know everything has gone a little haywire," he says.

As we leave lunch period, I think about how far me and Melo have come. I realize how comfortable we are here now. I had never been real sure about Tania before. I had never met a Puerto Rican like her, one with money, and she talks just like the white girls at the Whitney School and she looks white. Me and Melo have been to her house plenty of times, but we've never invited her over to ours. Not even yesterday. But now, I imagine it's something we could do.

. . .

Since I've been at the Whitney School, my guidance counselor, Ms. Kennedy, has been on me to do well in my classes and take advantage of the education I'm getting. This is my guidance counselor from the program me and Melo are in. The program gets smart kids from certain neighborhoods to go to these rich kids' schools. Ms. Kennedy grew up in Harlem, went to a boarding school, and was one of the few Black students there, so she thought it was a good idea for me and Melo to go to the Whitney School together. So we could have each other's backs. Thank God for Melo. Without her, I would feel completely lost. But me and Melo are lucky in that we got to stay in the city and didn't have to go to boarding school like some of the other kids in our program.

Ms. Kennedy has been like my academic mother, the one who looks out for me in terms of school stuff, and she likes to sometimes give me regular mom advice too. She says that once I get to college, I can meet a boy on my level, that I shouldn't waste my time with these boys from my neighborhood, that they aren't going anywhere. What has happened with every guy that I've met since being at the Whitney School is that we've just had little in common. Like with all the boys before Anthony, things started to go badly between me and him. I try to talk to him about the things that interest me—art, lacrosse—but he doesn't get any of that stuff, and he just stopped trying. The only thing we can agree on is hip-hop.

But I still see things in Anthony that other people don't.

• • •

I've been studying for the PSATs, so I've used that as an excuse to stay away from Anthony. I told him it would just be a few intense weeks when I would have to be on lockdown. While this is all true, I'm also giving my mini-Santería time to work. My mother refuses to answer any of my questions about Santería, and the closest I came to learning about it was when I was thirteen. I begged my mother to send me to PR after I got accepted into the Whitney School.

"She's older now. I don't know." I overheard my mother hesitating on the phone while talking to my tía Chucha in PR.

My tía won her over, though.

When I was in PR, my grandmother, who hadn't seen me since I was six, examined me, held me by the shoulders, and finally said, "Tu eres la hija de Changó."

"Mai, you're going to scare her, and you know what Carmen said," my tía Chucha cried out.

"What? What does that mean?" I whined. It was clear my tía and grandmother had big mouths, and I was excited at the prospect of all these family secrets tumbling from them. But with a quickness, they got as tight-lipped as my mother.

I could see the relief on my mother's face when I got back home the following week. She was in a talkative mood as she helped me unpack, so I thought I would try again. "Can I ask you about abuela being a Santera?"

My mother freaked out. "You didn't see anything, did you? Your tía Chucha told me mami doesn't do that anymore."

"No, they wouldn't tell me anything. It just slipped out one day. Someone said something about it."

My mother took a long breath and shook her head. "I just don't like to talk about that."

"Why? Did you see something?"

"Yeah, yeah, I did."

I let my questions sit in the air in the hopes that she would answer a few of them.

My mother started to pick at the crusted stains on her sweatshirt. "I used to see my mother do the consultas. The women were in so much pain because of love, and the men were so desperate for money. It was just sad."

"What did abuela do, exactly?"

"Ceremonies. She would do the ceremonies. Orishas would come and take over your body. Whenever they wanted." My mother got quiet.

Then, in a soft, sad voice, she said, "I hated the next morning. Having to clean up all that blood from animals sacrificed the night before."

I pressed her for more information, but she closed the suitcase and the conversation.

As she left the room, she said in a firmer voice, "I left Puerto Rico as soon as I could because of that. Your grandmother was pissed. Said I would let our family traditions die. But the truest thing she said was because your father had been initiated as el hijo de Changó, and I hadn't been initiated, he'd have all the power and I'd have none."

• • •

I don't know how to build an altar, but I clear off a corner of my desk and place on it a picture of me and Anthony, the candle, and a picture of my mother when she was seventeen. It's black and white, so it doesn't capture the prettiness of blue seas and pink houses. She sits on a horse in the middle of Arecibo, the town where she was born in Puerto Rico.

There is a car coming toward her in the background, but she smiles for the camera with glorious brown hair at her side. Tía Chucha told me that I looked just like my mom when she was my age. I love how audacious my mother looks in this picture. It's in my room now because my mother got tired of me always digging through her photos to find it, so she just gave it to me one day. From this picture, I know that she imagined a different life for herself. That even though she may not have had grandiose plans for her life, never dreamed of being somebody important or rich, she did not imagine the life that she has for herself now. She never wears makeup. She never tries to be the pretty girl captured in this picture. She's quiet. When she comes home from work, she sits in the living room and watches TV. Her life revolves around herself. I sometimes come in and watch in silence with her. I like being with her because I think that if I am present, even if I am quiet, maybe she can remember, remember how she used to be.

. . .

"Changó has three girlfriends, well one is his wife, Oba, Oshún, and Oya," I tell Tania and Melo.

"Yup, that sounds like you," Melo adds.

"Shut up," I respond. I've invited them for a sleepover because I was finally able to fix up my room. I've always envied Tania's room. It's like one you see in movies. There's a bedskirt, ruffled pillowcases, and an intricate beaded duvet that covers a down comforter. I couldn't afford all that, but I was able to save enough money to buy a bed-in-a-bag set. It's not the same quality, but everything finally matches, and it's not a hodgepodge of pilled blankets and thin sheets.

"Three? Does he have a favorite?" Tania asks.

"His favorite is Oya, she's the most like him; she also rules lightning. But he's married to Oba, but I think Oshún loves him the most. She's always doing this illmatic shit to get his attention," I say.

"For real? Like what?" Melo asks.

"Well, she got Oba to cut off her ears and serve them in a soup to Changó. Oshún told her it would make Changó stay."

"Dammnnn. I guess that does sound like you," Melo says to Tania.

"I would never be that mean," Tania says innocently.

"Wait a minute, hold up, Oshún is the goddess of love, right? Why can't she keep Changó?" Melo asks.

I put my index finger up in the air, take a long look at my book, but I can't find an answer to that question.

. . .

I am super excited to take Anthony with me to the Ritzy, our annual fall ball at the Ritz-Carlton. Plus, I haven't seen him in weeks. Me and Melo have never gone, but this year we were determined to go, so we saved up all summer long. He's excited to go with me. This is the first time he's seeing my other world. I've told him about what the people are like at the Whitney School, but there is a big difference in me telling him and him seeing it for himself.

As soon as we sit down, Tania comes over and says, "Quick, what does 'sycophant' mean?"

In unison, me, Melo, Chris, and Steve say, "Bootlicker."

"I'm glad everyone has been studying," Tania says.

We are all taking the PSATs next month, so that's all we have been talking about at school. Every time we see each other, it's pop quiz time. I hope Anthony doesn't think it's retarded.

"Yeah, too much," Steve says. "I hate all this pressure. Tomorrow morning I still have to meet with my Kaplan tutor. I tried to get out of it, but my parents wouldn't let me."

"Damn, I'm skipping tomorrow. I'll be too sleepy to pay attention. But I feel guilty too," Chris says.

"I heard that years ago, the teachers arranged for someone to come into the school on the Thursday after the Ritzy, to make up for the missed session tomorrow, since so many of us don't go," Melo says.

"I wonder why they don't do that anymore. That would be super helpful," Tania says.

"Anthony, are you taking the PSATs too?" Steve asks him.

"Not that I know of. Is that a citywide exam? Xaviera's been talking about it, but I just thought it was something y'all were doing," Anthony says without looking directly at Steve.

Chris looks down at his plate, Steve rolls his eyes at Melo, and Tania is trying to hold in her laughter. My face starts to prickle. I start to feel waves in my stomach rolling over and over again, then falling away. I don't want to look at him, so I stare at the students dancing to "I Will Always Love You." Oshún is the goddess of love and marriage. When a woman wants a man, she consults Oshún. She should buy an image of Oshún in her Catholic form, Our Lady of La Caridad del Cobre. Buy a yellow candle. Place a picture of the man she wants on a small plate and pour honey over it. Oshún has an arsenal of herbs, vegetables, and magic that will always make a man succumb to a woman's desire.

Yet Oshún cannot keep the man she wants.

I find that remarkable.

If she fails herself, what of the rest of us?

I imagine Anthony at the Puerto Rican Day Parade festival. I taste the alcapurria. See his smile.

When I look at Anthony again, I will that shame away.

. . .

When I get home from the Ritzy, I sit in front of my altar and think about my grandmother. I hadn't seen her in years when she died. I wish that I had spent more time with her to see what this gift actually is, to see if I have it. I like thinking about how there is this one thing in the world that could set me, us, apart from other families. But it's just been cut off, and I wonder how my mother had the power to break away from our family and not from other things. Because it seems to me that loving my father has been the more detrimental choice. Even though she was the one that broke up with him, she's never really left him.

. . .

A few weeks after the Ritzy, Anthony takes me to his mother's birthday party so I can meet his family. Everyone is going to be there, his mother, his three sisters, and a bunch of cousins. I make sure to look really pretty and be extra nice to his mother. I even say the couple of words that I know in Spanish to her. Anthony walks me around the room and introduces me to everyone. He seems so excited to have me there, and I think back to the first day we met. He tells everyone how I go to some fancy school, and I like how proud he seems of me. Then his cousin Angela from the

Bronx has a stank face before she even meets me. She has red lipstick on and blond highlights in the front of her hair and weighs at least three hundred pounds. She has gold doorknockers with "Angie" written on them, and I know she's going to be trouble before she even opens her mouth.

"So you're Anthony's new girl," she says.

"Yeah," I respond in my most stank East Harlem voice.

She sucks her teeth at me and is like "You talk funny. Where you from?"

"I'm from across the street."

"Oh, I thought you might be from Park Ave or something. Why do you sound like a white girl?"

I hate—*hate*—when people tell me I sound like a white girl. This is the moment I always dread. Ever since I have been to the Whitney School, it's like everyone I meet knows I have gone through some life change and this is the inevitable outcome. I try to calm myself down, as I am surrounded by Anthony's family and I don't want to be a bitch, but at this point Anthony starts laughing.

"Yup, you do sound like a white girl. I was trying to figure that out this whole time," he says.

"I don't sound like a white girl. I'm just educated." Now that shuts them both up, and they both start mad grilling me and I am pissed. I look at Anthony and I feel like an asshole and like he just spit on me, all at the same time. And I'm not sure what I should feel more. Never before have I put up the educational differences between me and Anthony, at least not to him. And now I think that it might be true, what Ms. Kennedy said, that you can never go back, and the moment I walked through the doors of the Whitney School, things would never be the same again.

There is another story about how Changó went from being a man to being a god. He was killed as a baby. But he was the first child born to the new generation, and on his thirteenth birthday, he should have spilled his blood on a tapestry that denoted the birth of a new era of men and leaders. So to honor his lineage, his people made him a god. The Changó in this story is not the young warrior full of braggadocio. Lost from his mother, father, sisters, and the people who would have taken care of him, and lost from the women who would have loved him, this Changó seems melancholy. He lives the life of an orisha, high in the sky. Not a better life, though, as nothing sticks to him. This one remains lost.

. . .

"She called me a white girl! That stupid, fat bitch called me a white girl. Can you believe that? I wanted to deck her. She's lucky she's Anthony's cousin."

"It's mad annoying. I mean, I could see why they could call Tania that because she does talk like a white girl, but us . . . naw, I don't think so."

"But what pissed me off was that Anthony just stood there laughing like what Angie had to say was the funniest shit ever. Man, I wanted to punch him too. I mean, I'm his girl."

"Yeah, well, it's like Ms. Kennedy always says, we can't be going out with these boys from around here anymore. I mean, sweetie, at the end of the day, you're going to go off to college, hopefully an Ivy League one, and what are you going to do with a guy like Anthony?"

"Well, am I going to go out with some white boys, some corny dudes from our school? That's not my style and never will be."

"No, but I think that Ms. Kennedy is right, we will be different people at the end of this, no matter how much you want things to stay the same. Like someone like Chris is cool. You know, someone from the hood, but who at the end of the day will end up in the same place that we will."

"I hate how everybody treats us like we're different. It's like they assume we think we're better than them, and that's not even the case. I mean, we go to school every day and we see how different we are, and then we come home and it's the same shit."

"Yeah, I hear that. But when you're thirty and successful, will any of this matter?"

"Yes, yes, it will matter."

"No, Xaviera. No, it won't matter. You won't even remember Anthony."

. . .

I've been confused about what I should do about Anthony. I'm not sure if I can make this work. I haven't seen him in weeks, and I figure it's only fair to make a decision. He's called me once since the party. I never called him back, and he didn't try again. But tonight, I decide to go and find him.

I run into him at Jefferson Plaza with Diana and David—two kids I went to junior high school with. I am happy to see them, as I haven't seen them in years. Anthony kisses me and the mix of beer and gum tastes sweet in my mouth. He asks me how my classes are going, if I've gotten all my studying done. He continues to drink his forty. He doesn't mention the whole party thing at all. And in my head I keep making excuses for him; I decide to wait until we are alone to see if there is anything he will say about it. We drink, laugh, and bullshit for a while, then Anthony grabs my hand and takes me to the back of the projects.

"So what's up, you've been really busy lately. Is there anything wrong?" he asks.

"No. You know, school's hard."

He mumbles, "OK." And he leaves it at that.

In my imagination, he would push more, trying to find the truth of the matter. He would know that I was not being completely honest and would know that I want an apology.

"Well, I've missed you," he says.

That makes me smile. He rarely says that anymore. And that makes me feel a whole lot better. He grabs my hand and leans down to kiss me. He shoves his hand in my hair. Runs his hand up and down the front of my shirt. He gasps for air, then clenches my skirt in his hands and rushes in. My arms wrap around his neck, and I squeeze my eyes shut. I think about the first time we met, . . . trying to conjure up any happy image, . . . anything to resuscitate. And I wonder if it is like this before someone dies. I look behind him at the playground me and my cousin Jessy used to play in. My eyes trace the familiar scrawling of the hopscotch squares. 1, 2, 3, 4, 5, 6, 7, 8, 9, 10. Where would my rock land now if I threw it?

• • •

I walk around the neighborhood for an hour by myself after leaving Anthony. I know what faces me when I go home. On the streets, I have to retain my composure. I can't cry. I asked Doña Serrano for love, but it's really me who doesn't love. I see couples walking down hallways, holding hands, talking about first loves, and I don't love anyone. No boy, ever. I like them, but I never truly feel what I think I am supposed to. For me, there always comes a moment of rupture, a moment when I just can't look at them the same way. Sure my heart palpitates, but it always seems like I love someone who is never there.

But I don't want to be like my mother, weighed down by this love that can't be fixed, that is always rotten. Or like my father: careless with a human heart. When I leave, it's usually because of something I can't name. Something that lets me know that what we are doing is no longer right, no longer good enough. That moment has come with Anthony, even though I tried to stave it off.

I end up by my old elementary school, and through the gates, I stare at the front steps. The first place I was ever kissed. I remember how that first kiss felt like a starburst, and nothing has sincerely felt like that since.

I muster the courage to go home.

Luckily my mother is not up when I come in. By the time I reach the altar on my desk, a torrent of tears has washed down my face. And I no longer care about what is right or true. I throw myself on my knees in front of my altar. "Please, Changó, make me love him. Make him love me. Please, Changó, don't let me be all alone in this world. Please, Changó. . . ." My words spew out of my mouth faster and faster. "Please, Changó. . . ." I don't want to be alone anymore. I beg until the tears fill my mouth. I punch my open hand and eventually have to put a pillow over my mouth to make sure that I don't wake my mother up. I bang my head against my mattress, then I lean against my bed until I have the strength to crawl in it. When I do, my mother knocks and comes in.

"What's going on?" she says softly.

I shake my head because I can't answer.

"Is it about the boy?" She guesses.

I nod my head.

She comes over and gets in bed with me and pulls my body up against hers. "I know. I know," she says as she kisses my forehead.

She holds me for a long time before she speaks again. "That picture," she says as she clearly stares at her photo from Arecibo. "Your father took that picture. He captured me in a way that I never would be again." She sighs and strokes my hair as my body hiccups against hers.

"Did you ever regret leaving him?" I ask.

My mother puts her chin on the top of my head. "It's not regret . . . only because whatever you want the most is probably already gone. I wanted your father like Oshún wants Changó. At the end of the day, that's why I didn't want to get initiated. I didn't know if I could be like Oshún, if I could resist using all that power for myself. Oshún, whatever she really wants, she doesn't want it through magic."

I see Oshún in her abode surrounded by all her accoutrements of magic. I see how she has loved him, danced for him, spread honey on his lips. And I see her stop. That is as far as she goes. Then I know Oshún does not fail herself, she could do anything to win Changó. Instead, she chooses to chase, tempt only for so long, and lets him walk away. Because what must be cajoled will never stay, and she has never wanted to be the third wife, third love.

I nod my head, and my crying calms down.

When I first read that Changó exchanged the power of divination for the power of dance, I thought it was stupid he would make that trade. But I can see it now. Dancing is a way to connect with people, to touch them, a way to find his way back to a gaggle of bodies in unrest, bodies moving and crushing on top of each other. And maybe Changó is just like the rest of us. He wants to be touched amid all those shifting bodies, and he wants someone to stop and hold him too, and for just a few minutes in time over and over again, he doesn't want to feel so lost.

I think about Anthony. I think about it all, and I give each its destiny back.

JENNY'S DOLLAR STORE

K-Ming Chang

Because Jenny only hired Taiwanese girls, I lied about my father, my mainland surname. I said I'd taken the name Zhang to blend in, and she believed me. *Don't ever think you have to be like those dogs*, she told me, though she loved dogs and owned two mutts, both named Daughter. She opened the store every day with Daughter and Daughter lapping at her radish calves, foaming pink all over her feet. We tossed boxes and Styrofoam peanuts to the dogs, tasking their teeth with cardboard feasts. Jenny's Dollar Store sold most things legally, like thumb-sized flashlights and box macaroni and house slippers (cotton) and outdoor slippers (plastic) and rattan furniture and lighters, but she also sold New Year's firecrackers shipped from her nephew in Miaoli, hidden in a suitcase half full of Styrofoam-stuffed pineapple cakes. In the spring, she sold Daughter's yearly litters, puppies the size of my fist with eyes slicked shut and no teeth yet and blood mucus purpling their fur. Jenny kept the litter in a laundry basket so cramped that a couple of the puppies suffocated to death beneath a squirming quilt of siblings.

What should I do with them? I said about the two dead puppies. Jenny looked at me from the canned food aisle, her full-face visor always lowered over her face in the afternoon, even though the windows of the store were too dusty to breathe light and I wasn't allowed to wipe them with anything but wads of newspaper. *Throw them in the dumpster*, she said, so I knotted each of them into a separate plastic bag—it seemed disrespectful to bag them together—and swung them into the dumpster we shared with the Shanghainese restaurant next door. *The only thing mainlanders want is money*, Jenny said about the restaurant, though I once saw her steal empty cans of wanglaoji out of their side of the dumpster to trade for quarters at the recycling center.

Jenny had worked at this strip mall since I was a little kid, and I used to watch her smoke while squatting on the sidewalk, her visor trapping the smoke and corralling it close to her face, blurring her away. Back then, Jenny was a teenager and there was a laundry next door where Abu folded clothes until late, tucking in the sleeves, surrendering the waist. I would sit on top of the washing machine as it bounced my bones and marvel at how Abu could fold a dress so delicately that when you unfurled it, there wasn't a single crease in it, no sign that it had once been any shape but standing.

I don't know how this bitch keeps getting pregnant, Jenny said, pointing at the dog with two blonde spots on its ass. When she left the store for her sidewalk smoke break, I flipped Daughter and Daughter onto their backs and saw that only one of the Daughters was a bitch. The Daughter that was a boy stood up and licked my wrist, his tongue thin as a whip. One of his ears was torn, and I touched it with my thumb, the serrated edge of the wound, the curdled veins. He shied and spat, swinging a rope of spit at me, barking once, and Jenny stuck her head back into the store to say I shouldn't touch her daughters. With her visor down, I couldn't see her face, only the smoke bruising her shield of dim plastic, fogging her features. She was joking, but I wondered if she'd heard about me, the dyke, the damned, the one who was once caught naked in a creek bed, a girl on my breath.

Jenny told me to come in early the next morning to hang a new banner she'd ordered from Taobao. It was a plastic tarp, blistered by heat, with a pixelated stock photo of an ocean wave. *WATER SOLD HERE*, it said. *THE BEST TASTE IN TOWN*. When the water store in the strip mall went out of business last month—there were rumors that the water caused hallucinations and induced two women to stab each other in the shoulders—Jenny decided to fill up five-gallon jugs with her hose at home and sell the water at the store. *The best taste in town? Water tastes like nothing*, I said, climbing down the rusted ladder. Jenny was leaned against the concrete column, Daughter and Daughter wedged between her calves, her visor already lowered even though it was dim, the sky sputtering on like a stove. *Don't make fun of me, dog ass*, she told me. *All water has a taste.* Back in Taiwan, she told me, she lived next to an old abandoned prison with a wishbone-shaped river behind it, and the water tasted like blood, not the rusty old kind of blood, but the kind so fresh it feigns being sweet. She told me the Nationalists used to build prisons next to rivers because it made it easy to get rid of bodies: The prisoners were shot on the banks so they'd fold into the water and be recycled out to sea. *Easy*, she said. *Practical, that's what those people are.* You didn't even waste bullets, she told me. String all the prisoners together, and shoot just one of them. Then they'll all fall into the water and drown. Nothing wasted. This was how Jenny justified selling expired cans of soup and boxes of frozen pizzas that the dogs gnawed through.

There will always be someone, Jenny said, *who will eat anything.* You wouldn't believe where my mouth has been, she told me. Or maybe you would, she said, laughing, and I walked behind the counter, opening the register even though I knew it was empty. Because her face was visored, I looked at her neck instead, the purple vein that rivered through it. She wasn't any lighter skinned than me, despite always dueling the sun, and her arms were laddered with dark scars, a pattern I recognized: Abu had those scars from years as a cane cutter, all those blade-edged cane leaves snipping her skin to coils of ribbon.

Jenny shouldered boxes out of the storage room. She claimed never to need help, but her lungs filled with smog whenever she bent. She coughed into a mug behind the counter, full of honey-thick phlegm. When I pried open one of the boxes, it was crammed full of costume boas, neon feathers snowing onto the floor, the dogs leaping to snag them midair. She tugged one out and untangled it, telling me to hang them on the back wall where we sold packaged Ping-Pong sets. All the boas smelled like smoke, and some of the feathers were charred at the edges, ash-silver. *I got them at a fire sale*, she said. *A factory blew up.* I joked to her that they were phoenix feathers, but I didn't think she understood. Turning toward the back wall, I whisked one around my wrist, flirting with flight, even though I knew the feathers were synthetic and had never been part of any sky's lineage. Outside the store, Jenny was talking to a teenage girl about firecrackers. Daughter and Daughter circled my legs, barking up at me like I was some bird they were hunting down from a branch, and I laughed, lassoing the Daughters close with my boa, feeding them feathers and forgetting about flight.

It was the only thing I ever stole from her. When it was time for me to close the store, I coiled one up, yellow and glittered, and shuttled it into my purse. At home, Abu was asleep with her face down in a real estate exam prep book, red-dyed sunflower seed shells littered in a blooded halo around her head. *That's where the wealth is*, she always said. *Land. That's the business we need to break into. When everything else is gone, that's all that will be left.* I reminded her that her family had once lost land after the Nationalists took it away, that there was nothing permanent about dirt, but she waved both her hands at me and spat a red shell into her palm and said, *Yes, yes, but it's different here.*

When I woke her up, tickling her cheek with a stray yellow feather from my balding boa, Abu said without lifting her head, *I don't like you working for Jenny.* Their histories were twinned, symmetrical as wings—Jenny came to LA the same year as my mother, on the same China Airlines flight but in opposite aisles—but unlike Abu, Jenny had her own store, plus a firecracker supplier, and though Jenny had no husband or daughters, even my mother conceded that dogs were probably preferable. I pinched the red shells off the pages of her book and cupped them in my palms, each seed still glowing with my mother's spit, bright as a lit matchhead. *Go to bed*, I told her. I saw that the corners of her textbook pages were folded neatly, each dog-ear symmetrical, and remembered how precisely she re-pleated pants at the laundromat, sealing each crease with steam. *Let me study*, she said. *Don't turn off the lights*, she said. *OK*, I said, draping the boa around her neck. *This thing is tickling me*, she said, shrugging. *At least it'll keep me awake.*

Back when Ahma was alive and we shared our yard with her chickens, before we buried her ashes in an abandoned lot, Abu was the one who sent me out to snatch a hen for slaughter. They fled my boneless fists, and I always came home with only feathers. Abu laughed at me for chasing the chickens, my knees rolled in a salty batter of mud and scabs. Finally, she told me that the only way to catch a chicken was to forget about outrunning it: *Don't try to grab at it from behind, just sneak up close. Swing your shadow over it. Straddle it and it will squat for you, thinking you're a rooster trying to mount it.* It worked, and when the hens squatted below me, I plucked them up, passive as stones, and later I convinced the neighbor girl to play Catch a Chicken with me. *You be the hen*, I said, *I'll be me.* She got on her hands and knees, and I squatted over her, tickling her belly until she flipped over, laughing until laces of spit crisscrossed the air and lashed me. Ahma watched from the kitchen window and threw open the door, told me to get my melon ass back inside. *You're not a rooster*, she told me. She said to Abu, *Your girl. Someday she'll do something unnatural with her shadow.*

I told Jenny this story on a slow day. The back of my shirt was mirrored with sweat, and I avoided looking at the back wall where the boas were. I'd tried to take a color too common for her to notice its absence, all those yellow and orange boas swinging from the rack like limp necks, twisted dead by my hands. Jenny laughed at the story, smoking behind the counter with me. She was using the tip dish as an ash tray, since no one gave us any tips anyway. *You're a rooster for sure*, she said, *a real cock*, and I looked at the two of us on the TV screen's security footage, my silhouette small as a thumb, smearing hers into shadow. *I gotta get better cameras*, she said, *I can't even see my own face.* I tried to remember if I'd turned my back to the camera before wadding the boa into my purse.

Jenny turned to me on her stool. Her bleached-copper hair touched her shoulder blades, glittered faux gold in the fluorescence, and there were two moles on her chin so close together it looked like they were either fusing or splitting apart. I wanted to reach out and decide with my thumb-nail, delivering the mole into two, mother and daughter. Around her neck was something new, a pewter crucifix on a chain, dead against her chest as if nailed there. Jenny saw me looking and smiled with one side of her mouth, hiding the hole on the right side where she was missing a molar. *I decided to go to church*, she said, laughing. I told her that my mother used to go to church in Taiwan just because the missionaries gave out free bags of rice at the end of the sermon. *Are you trying to convert me?* I asked her. Jenny laughed again and said, *You an aborigine too? Then you know. When the missionaries came, they gave us Bibles. Then they caught us ripping out the pages to use as toilet paper. Whipped us for it.* I nodded and said I'd heard the story before. When my mother told it, it was a story about how our people couldn't read, how they were so pig-brained, they smeared shit all over the Good Book, God's Word. The way Jenny told it, it was about practicality, how our people believed the only language worth knowing was the body, how holes are what make us holy.

The pewter crucifix looked blue-black in the light, bruised. I reached out and pressed my thumb against it, pinning it in place, and Jenny flinched away. Her heat hustled up through the medal, singeing my thumb. The pendant swung between us, a hollow man with holes in his wrists or his palms depending on what version of the story you believed. Depending on your definition of punishment. On the pad of my thumb, silver dust. I licked it off: bitter as blood, buoyant on my tongue. Not real pewter, but some kind of painted tin disrobing its color, revealing a duller gray beneath. Jenny stared at me, the cross at her neck rising up and down with her breath. One hand braced on the counter, one hand in a fist beside her. I wish I had known what was on my face when I touched my pulse to her pendant. What was beneath my face, that paint. *Sorry*, I said, and stood up from my stool. But the word lodged itself into silence and didn't loosen.

Jenny turned her back to me and pretended to be looking at the TV screen, though there was no one in the store but us. The girl would come back later, the one asking for firecrackers, and Jenny would wave her away. *But you promised me*, the girl would say. *Go away*, Jenny said. I had never once seen her turn away a customer, not even the time a man came in asking to buy Daughter and Daughter, saying they were the right kind of dog for fighting. *Look at these teeth*, the man had said, prying one of the Daughters' mouths open, gripping its gums. Daughter whined, bucked its head, tongue tamped back by the man's gold-ringed thumb. Jenny didn't chase that man away, just asked him if he wouldn't rather buy a puppy and raise it on hunger, not like these spoiled Daughters who have never once fought for anything? Later, Jenny spat on the sidewalk and said to me: *Dogfighting? I'm a barbarian, but not that kind of barbarian.*

But that day, after turning the firecracker girl away, Jenny walked into the storeroom and claimed to be sorting things, her chest pebbled with sweat even though she was barely moving. My thumb was still wet from when I'd licked it, the dime-colored stain still there, metallic. Always my love took the form of rust. One winter, a girl. It was back when the Wangs were always fighting next door, and Abu opened the door so we could eavesdrop better, pretending to be airing out the stink of frying fish. Wang Taitai was accusing her husband of stealing the cash she kept in her pillowcase, and Mr. Wang was calling his wife a bucket of rice worms. The Wangs had a daughter who came back from college, a girl my mother always compared me to—she wore her skirts knee-length, and her skin was estranged from the sun—and Wang Taitai begged me to pick her up from the airport because her husband had driven away in their Subaru. So I picked her up in the morning, her black hair bordering on blue in the sunlight. On the car ride home, she asked how my mother was, if I ever graduated, if her father was home, if he, if he. When she was done talking, I asked her if she remembered that time we played Catch a Chicken in our yard. I had kissed the back of her neck, licked along her hairline. She straddled me in the mud and fed a worm up my nostril, and I laughed, snorting it in, coughing until she reached down my throat and tugged it free, slick with me.

Without turning her head, she nodded. Yes. Then she reached out her hand, still not looking at me, and rested it in my lap. It bounced against my thigh as I pulled onto the off-ramp, and then it opened like a wing to fold over my knee. When I pulled up to her house, squat and heat-warped like all the houses on this street, she lifted her hand from my lap and left. She turned back and looked at me once through the passenger window, and I knew it was because it was tinted: She couldn't see my face but I could see hers. I backed up the car ten feet, in front of my own home now, and before I unbuckled, I saw a stain on the passenger seat. I bent my head to it: blood. A bright wing of it on the fake leather. I spat on it, rubbing at it with my sleeve, measured it against my palm like evidence of my own sacrifice. Then, before I conceded that it would be permanent, I licked it once, tugging the blood onto my tongue.

At the end of the day, when I'd finished wiping Jenny's windows twice with wadded-up newspaper, I knocked on the door of the storage room and asked if it was time to lock up. *You can go home*, Jenny said through the door. The rustle of plastic, then something metal and hollow falling to the ground, harmonizing with the silence. *OK*, I said, but didn't leave. I waited until Jenny opened the door, one of the costume wigs from inventory squatting on her head, a yellow like the boa I'd stolen, a canary singing its prophecy. I laughed, stepping back. Jenny looked at me and nodded to the door, Daughter and Daughter darting between her legs, fur oiled in this light.

I said you can go, she said, but pulled the door open wider, stepping back to let me in. I entered. Jenny shut the door. We stood facing each other, one of the Daughters nudging its wet snout against my knee. I pushed Daughter away with my foot, stepped closer. Jenny brought her hand to her throat, but the crucifix wasn't there. I looked at the floor, wondering if it had fallen off somewhere, if that was the hollow sound I'd heard earlier, and then Jenny placed her palms on my cheeks and lifted my head. *Turn off the lights*, she said to me, her face so close I almost crossed my eyes. She was taller than me, and I looked at the converged moles on her chin, wanting to bite them off like salted pearls and roll them in my mouth. Reaching behind me, I flicked off the lights. Our teeth were the only light to see by. Daughter and Daughter camouflaged with the dark, the white spots on their rumps rippling and conjoining like constellations.

Her hands beneath my shirt, roaming the rungs of my back, the nick on my hip where a rooster spurred me. There'd been a rooster one summer, bought on Craigslist by Abu, and the rooster had hurled itself at me every time I went out to catch a hen. *There can't be two roosters in a flock*, Ahma had joked. *One of you has to go.* Jenny's thumb snagged on the scar, digging at it as if she wanted to flip it like a coin. My mouth on her neck, the basket of her breast, the beading of her nipples. There were neon feathers scattered on the floor like the aftermath of a slaughter, and I reached down to grab a handful, stuffing them into her mouth. She chewed them in the dark as I touched her, spitting them into flight. With my tongue, I wrote over the scars on her arms, the calligraphy of cane leaves.

We left late that night, and in the morning, when I came late, the store was locked, no one inside. I pressed my face to the windows, knocked, realized I didn't know Jenny's phone number or where she lived. I thought she inhabited the store the way grief inhabited a body. I thought she was born there. She had called me last night by my Tayal name, Savi, Savi, Savi, and I wondered what inside me still answered to that sound, how to name this need that preceded me.

I sat on the sidewalk with nothing to smoke, listening for the whine of Daughter and Daughter when they used to nudge my fists open, seeking something sweet.

It was two days before the store opened again, and when I drove by, I saw Jenny inside with a customer, the windows lacy with dust now that I wasn't wiping them. She turned her head and saw my car outside the store, idling, my windows rolled up. In the empty seat beside me, the stain was already almost gone. Abu, after all her years working at the laundry, would tell me that spit really was the best way to get rid of a fresh stain, but she didn't know about an old one. She didn't know what to do with something that had always been there, a birthmark, an island, Jenny's story about the Bible, each page already stained with our names.

I drove away. Jenny recycled rumors about me later, about how I'd stolen from her and that's why she fired me, yes, who steals something as cheap as that, so tacky, so typical, and I didn't go back. At home, Abu gave up studying for her real estate exam and decided instead on becoming a landscaper. She told me all kinds of facts, like how overwatering a plant prevented it from staking its roots deep enough: all of its roots bobbed to the surface, shallow, denied by the dirt. *Who knew*, my mother said, *you could kill a thing by giving it everything.*

Sometimes I drove through the parking lot, windows down in case she wanted to see me, remembering when we would stand together on the sidewalk and the Daughters would lay down behind us like our shadows but full of blood, knotting themselves together in sleep, undone by our touch.

CLEANING LENTILS

Susan Muaddi Darraj

On Wednesdays, Sits's house smelled like lamb stew. On Saturdays, like chicken marinated in sumac and lemon, the meat so tender it fell apart under the fork's gentle probe. That was it for meat—just two days a week. On the other five days, there were lentils: brown, green, or red, mingled with sharp onion and sweet basil, simmering in her blue enameled pot.

It made Hiba sick to her stomach. All of it.

The whole world conspired to make her fat. That's what it had to be. When she thought of her gigantic ass atop legs that had no calves, her ass below a flat torso, it disgusted her. God and the ancestors had pranked her, sending all the curves to the wrong damned place.

Sits had given her a bedroom on the third floor. She'd called Sitti Maha "Sits" since she was a baby—it was a family joke now, but Hiba had never stopped using it. Even up here, the floor was tiled, so her bare feet—even they looked thinner now—froze.

Sits swept the whole house once a day; three times a week, she dumped a cup of lemon juice and a half cup of olive oil into a bucket of soapy water and mopped all three floors. She even covered her hair when she cleaned. Instead of her usual white linen veil, cleaning day meant she wore her orange bandanna that read "Mick's Bike Shop" in thunderbolt lettering. She explained to Hiba that some nice boy in a black leather jacket had been handing them out on the street. She'd asked for one, and he'd smiled and gave it to her.

"He was laughing at you."

"No. I don't think so. He asked me about this." She pointed to the rough cross and the lamb inked on the inside of her wrist. "He wanted to know who did it," she said and shrugged. "I told him in the old country, and maybe Jesus had one like it."

"I think he thought you were silly."

Sits shrugged, but she had a strange look on her face, like Hiba was a stranger.

She didn't know. She couldn't know. Hiba, coming off her own humiliation, lingered on Sits's ignorance of hers.

Seedo took care of the outside. Wasn't much of an outside, though. Her parents' lawn was one acre, bisected by a winding, curling driveway. The front lawn of Sits and Seedo's house was Thatcher Street, which had four potholes that the city promised to fix and never did.

Thatcher Street and potholes and row houses and homeless people were why Mama had refused to live anywhere but Wentworth when they'd gotten married. That's where Hiba had grown up, and it was very expensive. When Seedo once talked to Mama about how much she spends, she snapped, "Demetri is a rich man." And she'd added, "Why do you think I put up with him?" She didn't know they heard that, Hiba and her sister Mina, but they totally had. So Hiba had grown up in the posh neighborhood, where the grocery stores had cafés and restaurants inside, where your neighbors lived half a mile down the road, where men on machines came to trim the grass. In the suburbs, the girls were all skinny. They all dieted starting in middle school, talking about Atkins and Paleo on the bus. Two girls, Mary Thomson and Jennie Stonefeld, were always fainting and loving the attention, but it was because they needed to eat. Alexis Moore was more yellow than white because she was so damn hungry. Here in Baltimore, the girls were more varied; Hiba watched them walking to and from school—tramping down the sidewalk in their boots, lugging their backpacks. Some of them thin, some athletic and muscular, some round and chubby. But here, the fat girls wore tight leggings like the skinny ones, and they didn't seem to give shit how they looked.

Everything was strange here, but Hiba liked it. Here in Baltimore, the grocery store was a corner deli, where they sold one kind of milk, one brand of toilet paper. The only fruits came in cans in heavy syrup. Sits walked eight blocks to the open-air market for the fresh stuff, and once a month, she and Seedo took the bus to the other side of the city. There, between a synagogue and a strip of car dealerships, there was an Arabic grocery store, where they stocked up on sumac, warak, cumin, and lentils. Hiba never went with them. She hadn't ventured past the front door since she'd arrived, but when they came home, loaded with bags and bags and Sits's metal shopping cart, she did help carry the lighter bags inside and stock the tall pantry in the kitchen.

"Why doesn't she go out?" asked the tall lady who lived across the street, the one with the flat-ironed blue-black hair and the penciled eyebrows. Her name was Liz, and she talked to Sits all the time, conversing across the narrow street. Hiba could hear them from her bedroom. She was so tired, but still giggled when they shouted to be heard over a car rather than pause their conversation, their voices rising as the vehicle chugged closer. "Did you get the COUPON FROM THE RITE AID that came in the circular?"

"She visiting us." That was Sits's voice, so gentle but firm. "She student in za college."

"But it's November."

"She on a leetle break now."

The backyard of their house was something. Hiba had grown up with a ten-acre backyard, and she'd never once sat in it. There had been a small playset with a slide, but Mama had had it torn down years ago, when Hiba finished fifth grade. "No need to keep junking up the yard," she'd said.

Seedo and Sits's yard was just a rectangle of cement with a table and a lounge chair and a crucifix on the brick wall. In one corner, there was an apple tree, slender and fragile, growing out of a stack of black rubber tires, their centers packed with dirt like filled donuts.

But she came out here every day. And sat. Sometimes she cried; she thought about Snapchat and the texts and the whole last month and how she'd been brought to this. She was in Baltimore, for God's sake, living with her grand-parents, who didn't even have Wi-Fi.

. . .

Hiba sat in the lounge chair one evening and pulled her long sleeves over her wrists, cocooned in a sweater that had become oversized but that only last year had fit snugly over her breasts. Sits found her there and set two cups of coffee on the table.

"Your parents called again." She spoke to Hiba in Arabic only.

Hiba answered in English. "I don't care."

"Ou wella bi him nee," Sits assured her patiently. *I don't care either.*

Hiba didn't bite. Sits had been trying all month to make her speak Arabic, since she'd shown up on her steps with her Coach suitcase and Tory Burch sandals on her feet. She'd also been trying to feed her obsessively. Mama must have told Sits about her weakness for rice, so Sits served it with every meal, either plain or, when that didn't work, colored with saffron, glittered with sautéed pine nuts, even sprinkled with cinnamon. But Hiba wouldn't touch it. She barely ate any of Sits's food at all, just pushed it around, made small hills of it on her plate, sitting quietly because Seedo insisted if she wanted to stay there, she had to join them for breakfast, lunch, and dinner. She didn't have to pray, but she had to fold her hands and lower her eyes respectfully while they did.

"Any other rules? Anything else I need to do to stay here?" she'd asked that first night, sitting angrily on the kitchen chair, her forehead beaded with sweat. She'd brought a Get Out of Jail Free card, stashed it in her room. But she would let them talk, and say whatever they wanted, to think they were in charge.

"You can help with the chores, if you feel up to it," Seedo had said in Arabic. He was a tall, stout man with a beefy chest and a thick white mustache. "Your grandmother is seventy-six now. I'm eighty-two. The garden needs work. The dusting needs to be done."

"Why don't you just hire someone, like my mom does?" She'd stared scornfully at Sits's hands, the back of which were stretched and shiny like wax, the veins bulging on her forearms. Hiba's nails were usually polished and neat, because that's what Mama expected. She'd had her first mani-pedi when she was ten, and every two weeks since. Here, though . . . here was different. Hiba's nails were chewed and bitten, eaten away the way she wanted to devour herself, devour her pain. It made her laugh to think how Mama would grimace if she'd seen them.

"Hire someone? To clean my own house?" Sits had looked incredulously at Seedo and chuckled. "Istaghfirallah." Seedo smiled too, his white mustache curving like a tuft of snow settling on a tree limb.

"Fine. I'll do chores. Anything else?"

"Yes." He stared at her somberly. "In this house, we pray. I know you don't, so izz OK." He shrugged. "But we also smile. So you have to smile at least once a day." He grinned at her, his eyes disappearing into his cheeks. "Seeing you in our house is like waking up to a dream, my angel."

She thought about his words now, as she sipped Sits's coffee. Her grandparents spoke in casual poetry, dropping phrases like "You're blooming today" and "You bury me because I love you so much." They always always always called her habibti and ya ayooni. My love. My eyes. The fact was that she wasn't used to this, this awkwardly normal way of discussing intense emotions.

Her mother only used flattery on board chairmen, her father only on waitresses. But with Hiba, they were like teachers, where "caring" also meant assessing you, grading and judging. "Watch your expression," Mama liked to snap. "Head high. Remember who you are." How could Hiba tell her she longed for any memory of who she was, any memory at all.

• • •

Jennie texted her on the Saturday of her third week.

You OK. Haven't heard from you.

> *Staying with relatives. Taking the rest of the semester off.*

Dina's taking over your space. Wanted to see if you're OK.

> *All good. Just need time off.*

Glad you're OK. Your rents OK with time off from school?

> *Don't care.*

K.

> *Yep.*

She's loving all the extra dorm space. Bitch.

> *I bet. Bitch.*

He's in there every night. Probably eating it.

> *Daniel?*

Yeah. He'll fuck anything that moves. You saw the shit he posted that time?

> *Yeah.*

That poor girl.

> *Yeah.*

• • •

During week three, Sits told Hiba to help her clean the windows. This meant moving all the knickknacks—the porcelain Victorian ladies, the picture frames, the vases of plastic flowers—off the windowsills and wiping them down, then standing on the sill and windexing the glass top to bottom. At her parents' house, there were windows that were twelve feet tall, which men came with ladders and sponges on poles to clean. But Hiba obeyed Sits, because when Baba had told her "Enough is enough" and "Get your pathetic ass out of my house," it was only Seedo who'd said "Come."

There was one photo of herself, her sister Mina, and their brother Amir, all in their Christmas outfits, flanking her parents in front of the tree. Mama's "Macy's tree," Hiba always called it. She must have been about ten in the photo, and she looked like a goddamn whale. Her sparkly gold dress made her look bloated, especially next to Mina, who always wore sleek black dresses at the holidays. Hiba picked up the photo and carefully moved it to the side, then climbed up on the sill.

She stood carefully, aiming the spray bottle of blue cleaner up at the top. She started to rub the bubbles with her towel, when Sits stopped her. "No," she said in Arabic. "We don't want streaks." Then carefully, she coached Hiba how to wipe down, down, in one smooth motion, then move back to the top of the window. When it was finished, she stood there, her body in the window frame, and looked down at Thatcher Street, at the girls playing double Dutch. One of them, with long, blue-tipped braids, was in the cage now, her chubby stomach and thighs bouncing as she jumped. Her mother sat on her stoop, smiling and clapping along with the beat for her. When she messed up, her ankle catching the rope, her mom clapped even harder and shouted something that made the girl flick her braids and smile. Hiba wished she could go down to the street and rewind it, to hear the words that the mother had said.

"Khalasti?" Sits asked her. "We have two more rooms."

"One more second."

"What's wrong?"

Hiba continued looking at the girls. "Can you throw away that picture of me?"

Sits picked it up. "No, I love it."

"I wish you would." She climbed down carefully, her arms not as steady as they'd been in the past.

Later that night, when all the windows sparkled and Sits and Seedo had gone to bed, she carefully removed the photograph from the glass and completely and cleanly cut her body out of the picture.

• • •

One day, Seedo requested her help. "I'm tired," Hiba said, lying down on the couch. She slept here a lot in the midday, wrapped in the numerous blankets that Sits crocheted. Her favorite was one of multicolored, mismatched yarn. "This one is so warm, but the pattern is strange."

Sits had shrugged. "I had a big box of leftover yarn. So I kept crocheting until I had none left." Hiba loved that she could understand Arabic better since moving in with them. Now Sits looked suspiciously at Hiba. "You know, I made you a blanket when you were little. For your tenth birthday."

"I don't have a blanket from you."

"A big light-blue and gray one?" Sits stretched out her arms. "It's for a twin bed—so big."

But Hiba had never seen it.

"Humpf," Sits had snorted, then gone back to stirring the lentils in the pot.

But Seedo made her shed the blanket, put on an extra sweater, and come outside. He wanted her to work in the garden.

"You don't have a garden," she explained to him calmly. He raised a palm to his heart and looked offended. "Ilsanik," he chided. Your tongue. But he was laughing, and she laughed too. It felt so strange, how much they laughed. They didn't have cable or Netflix, or goddamn Wi-Fi, but they told each other jokes and laughed all the time. One day, Seedo had said he felt like eating lamb, and Sits had reminded him it wasn't Sunday. "But I feel like having it," he said stubbornly, winking at Hiba, and Sits's response had been a cool, "I'll make it at your funeral."

"What am I supposed to do?" she asked, as he handed her a trowel.

"Dig holes here, about six inches apart," he instructed her. "And we're going to plant these." He pointed to a flat cardboard box, like the kind they hauled apples in from the outdoor market. It was filled with clumps of dirt.

"You're going to plant dirt?"

He looked up at the sky. "They claim she's in college, heavenly father," he spoke to the clouds.

She tried not to, but in spite of herself, Hiba giggled.

His head snapped forward, and he winked. "This is garlic." He fluttered his hand around the dirt in the box, shedding it to reveal white bulbs like curved ivory fangs.

So they squatted before the trough of dirt, and she used the trowel to dig holes. Her arms ached, and at one point, they shook from the exertion. Seedo said softly, "It's OK. It's good for you. This is like exercise. Make you strong."

"Make me have an appetite?"

He grinned and winked. "Your Mama—she's smart too."

Hiba turned her attention to the dirt. Everyone said that about Mama, but she wasn't smart, Hiba thought. She was just busy. She acted busy. She looked busy. Sitting on the boards of charity groups. Going to fundraiser galas anywhere between DC and Philadelphia. She always said Baba had made his money in real estate, not in something like medicine or law, so she had to make up for that lack of prestige in this way. Every time she said it, Baba stood and left the room.

Hiba had always hated Mama's charity work. Once she got a community service award at some fancy party in a ballroom, and she and Mina had to dress up and be shown off like an accomplishment. Their brother had been there too; this was before Baba had sent him to rehab for drugs. Mama hardly ever talked about Amir, and when she did, the story was that Amir had somehow betrayed her.

• • •

Hiba scraped her finger on something sharp, a shard of wood. The skin separated, and the blood ballooned out in a big, fat drop. "I'll be back."

"No, just wash it here, with the hose."

"No, Seedo." She shook her head. "I need a Band-Aid."

There was a shelf in the bathroom where Sits kept extra towels, cotton balls, Band-Aids. But she heard a noise in her bedroom and walked in. Sits had her hands in Hiba's top drawer, digging under the bras and T-shirts. Hiba could see her mattress had been moved, the sheets messed.

Sits slowly withdrew her arms. She held the bottle in her closed fist.

"What the hell."

"We were worried. We told you not to bring anything that could hurt you."

"I'm leaving."

"No," Seedo said from the doorway. "No, angel. You're staying here until you're better."

. . .

One day, when she couldn't take it anymore, she texted Jennie.

What's with Dina and Daniel?

*He posted a pic of them
trashed. From last week.*

Right before finals.

*I told her to be careful. He
posted the pic of that one girl,
he'll do the same to her.*

Good pt.

Idk. She's a bigger skank than he is.

. . .

One morning, Hiba's cheekbones pushed out against her skin. They'd been disappearing these past three weeks, as she'd been lulled into Sits and Seedo's quiet life. But now they were back, jutting out sharply, like marble, giving her face a distinct, sophisticated, sharp look. A look that said, "Stay away from me, or I will hurt you too."

She thought—not for the first time—that she looked scary.

Had she appeared like this to Daniel? She'd struggled so hard, and it hadn't been good enough anyway, but now she wondered if she had been pretty at all. Maybe he didn't care— the picture hadn't been of her face, after all.

When he'd leaned over her after, while she slept, what had he thought? When he'd raised the camera, what had he hoped to capture? Something gross? His caption had said, "At the beach, bitches." Because there she'd lain, like a big whale on a messy bed, her back to the camera.

Sits always liked to touch her face, to tug affectionately at her hair, to say "jameela"—beautiful—several times a day. That's how she was. Always touching. Seedo too—he kissed Sits's hand every time she brought him a cup of tea, patted her shoulder whenever he walked past her. Without thinking, it seemed. It's just how they were.

How had Mama grown up in this house? Hiba imagined her as a little girl, being carried on Seedo's shoulders, being wrapped in a handmade blanket on a cold night, having two people worry when she got sick. She imagined Seedo getting up early to sponge brown dye on Mama's school shoes then smooth it through the leather so it gleamed. Had she hated this life? Is that why she threw out any shoes with a scuff? Any sweater that sprouted a thread? This was not poverty—not the kind she saw in her textbooks, or the kind that they talked about at the galas on whose boards Mama served. No swollen stomachs here, no famine, nobody swatting flies and walking to the well for water. What had made her the kind of mother who assessed each one of them before they left the house, making sure their hair was stylish, their makeup right, their handbags and shoes Prada or nothing? A woman who'd once tossed away Hiba's craft bin when she'd started painting T-shirts with puffy paint for fun. Who'd insisted on hair relaxers to ease the frizz. Who had a manicurist on call at the salon in case she chipped a nail.

Sits noticed her cheekbones. She ran her waxy palm over them. "Ya rouhi, ya rouhi," she said. A few minutes later, Hiba watched her burn incense in a black cast-iron bowl and mutter prayers over it. She took the smoking bowl upstairs, and an hour later, when Hiba went to lie down in bed, she smelled its aroma everywhere—her sheets, her closet, her dresser—a sad, sweet smell, like something she missed.

She wanted to say to Sits:

You're so good to me.

I think you're beautiful. Your gray hair like steel, the wrinkles at the corner of your eyes, the shuffle in your walk—it's the purest beauty I've ever seen.

Sits, she wanted to say, *I hate the way I look.*

She focused instead on being here in this house. On the concrete moments. Touching the tiled floor with her bare feet. Listening to Liz shout at Sits across the street. When she was watching Seedo through the kitchen window as he hunched over the apple tree, tying it at one point to the fence to keep it from collapsing.

"You need to go outside and walk a little bit," Sits said during week five. She'd received an application form from her teachers to request an extension to turn in her incomplete work, but she hadn't filled it out. She hadn't even read through it.

She'd only been going outside to sit on the lounge chair, soaking up the light like a human solar panel. Sits had taken away all her long-sleeved shirts, but neither she nor Seedo said a word about her thin arms. She'd also hidden all the knives in an overly dramatic move, but Hiba didn't blame her. She heard Sits talking on the kitchen phone to Mama, asking her what she should do. "No, no, she can stay here as long as she wants. But I'm worried. Wallah, I'm scared for her."

It was really bright and sunny the day that Sits insisted. They walked to the produce market, and Hiba pulled a metal cart behind her.

"Look at these," Sits said, running her rough hands over a bin of cucumbers. "They're cheap and they're small, like the fakous we eat." She looked at the burly man behind the stall. "Hello, Mauricio," she said in her English.

Hiba stood quietly, her hands deep in the pockets of her hoodie. The sun filled her eyes, and she didn't have shades, so she pulled her hood up and over her head.

"Your granddaughter?" Mauricio asked.

"Hiba. Yes." She patted her chest. "Ma do-tur's girl."

He nodded at Hiba, but she smiled back in a quick way, then ducked her head again. The glare was making her eyes water.

"My grandson . . . he help me too. Good boy, he works with me."

"That's good boy."

"How many you want?" He smiled at Hiba. "You need a lot. You gotta feed this one. She too thin."

Sits asked Hiba if she'd like to try them, and she nodded just to say something. She really wanted to go home, to her little clean room on the third floor, where everything smelled like lemon and wind, and lie down in her soft bed where the scent of incense lingered a week later. She didn't want to imagine Daniel in her old dorm room, climbing into Dina's bed the way he'd climbed into hers, kissing Dina and telling her she was beautiful, as he'd told her. He wouldn't ever. She was sure of it.

"How about these tomatoes? These look good to you, habibti?" Sits held up a dark-red one, like a softball. Hiba peered at it, squinting. "I'll get a few, yes?" Sits smiled and Hiba could tell she was worried. She'd gone back to not eating at all in the last two days, since Jennie's text. She'd picked at small fragments of her food, enough to keep the acid down, but her energy was draining. What had she eaten yesterday? she wondered as she watched Mauricio bag some tomatoes. Half an apple. Ten almonds. A piece of chicken the size of her thumb.

Jennie hadn't figured it out. Snapchat got rid of it, but surely someone . . . someone had figured it out. Her hair had been spread across the pillow . . . not many girls on campus had hair like her.

Farther down the stalls, she pulled Sits's metal cart as her grandmother loaded up on green peas, bananas, and potatoes. Hiba had not eaten a potato in two years, not since senior year of high school, at Jennie's graduation party. She wondered what Jennie was doing now. Probably studying for midterm exams. Maybe planning the Halloween bash on campus. Maybe sitting on the quad, eating her pho from the takeout place, not giving a shit that she'd gained twenty pounds since freshman year.

Hiba's head buzzed. As they turned a corner to visit a new row of stalls, the sun hit her harder than ever. This row didn't have the wide umbrellas that the others did, and the glare lasered down on her full-force.

"They have fresh apricots, habibti," came Sits's voice, seeming far away. There was a lot of noise, but from where? Hiba squinted through the yellow flashes before her eyes, swimming in heat, and registered—right before she collapsed—that Sits had started to scream.

· · ·

They told her that Mauricio and his grandson had lifted her like a feather into the back seat of Seedo's car. The doctor in the emergency room said she was severely dehydrated, and she found herself on an IV. They couldn't detect a vein in her inner elbow, so they punctured one in the back of her hand, then began forcing her body to accept calories.

Sits and Seedo sat on the chairs in her room, pecking away at the cell phone they shared. It was a flip phone, but they texted on it anyway, hitting the number keys repeatedly until it reached the letter they needed. When they left the room to huddle with the doctor, she took the phone they left on the side table. Using her free arm, she scanned their messages.

She sick. Come.

> *She does this all the time.*

Need you.

> *It's her drama. If we come,*
> *she'll know she won.*

Haram.

                                        She wants attention.

She desirv it.

• • •

Mama and Baba did not come.

Instead, they sent Mina.

Mina, a younger, less plastic version of Mama, swung into the hospital room carrying an expensive bag and wearing tight jeans and beaded sandals. Her eyebrows had been tattooed on her face that summer during a trip to Beirut with their cousins. Hiba hadn't been invited. She'd never been Mina's choice of a friend. Mina felt the same about her—she had no doubt. Mina, for sure, felt she'd been dealt a bad hand in getting a dud, depressive for a sister.

"The doctor said you're underweight," Mina said, perching on the chair. "Tell them you'll start eating more, and they'll let you go."

"OK. I will."

"Make it believable."

"Yep." She was too tired for Mina today. Or any day.

Her sister noticed the faded vinyl purse on the floor. "Is this Sits's?"

"She went for a walk with Seedo. They come at eight every morning and stay all day."

Mina saw the cooler with the wheels and looked at Hiba.

"They bring their own food," she explained. "They don't like the cafeteria food."

"There's Uber Eats. Or Grubhub."

"They have a flip phone, Mina."

"Fucking Christ." Mina snickered. "How do you deal with them?"

"They're fine," Hiba said, suddenly annoyed.

"You're so weird, Hiba." She readjusted herself on the chair. "You could have just come home. Mama and Baba aren't mad. Just embarrassed."

"Right. OK."

"Mostly Mama. Baba's worried about you and wants you to come home."

Mina's eyebrows looked like two sword blades about to cross each other. She looked like a monster, with her carefully lined lips and her skin coated in primer and contouring makeup. A clown in some sick nightmare.

She leaned closer to Hiba. "So. You had a boyfriend. And he dumped you. Big fucking deal."

"It was a big deal." She looked at Mina's manicured pink nails, thought about Daniel's fingers pinching her waistline.

"Get over it."

Hiba wanted the bed to either swallow her or snap together in half and kill her.

"There's a silver lining, right? You lost some weight. That's good. Now just don't overdo it."

The fingers in her right hand, where the IV pierced her tissue-like skin, looked like the chubby worms she'd had to dissect once. That was in high school, where she'd first realized she was fat. The soft curves of one's upper arm were no longer sweet. Having a butt that filled out your jeans meant you were a pig. Eating in front of other girls was a disaster. Everyone was on a diet, and nobody was ever hungry. She'd eaten half her sandwich, then a bag of chips one day, and by tenth period, her new name was "Hippa." She'd carried it through graduation.

But college was a new beginning. And she'd lost weight over that summer, getting in shape throughout her freshman fall. That spring of freshman year, she'd met Daniel, when she thought she was finally trim and fit. Except after she'd let him fuck her, her first time, on her bed in her dorm room, with Jennie in the next room, he'd run his palm over her belly and said, "You need to get this under control." She'd tried. Because she craved having someone like Daniel put his arm around her in the student lounge, in front of everyone, of having him kiss her on the quad while people walked past. For once, people looked at her like she was more than just a brown girl with frizzy hair, more than just the girl you asked for the class notes. She was attached to someone. She belonged to Daniel. And she wasn't about to give it up.

And then one morning he left, and after class she'd seen her picture—the picture of her bare ass in bed—on his Snapchat. He'd never called or apologized. The dorm buzzed for a week about whose ass it was. Jennie asked if it was hers, and she'd said no. It turned out he was fucking two other girls, so hardly anyone knew about her anyway. And the most pathetic part, she'd thought, before having a breakdown in her room and swallowing the pills, was that she'd almost been glad because that was the slimmest her ass had ever looked. She'd had pretty dimples in her cheeks, the way skinny girls did when their jeans hung low. When she'd woken up in the hospital, she'd refused to be released to her parents' home. Mama had looked almost relieved.

"Mama said if you want to come home, you should. She's just telling everyone you're doing some kind of yoga retreat thing."

Hiba decided that if the bed didn't swallow her or do her the favor of killing her somehow, she'd make herself disappear. She'd done it before, when she'd heard girls gossiping about her ass in study hall, or even when Mama had *tsk*ed over her taking a second helping at dinner. "God, that shit wiggles like Jell-O when she walks." "Do you really need that, Hiba? It will take you an hour on the elliptical to burn it off."

She'd cocooned herself in silence during those moments. Now she did it again by imagining herself in the small backyard, by the odd apple tree, in her worn hoodie, sipping Sits's coffee. She became the tree, slipping into the hollow center of the black tires, sinking into the soil. Mina's words couldn't scale this. Her sister talked, tried to wring a compromise out of her, but Hiba remained silent until Mina shook her head and finally left.

When Sits returned, she sniffed the air. "Who was here? Your mother?"

"Mina."

"I smell her perfume." She coughed. "Did she leave any in the bottle?"

Hiba stayed quiet, wriggling her fat fingers, making the skin on the back of her hand stretch painfully.

"It reeks of arrogance," Sits muttered in Arabic, then cried in alarm at the choking sound coming from the bed. "Habibti, what is it?"

Even Hiba needed a few seconds to recognize the sound of her own laughter.

. . .

"They want to come and see you. It's Eid al Milad." Sits was a Christmas maniac. She started decorating right after Thanksgiving with her embroidered tatreez tablecloths and runners.

"I don't want to see them."

They were sitting in the yard, and snow had dusted everything, even the leaves of the apple tree. It was still standing because Seedo had tethered it to the wall. But with its white coat, it glistened like an angel. It could be a Christmas tree, if she hung some decorations from it.

"You should," Sits said. She set two trays filled with lentils on the table, one in front of herself and one in front of Hiba, then began picking carefully through them. "Look for small stones or dirt."

Hiba obeyed, watching how Sits's fingers scurried across the pan, sifting and inspecting.

"How do stones get in there anyway?" Hiba asked, reluctantly pulling her hands out of her sleeves and stretching her arms across the tray.

"They just do. And I have to make sure they're clean before I cook them."

"My mother never cooks addas."

Sits snorted and paused to sip her coffee, then went back to picking. "Food is love. You have to pass your love into the food," Sits said solemnly, like she was reading from her Bible. "We lived during three wars. Lentils kept us from starving. Eating them reminds us of those days."

"Why would you want to remember? If they were such bad days."

"It's good to remember," Sits said, nodding. "So you can look at your life now and say *alhamdulilah*."

Hiba continued steadily picking, watching how Sits's fingers worked in acute, precise movements. She wanted, she realized, Sits to take care of her, to belong to her. Her grandmother's knuckles were big and knobby, flicking through the dry beans, clicking and shifting them across the wide aluminum pan, separating out the stones that would hurt you.

WHAT'S FOR SALE

Nicole Dennis-Benn

At Old Fort Craft Park, Delores links hands with the flushed-face men in floral shirts who are too polite to decline and the women in broad straw hats whose thin lips fix in frightened smiles. Before the tourists pass Delores's stall, she listens to the prices the other higglers quote them—prices that make the tourists politely decline and walk away. So by the time they get to Delores—the last stall in the market—she's ready. She pounces. Just like she does at Falmouth Market on Tuesdays as soon as the ship docks. But the tourists hesitate, as they always do, probably startled by the big Black woman with bulging eyes and flared nostrils. Her current victims are a middle-aged couple.

"Me have nuff nuff nice t'ings fah you an' yuh husband . . . come dis way, sweetie pie."

Delores pulls the woman's hand gently. The man follows behind his wife, both hands clutching the big camera around his neck as if he's afraid someone will steal it.

To set them at ease, Delores confides in them: "Oh lawd ah mercy," she says, fanning herself with an old *Jamaica Observer*. "Dis rhaatid heat is no joke. Yuh know I been standin' in it all day? . . . bwoy t'ings haa'd."

She wipes the sweat that pours down her face, one eye on them. It's more nervousness than the heat, because things are slow and Delores needs the money. She observes the woman scrutinizing the jewelry—the drop earrings made of wood, the beaded necklaces, anklets, and bracelets— the only things in the stall that Delores makes. "Dat one would be nice wid yuh dress . . ." Delores says when the woman picks up a necklace. But the woman only responds with a stiff smile, gently putting down the item, then moving on to the next. Delores continues to fan. Normally the Americans are chatty, gullible. Delores never usually has to work so hard with them, for their politeness makes them benevolent, apologetic to a fault. But this couple must be a different breed. Maybe Delores is wrong. Maybe they're from somewhere else. But only the American tourists dress like they're going on a safari, especially the men, with their clogs, khaki apparel, and binocular-looking cameras.

"Hot flash and dis ungodly heat nuh 'gree at'all," Delores says when the woman moves to the woven baskets. Only then does the woman smile—a genuine smile that indicates her understanding—the recognition of a universal feminine condition. Only then does she finger her foreign bills as though unwilling to part with them. "How much are the necklaces?" she asks Delores in an American accent. She's pointing at one of the red, green, and yellow pendants made from glass beads. Delores had taken her time to string them.

"Twenty-five," Delores says.

"Sorry . . . that's too much," the woman says. She glances at her husband. "Isn't twenty-five a bit much for this, Harry?" She holds up the necklace like it's a piece of string and dangles it in front of her husband. The man touches the necklace like he's some kind of a necklace expert. "We're not paying more than five for this," he says in a voice of authority that reminds Delores of Reverend Cleve Grant, whose booming voice can be heard every noon offering a prayer for the nation on Radio Jamaica.

"It tek time fi mek, sah . . ." Delores says. "Ah can guh down to twenty."

"Fifteen."

"Alright, mi will geet to yuh for fifteen!" Delores says, suppressing her disappointment. As she counts the change to give back to the woman, she catches her eyeing the miniature Jamaican dolls. Surely it must remind her of the types of people on the island whom she'd only get to see in a day—the people her husband captures with the camera slung around his neck, snapping pictures every so often at something he and his wife can marvel at later with their friends. He, too, surveys the table of the Rastas with long, oversize penises; the smiling women with tar-black faces and baskets of fruits on their heads; the grinning farmer carrying green bananas in his hands; the T-shirts with weed plants and a smoking Bob Marley with IRIE written in bold letters; the rag dolls wearing festival dresses that look like picnic table cloths.

"If yuh buy three items yuh get a discounted price . . . all these t'ings are quality," Delores says, seizing the opportunity. "Yuh wouldn't get dem anyweh else but right yah so."

The man takes out his wallet and Delores's heart leaps in her throat. "Give me two of those in a large . . . the tank in a small . . ." He points at the T-shirts. Once he makes his purchase, his wife, as though given permission to grab as many local souvenirs as possible, purchases a woven basket

("For your mom"), more bracelets with Rasta colors ("For Alan and Miranda"), and a couple of the rag dolls decked in festival dresses ("For their girls").

By the time they were done, they bought half of what Delores had. Only Delores can sell these souvenirs in a day, because unlike the other higglers, she knows she has a gold mine at home—a daughter she has to support—one who is going to be a doctor. She does it for her. Thandi. All the foreign dollars she stuffs inside her brassiere will be saved inside the old mattress on the bed that she shares with her mother.

. . .

Thandi waits to show Delores her drawing. Her mother comes home from the market and immediately begins to cook dinner, her stocky frame pouring over the small stove. Delores wipes her face with the collar of her blouse and stirs the cow foot soup. She mindlessly dashes salt and pepper and pimento seeds, talking to herself about the day's sales. "Ah told di man twenty dollah. Jus' twenty dollah. Him so cheap that him pull out a ten . . . say him want me to go down in price. But see here now, massah. What can ten dollah do?" She laughs and leans over and tastes the soup, her face scrunching as she reaches for more salt. "Eh, eh!"

"Mama, I have something to show yuh," Thandi says, taking small steps toward Delores, clutching the sketch pad filled with her drawings. The fire is high under the pot, and the house now has the smell of all the spices. "What is it now?" her mother says. "Have you seen yuh sistah since mawnin'?"

"No, Mama."

"Where the hell is that girl?" Delores turns to Thandi, her eyes big and wide like a ferocious animal. "Ah tell yuh yuh sistah is siding wid the Devil. Two nights in a row she hasn't been home. Is which man she sleeping wid now, eh?"

"I don't know . . . she neva tell me anything."

Delores laughs, throwing her head back so that her braids touch the back of her neck. She seeks the council of the shadows in the kitchen, the ones that lurk from the steady flame of the kerosene lamp. "Yuh see mi dying trial?" she says to the shadows. "Now she keeping secrets from me." She turns back to Thandi. "You tell yuh sistah that if she have a man, him mus' be able to help pay Mr. Sterling our rent. Our rent was due two days ago. Two days! And Margot deh 'bout, playing hooky wid god knows who . . . or what."

Thandi remains silent, hugging the sketch pad to her chest. It steadies her. She stares at her mother's back, the broad shoulders, the cotton blouse soaked with perspiration, the strong arms that look as though they could still carry her, the wide hips, the swollen feet shoved inside a pair of old-man slippers. She listens to her mother talk to the shadows crouched in every corner of their shack. Though they are shadows of inanimate objects, they stir with life, mock her. Thandi looks away from each of them, her eyes finding the flame in the kerosene lamp. How weak it seems, trapped inside glass. This little flame that has the potential of destroying the whole house. Thandi stares at it. She stares and stares, her own flame building on the inside, burning and burning until it's too hot to keep inside. "I want to draw," she says out loud. This incites Delores to stop talking and moving. The fire hisses under the pot. Delores turns around to face Thandi. "Beg yuh pardon?" The spoon is dripping to the floor.

"I said I want to draw," Thandi repeats.

"So why don't you sit and draw?" Delores asks. "See di table dere. Draw."

"I mean I want to do it for a living. I want to . . ."

"Hold on a second." Delores puts both hands on her hips, her big chest lifting as though filling with all the wind and words she would eventually let out to crush Thandi's dreams. "Yuh not making any sense right now. Yuh not making no sense a'tall, a'tall."

"I am really good at it," Thandi says. She opens her sketch pad and walks up to Delores. Her fingers tremble as she turns each page, showing her mother sketches after sketches. Her mother takes the book from her and examines the sketch of the half-naked woman standing in front of a mirror. Thandi is certain she recognizes the mirror. It's the one on the vanity. Thandi holds her breath as her mother stares at the image. What is she thinking? she wonders, almost asking this out loud. She has been waiting for the right moment to tell her mother about her plans to apply to art school. Brother Smith says she's good and after high school has what it takes to enroll in Edna Manley School of Art in Kingston. Thandi looks at the page her mother is looking at, wishing now that she had been more precise with parts of the sketch that now seem mediocre under her mother's gaze. She balances her weight on both legs, wringing her hands then putting them to her sides, since she doesn't know what else to do with them. Delores is silent for a long time. Too long. "What yuh think?" Thandi finally asks.

But Delores is shaking her head. "Yuh draw dis?" she asks Thandi without taking her eyes off the woman on the paper.

"Yes," Thandi responds. Her mother is staring into her eyes now. Thandi wonders what she's thinking. But Delores returns the book to Thandi without saying a word. She resumes cooking, stirring the pot of cow foot soup.

"I want to draw," Thandi says again. "I want to be an artist. Maybe yuh can start to sell my drawings to yuh customers." Thandi continues to talk as though talking to herself. "I'm really good at it. Brother Smith says I'm really talented. He said I could go to a school for art . . ."

But Delores stirs and stirs the pot, Thandi's words seeming to drown in the bubbling soup.

"Mama, yuh listening?" Thandi touches Delores's arm. "Mama, yuh hear me? I want to go to art school."

"I'm busy," is all Delores says. "I'm sending you to school to learn. So, yuh g'wan be something good in life. Nothing less. Don't come to me wid dis argument again, yuh hear? Yuh is no damn artist. We too poor for that. Yuh g'wan be a doctor. People can't mek a living being no ch'upid artist. Do you see the Rastas selling in di market making money wid dem art?"

Thandi shakes her head, her eyes on the floor. "But there are different types of artists, Mama."

"Different types of artist, mi backside!" Her mother seems unable to contain her annoyance now. "G'wan go learn yuh books, yuh hear! Yuh should be studying now. The CXC is jus' around di corner. Why yuh not studying? Yuh need all nine subjects to be the doctor yuh want to be . . ."

"That you want me to be." Thandi puts the sketch pad down on the dining table.

Delores stares at her. "Thandi, what yuh really saying to me?"

Thandi lowers her head and folds her arms across her chest. She cowers under the weight of the silence, her heartbeat echoing in her eardrums, her face hot. "Nothing," she replies.

"Who—who is filling up yuh head with all this, eh?" Delores asks.

"I have a mind of my own, you know," Thandi says. Clutching her sketch pad, she walks outside into the darkness that consumes her, leaving the back door open. "Where yuh going? Dinner will be ready soon!" Delores calls after her. But Thandi doesn't respond to this. She's too tired. Tired of everything. She leans against the back of the house and slides down to her buttocks, still clutching the sketch pad to her chest. All she wants to do now is close her eyes out here in the dark to quell her nerves, her shuddering breath. This simple act of defiance has incited the eruption of slight tremors inside her. She's not sure if it's caused by her rebellion or by this need—this passion that has caused her to fail all her other subjects as though it has possessed her, transformed her. For the old Thandi would never have voiced her desire to Delores and walk out of the house that way. Her chest heaves and sighs as though struggling to hold on to her last breath, struggling to hold on to pieces of her old self in case she goes insane.

· · ·

Thandi disappears outside into the darkness, taking all of Delores's breath with her. The girl must be smelling herself now, Delores thought. "But ah who filling up har head with all this rubbish, *eh*?" she asks this to the shadows. She wants to know. She has to know. Not her Thandi. She can't be losing her Thandi now. She's supposed to be the good one, different from her sister. Had Thandi not been such a good girl all this time, Delores would've knocked her in the head with the spoon she uses to stir the soup. But Thandi's eyes held in them the same glint of that thing Delores saw in Margot's eyes years ago on that day when the ship docked; the same glint that made Delores swallow the hardness lodged in her throat. She had to look away from it in case it struck her down like lightning.

She cannot get the sketch of the half-naked woman standing in front of a mirror from her mind. The resemblance between Delores and the woman in the sketch is uncanny, almost like a picture taken of her—same face, same eyes, same mouth, same sagging breasts resting atop the high bulge of her belly. She remembers the earnestness in her daughter's eyes when she looked at her and the slow smile that spread across the girl's face—one Delores hasn't seen in a long time since Thandi is always so serious. Her daughter's face had transformed before her. So much so that Delores had to look down at the drawing again to see what the magic was. She didn't know whether to feel proud or self-conscious; for in the sketch Delores saw everything she thought she had hidden so well, tucked away in the folds of years, heaped upon each other like steps that she takes one at a time. In her daughter's drawing, she saw the lines in her face, the weight of life revealed in prominent features like her double chin. She saw an ugly woman—an ugly Black woman with bulging eyes too wide to be gazed into before looking away and a nose too flat on the broad face. In this sketch she was not human, but a creature. This is how her daughter sees her—bull-faced and miserable. All Delores's secrets and insecurities are exposed in the gaze of this child.

Delores sits down, her bottom hitting the chair with a loud thump. A wave of exhaustion hits her. She feels again for that lump in her right breast that she felt for the first time this morning. "But what is this blasted thing though, eh?" she asks the shadows that fill the room, her only companions as of late. There's no man to talk to. No children to confide in. Silence fills the house, giving way to the crickets that serenade her from outside. She thinks nothing of the lump. She hasn't looked at her breasts, much less touched them in years. So when she felt the small, round hardness, which reminded her of one of those smooth stones at the bottom of the river, right under her arm, she brushed it aside. She wouldn't let it slow her down. She would sell her soul if she had to. Though, certain pains haunt her still. They become encroached in her joints, become embedded in the lines in her face, around her mouth and under her eyes that bulge like that of a bullfrog's, giving her a perpetual startled look. And so whenever Delores looks in the mirror, she sees little reminders of those pains etched in the aging of her face, making it look older at forty-six. Those memories that tug at her skin with all the weight they carry. All the guilt that resonates whenever she thinks of the look in her daughter's eyes sixteen years ago.

Thandi's drawing reminds Delores of this pain. It started the day she took Margot with her to the market. The girl was barely fourteen at the time. In the summers when Margot was out of school, she would help Delores carry the things to Falmouth and spread them out so that Delores could sell. While Delores sold items to tourists, Margot would help count the change and wrap the fragile items in newspaper. One day a tall, dark-haired man walked into Delores's stall. He was wearing sunglasses, like most tourists tend to do on the island. When he walked into the stall, he had a presence about him, an air Delores associated with important people—white people. Except, he wasn't white. A mixture, maybe. A mulatto kind. He wore a button-down shirt that revealed the smooth dark hairs on his chest. When Delores peered up at him, he was peering down at Margot. He turned to Delores, his eyes hidden behind the shades. "How much?" he asked in a voice that sounded to Delores like thunder.

"Di dolls are twenty, sah. Oh, an' di figurines guh for fifteen US, but ah can give yuh fah ten. An' di T-shirts! They're unique, sah. One of ah kind! Only fifteen dollah."

"No. Not those things," the man said, returning his gaze to Margot. "I'm talking about her." He used his pointy chin to gesture to a skinny Margot, who, at the time, had barely started menstruating or growing breasts. Delores looked from her daughter to the tall stranger wearing the sunglasses. "She's not on sale, sah."

The man pulled out a wad of cash and began to count it in front of Delores. Delores counted six hundred-dollar bills. She was blinking so fast that her eyes grew tired from the rapid movement. She had never seen so much money in her life. The crispness of the bills and the scent of newness, which Delores thought wealth would smell like—the possibility of moving her family out of River Bank; affording her children's school fees, books, and uniforms; buying a telephone and a landline for her to call people whenever she liked instead of waiting to use the neighbor's phone.

All these possibilities were too much to swallow all at once. They made her stutter her next response. "Sah—but she—she's only fourteen."

The man placed the bills in front of Delores. She tore her eyes away from the stack of hundred-dollar bills sitting there on her table to look into the terrified eyes of her daughter. Margot was shaking her head slowly, mouthing "No," but Delores had already made up her mind the minute the scent of the bills hit her. Her eyes pleaded with her daughter's and also held in them an apology. "*Please undah-stand. Do it now and you'll tank me lata,*" Delores hoped her eyes communicated. She nodded to the man wearing the sunglasses when Margot looked away, defeated. The man took Margot somewhere—Delores didn't ask where he was taking her. It was in the direction of the ship that had docked for the day. The girl followed behind him, her steps feeble, uncertain. She never looked behind her to see the tears in Delores's eyes.

When the man returned Margot later that evening, she never spoke to Delores. She never spoke to her for days, months. Delores had left the market that day with six hundred dollars plus a tip that the man added. ("*She's a natural, this one,*" he said to Delores with a wink like a schoolteacher giving a report on performance. It was the first time Delores had seen his eyes, which were a shade of green that reminded her of those lizards that changed color in the grass.) Delores stuffed the money in her brassiere. At home she hid it inside the mattress where she hid all her money. She hid it so well that she never realized when the money disappeared. It wasn't until her brother, Winston, who was living with them at the time, announced months later that he got a visa and a one-way ticket to America that Delores wondered where he got the money. She never thought about the bills the stranger peeled out of his wallet that day and placed on the table in her stall; her mind must have tucked the memory away as covertly as she hid the money. Immediately after Winston's announcement Delores ripped the sheets off the bed and stuck her hand inside the hole underneath the sponge layer. Nothing came up in her tight fist. The realization burned her stomach and spread across the width of her belly like the pressure of a child about to be born. Delores almost collapsed, not with the fury and raging anger she harbored for her brother, but for the loss of her daughter's innocence, which, she realized too late, was worth more than the money she lost and all the money she would ever gain.

Now Delores sinks into the chair around the dining table. The shadows converge on her, their wings spread in an embrace. She's one with the darkness. For this terrible sin she committed is unforgivable. Thandi might have seen this too. She captures everything. And all Delores is to her is this ugly dark woman capable of nothing but fits of rage and cruelty. No wonder Thandi hates her now. And then there's Mama Merle, sitting outside on that rocking chair. The old bat will spend another day wishing her beloved, good-for-nothing son home, while Delores will continue breaking her back to provide for the family, doing what she does best: survive.

· · ·

The sky opens up, giving way to the golden shower of the sun. Its spherical shape is hidden behind its luminous rays that cap the hills and mountains. There is very little one can do to avoid the sun when it's at its peak, hovering above the land with a searing, watchful eye. And with the sun comes that heat. They go hand in hand like John Mare and his old donkey, Belle. So arresting is the heat that people have to stop what they're doing every so often to preserve the little energy they have. Or if they must keep moving, they have to slow down at a snail's pace.

Way down Mercy Lane, the barren fruit trees wilt and the grass browns with all the moisture sucked out of them. Dogs lay on their sides with their tongues out, goats lean against the sides of buildings or fences, and cows move about with exposed rib cages, gnawing on bristle grass. Children crowd around standpipes to bathe or drink from the little water that trickles from them, while some accompany their mothers to the river with big buckets.

Meanwhile, idle men hug trees for shade, pressing flasks of rum to their faces. Some chew sugarcane or cut water coconut open with machetes to quench their rabid thirst. Church people mumble prayers against Satan, wondering if the world is coming to an end. Verdene Moore and the likes of her (the battyman and sodomites) could be behind this for all they know. All this heat and no rain mean all things living will eventually die. So the God-fearing people become intent on staking their claim in heaven, while the sinners put their hands to their heads and cry, "Jesas 'ave mercy!"

Crops are ruined, forcing the market vendors out of the market with nothing to sell. The normal meanness that the heat and the sun brought is compounded by the anxiety of hunger and bitterness. The children sit inside houses on cardboard boxes, sucking ice and oranges, careful

not to provoke mothers who are now prone to throw fits of
rage while scolding. Teenagers escape to the backs of schools
and churches and to the river to seek reprieve from the heat,
their own heat more glorious, spontaneous.

Only vendors like Delores who sell in the market have to
bear the heat. For money has to be made. Even at their
own risk. The sun and heat penetrate the blue cover above
Delores's stall, making it feel like the inside of an oven.
She fans herself with an old *Jamaica Observer*. Her bright-
orange blouse is soaked with sweat, like someone threw
water and drenched her under the armpits, across the belly,
all the way down to her sides. The heat seeps into her
skin and stays, pushing out beads of perspiration like tiny
fountains beneath the hairs. Two vendors couldn't take
the heat, so they packed up their things and went back
home. The others, including Delores, sucked their teeth:
"Dem really aggo give up a day's work because ah di heat?
Ah nuh Jamaica dem born an' grow? Wah dem expec'?"

Delores wipes the sweat off her face with a rag she tucks
inside her bosom. She prepares for business as usual. Mavis,
who has a stall next to Delores, is fully covered from head
to toe. She reminds Delores of one of those Muslim women
she sees sometimes—on very rare occasions—walking in
the square with their faces covered.

"Di heat is good fi yuh skin . . . mek it come quicker,"
Mavis says, adjusting the broad hat on her head. Delores
sucks her teeth at the woman who has been trying different
skin-lightening remedies since Delores knew her. Delores
has already dismissed the woman as off. For only off people
do those things. People like Ruby, who used to sell fish and

is now selling delusion to young girls who want more than apron jobs. Poor souls think a little skin lightening will make the hoity-toity class see more than their shadows slipping through cracks under their imported leather shoes.

"Why yuh nuh try drink poison while yuh at it?" Delores asks the woman.

Mavis rolls her eyes. "If me was as Black as you, Delores, me woulda invest me money inna bleaching cream. Who want to be Black in dis place? A true nobody nuh tell yuh how Black yuh is . . ."

"Kiss me ass, gyal! An' g'weh wid yuh mad self!" Delores throws down the old newspaper.

Just then John-John stops by with his box of birds he carves out of wood. He sees the women arguing, sees his opportunity, and seizes it by defending Delores. "Ah wah Mavis do to you, Mama Delores? Here . . . sidung an' let me handle it. G'weh, Mavis, an' leave Miss Delores alone. Yuh nuh have bettah t'ings fi do? Like count out di ten cents yuh get fi yuh cheap t'ings dem? Yuh son sen' yuh money an' t'ings from foreign, yet yuh stuck inna dis heat? Fi wah?"

Mavis whips around to face him now like a player caught in the middle of a dandy-shandy game. "A an' B having ah convahsation. Guh suck yuh mumma, yuh ole crusty, mop-head b'woy!"

But John-John puts down his boxes of birds, a smile hinging on his face as though he's enjoying this exchange. "Every Tom, Joe, an' Mary know seh yuh nuh get no barrel from foreign. A lie yuh ah tell. When people get barrel dem come moggle in dem new clothes. Yuh dress like a mad 'ooman, an' yuh look like one too wid dat mask pon yuh face!"

The other vendors in the arcade holler loudly with their hands cupped over their mouths, shoulders shuddering, and eyes damp with tears. Mavis adjusts her hat and touches her screwed-up face with the bleaching cream lathered all over it like the white masks obeah women wear. "A true yuh nuh know me," she says, her mouth long and bottom lip trembling. "Me son sen' barrel gimme. Ah bad-mind oonuh bad-mind!"

"Nobody nah grudge yuh, Mavis," Delores says. "Him jus' a seh it nuh mek sense if di clothes yuh son sen' look like di washout clothes yuh sell. There's a discrepancy in what's what!" The other vendors' laughter soars above the stalls, flooding through the narrow aisles where the sun marches like a soldier during a curfew. Delores continues, "Is not like yuh t'ings sell either. Usually di tourist dem tek one look, see di cheap, washout, threadbare shirt dem then move on. Not even yuh bleach-out skin coulda hol' dem!"

"G'weh!" Mavis says. "A true fi yuh pickney dem nuh like yuh, mek yuh ah pick pon me!" Satisfied after delivering the final blow, Mavis retrieves into her stall with a smirk Delores wishes she could slap away. But she couldn't move fast enough, because John-John is already holding her back. Her hands are frantically moving over John-John's shoulder, wanting to catch the woman's face and rip it to shreds. For that smirk holds the weight, the scorn, of her situation. It holds the memory of Thandi's drawing. All week her movement has slowed because of it. Setting up her items took longer than usual. She's always the first to have everything presented well enough for the tourists to come by, but that week she struggled with the simplest task of covering the wooden table with the green-and-yellow cloth. All because of Thandi's sketch. One of the figurines had even fallen, breaking in half during setup this morning. Nothing went right. The thought of spending the entire day selling felt like she was carrying an empty glass pretending to have liquid in it. She confided this to Mavis, because she wanted someone to talk to at the time. How she has been selling for years now and has never felt this way. How Margot, and now Thandi, couldn't care less if she dies in this heat, a pauper. And now Mavis calls her out. Mavis of all people. Mavis—with her crazy, lying, bleaching self—knows that Delores's children hate her. Mavis—the woman with nothing good to sell and who can never get one customer to give her the time of day—knows Delores's weakness. And now the woman has everything over her. She knows it. That smirk Delores itches to slap off her face says it all; and even if Delores succeeds in slapping the Black off the woman (more than the bleaching products she uses could ever achieve), it won't erase the fact that Mavis probably has a better relationship with her son than Delores would ever have with her daughters.

And now John-John releases Delores. "Yuh mek har know who is in charge, Mama Delores! A good fi har," he says. "Nuh let har get to yuh dat way." Delores ignores him and plops down hard on her stool. She picks up the *Jamaica Observer* again to fan with as John-John surveys her table, checking if she sold any of his carved animals since the last time she saw him.

"Notin' at'all?" he asks when she tells him. He sits down on the old padded stool in Delores's stall and runs one hand through his dreadlocks, visibly puzzled. Delores is the best haggler out here, so her news of no sale all week is sure to cause an alarm, even to the most envious vendor.

"Yuh see people come in yah from mawnin?" she asks John-John in defense. "Sun too hot." She doesn't tell him that lately she hasn't been in the mood to do the regular routine—linking hands with tourists, courting them the way men court women, complimenting them, sweet-talking them, showing them all the goods, waiting with abated breath for them to fall in love, hoping they take a leap of faith and fish into their wallets.

John-John shakes his head, his eyes looking straight ahead outside. "We cyan mek di heat do we like dis, Delores. No customers mean nuh money," John-John says. His body is sluggish on the stool, his movements slow. His jaundiced eyes swim all over Delores's face. "Wah we aggo do, Miss Delores?" he asks.

"What yuh mean what we g'wan do? Ah look like ah know?" Delores fans herself harder, almost ripping the newspaper filled with the smiling faces of politicians and well-to-do socialites on the front page. She wants John-John to leave her alone to her own thoughts and feelings. But the boy can talk off your ears if you let him. He would sit there on the stool and talk. Sometimes this interrupts Delores's work, because tourists would see him in the stall and they would politely walk away, thinking they were interrupting something between mother and son. "Well, Jah know weh him ah do. Hopefully him will sen' rain soon," John-John says.

"Believe you me," she says to John-John, who now squats to diligently paint one of his wooden birds. "Tomorrow g'wan be a new day. Yuh watch an' see. Ah g'wan sell every damn t'ing me have."

"Yes, Mama Delores. Just trus' an' Jah will provide fah all ah we," John-John says. The pink of his tongue shows as he works on perfecting the bird's feathers. He has been working on that one bird since last week. Usually it takes him only a few hours. When he finishes the bird, he separates it from all the others that he wraps one by one in old newspaper to place inside the box. Delores picks up the bird he just finished. It's more extravagant than all the others, with blue and green wings skillfully outlined with black paint, a red and yellow underbelly, and a red beak. The eyes are sharp, the whites in them defined with small black pupils. It looks like a bestseller. Delores already prices it in her head. She guesses fifty US dollars. More expensive than his other bird designs. Tourists buy them up like bag juice. So it's not like this one won't sell. John-John gives the birds to Delores to sell for him. He collects half of what she makes for the sales.

As Delores examines this new bird, she thinks of the parrot she once saw at a place called Devon House in Kingston—a colonial mansion with a beautiful garden that had just opened up to the public. The year was 1968. It was her first trip to Kingston at seventeen years old. She left three-year-old Margot with Mama Merle and rode on the country bus to town all by herself. Initially she went to look for work as a helper; but on a whim, she decided to venture to that new place people were raving about in the newspapers. Delores wanted to see it all so that she could write home with exciting stories. So she wandered from Half-Way Tree, where the country bus dropped her off, all the way up a busy street called Constant Spring Road. With a few wrong turns and stops to ask for directions ("*Beg yuh please tell weh me can fine Dev-an House?*"), she made it. It would take seconds for the nice Kingstonians she asked to understand her heavy patois and point her in the right direction, their patois milder. Their streets had names. So it wasn't hard getting to the place. Once she arrived she was taken by the Devon House mansion and the garden surrounding it. It was just as beautiful in real life as it was in the papers—white paint glowing in the sun, big columns and winding staircases, a water fountain. But more than the house were the parrots. They seemed suited for their habitat too—(before the officials moved them to Hope Zoo)—flying from tree to tree with colored wings through a lush garden of champion and oak, mahogany and birch, palm and Spanish elm, lignum vitae and stinking toe—every tree you could think of! And Delores knew them all. There were lots of colorful flowers too—hibiscus, Petrea, white lily, heliconia, bougainvillea—most of which held droplets of rain. Some flowers Delores had never seen before—had no idea they even existed in those colors. Delores followed the birds until she got to the courtyard where genteel Kingstonians sat, enjoying the outdoors under the shade of fancy umbrellas and broad hats with trimmings. As if caught in a limelight on stage, Delores fidgeted with her Sunday dress—the bright-yellow one with lace and puffed-up sleeves that she wore to nice events and places. She felt like Queen Elizabeth in that dress, especially because she had a pair of frilly green socks to match and a shiny pair of flats with buckles on the sides that never showed any specs of red dirt. The only thing missing was a pair of gloves.

And the Kingstonians—ones looking significantly different from the ones she stopped to ask directions on the way—must have thought so too. For a hundred pairs of eyes followed her when she walked by, frowning pale faces transforming into amusement. She must have made a good impression to be stared at that way. So caught up she was in how rude these Kingstonians were, staring like that without shame (*Damn bareface!*), that she didn't notice the pile of dog mess. She stepped right in it; and in her shock, she stumbled into the path of Catholic school girls. They were probably on a school trip, gliding in a straight line across the court-yard like swans being led by a mother swan—a nun who walked with her head tilted to the sky as though confident that the girls wouldn't wander off. The girls gasped when Delores stumbled in their path, immediately corking their small noses with delicate pale hands. The way the girls snickered as their eyes roved over Delores's dress made it seem as if the dog mess was smeared across it. Right then Delores hated her dress. But it was her shoes and socks that incited the most laughter. And then the nun, as polite as she thought she was, smiled at Delores, her pinkish face glowing like a heart. "You must be lost . . . Are you here with the group from the country? They're by the picnic tables." How did she know Delores was from the country? That morning Delores thought she did a good job putting her outfit together in preparation for a day in the big city. But the girls were all snickering among themselves, shoulders hunched and pretty heads jerking back and forth, moving their lengthy ponytails secured by white ribbons. Delores should have known better to listen to her mother. *"If me was suh big an' Black, me woulda neva mek scarecrow come catch me inna dat color. Yuh bettah hope di people inna Kingston nuh laugh yuh backside back ah country."* Mama Merle was right. Maybe bright colors weren't for her. The girls' laughter followed Delores all the way back through the gate like the smell of dog mess she never stopped to get rid of. She was too afraid the laughter, exacerbated by her mother's pointed words, would catch up with her and maul her (*"Country Blackie, guh back ah country! Country Blackie, guh back ah country!"*), worse than a swarm of flies.

It was as though a veil had lifted from her eyes. For when she looked down, all she saw was her Black skin and how it clashed with the dress. With her surroundings. With everything. It had collided with the order and propriety of the colonial mansion that day. And the uniform line of those high-color Catholic school girls. On her way back to River Bank, anger loomed large in Delores. She wasn't sure why, though. Why those high school girls affected her so. Something about that trip changed her. On the bus ride home, she became cynical, mocking everything—the sea green of the nauseating sea, the sun that sneered in the wide expanse of a rather pale sky, the mountains and hills drawn haphazardly across it, the indecisive Y-shaped river that once swallowed her childhood, and even the red dirt from the Bauxite mines caked under her worn heels seemed like a wide-open wound that bled and bled between the rural parishes.

Now Delores looks at this bird John-John has created—a creature of the wild that he too had probably seen and fell in love with. Delores frowns. John-John looks up and sees her staring at the bird. He gives her one of his clownish smiles, his front teeth lapping over each other like the badly aligned picket fences around Miss Gracie's pigpen. "Ah see yuh admiring me work, Mama Delores." He's only a boy, Delores decides. In time he will begin to see the ugly in everything and everyone.

He raises the bird to Delores, and she takes it. "Yuh didn't have to . . ." she says, her heart pressed against her rib cage, since no one has ever given her anything. She always wondered if she'd ever see anything like those parrots again.

"Is fah Margot . . ." he says. "Tell har is a gift from me . . . ah made it 'specially fah her . . . the prettiest one in the lot . . ."

Delores's hand shakes, and the bird slips from her fingers and drops with an impact that breaks its beak. She's not sure now if it slipped or if she heard Margot's name and flung it. The smile fades from John-John's face. He says nothing. He only sits there, his shirt open, his hands on his knees with his legs wide. He looks down at the de-beaked bird on the ground.

"Me nevah mean fi bruk it," Delores says. She bends to pick it up, but John-John stops her. "Is OK, Mama Delores. Nuh worry 'bout it. I an' I can mek anothah one." But the shadow hasn't left his face, and his eyes barely meet hers. She knows he has been working on this one for a while. She knows it probably took him a long time to choose the right colors.

"Ah can always mek anothah one . . ." John-John says again after a while, his eyes focusing intently on something in front of him. ". . . maybe if ah start now, ah can give it to you tomorrow . . ."

Delores is silent. She knows if she agrees verbally, it would give him too much hope. Delores lifts her tongue and tastes the dry roof of her mouth. She takes a sip of water from the plastic cup that grew warm sitting there on the table. It doesn't help. A wave of exhaustion comes over her that makes her lose focus. Like all other things that slow her down, she thinks this too will pass. Only this time, she's not certain what exactly she hopes will pass first—the drought, the fatigue, or that dark, looming thing that has been present inside her since the trip to Kingston. She has held on to her anger all these years, knowing very well what she would say to those girls if she ever sees them again. She could still hear the voices that chased her that day— *"Country Blackie, guh back ah country! Country Blackie, guh back ah country!"* Though the voices were all in her head, she knew the girls were thinking them. She knew they wanted to chant those words along with the ghosts. After decades of stagnancy, the words become molten inside her—a dark, murky substance that poisons her veins. For the times when it doesn't seep out in the form of toxic air, the residues blacken her heart, which expels her rage like a dark diffuse cloud under water. "She can come collec' it harself . . ." Delores finally says to John-John. "Ah can't speak for Margot . . . Margot is a big 'ooman. She know what she like an' what she nuh like. If yuh want my humble opinion, not a bone in dat girl's body is deserving of anything yuh can sell fah good money tomorrow."

EMPEROR OF THE UNIVERSE

Kaitlyn Greenidge

Bobby brought you back to me today. You look almost the same, maybe a little different around the mouth. Your lips are too hard. Bobby tells me that can be fixed. "Light a candle," he says. "And hold it to his mouth. Not right up close, but under the chin. When you see him start to sweat, take your fingers and press his lips around any way you want. That'll do it."

I don't want to try it at first. It's taken so much out of me to get you back. To have you again, to see your face. I don't want to mess all that up. Imagine if I made a mistake, if my hand was nervous or the candle too strong, and your mouth smeared, or worse, you got wounded. I say, "Thanks, Bobby, maybe I'll try it."

Bobby says, "There's no use in being unsatisfied, Miss Lillian." Then he leaves us alone together.

• • •

Your first morning back, we sit at the dining room table, just the two of us. Even though it's breakfast time, I make you your favorite meal: red beans and rice and sausage. It took me forever to learn how to make it. Before we were married, I was not a kitchen girl. I was the girl who made a point of hanging out with the men while everyone else cooked. I would come into the kitchen in my tightest dress, my nails all painted red, and say, smiling into the other women's sweaty faces, "I just don't know how you all do it."

After we married, none of your sisters, not even your mother, would teach me how to make it. They figured you married a girl they didn't like, your stomach should suffer. They thought maybe if you had to eat my cooking night after night, you'd run away from me, to the table or the bed of somebody better. But they underestimated me. I taught myself how. I was too proud to ask my own mother. Any girl with half a brain knows how to make red beans and rice and sausage. The first tour you did, after we were married, when you were away with the band, I made it every night for a week. I ate burnt, bland rice and soggy sausages till the tips of my fingers smelled like salted meat. And I got it right. I got it right.

The first time I made it for you the right way, it was the middle of the night. You'd just come back from the final stop of the tour, from Mississippi, I think. You were still in the tuxedo you wore on stage. I was in bed. You jumped on top of me to wake me up, like you used to do, but before we could start anything, I took your hand and I said, "Wait."

I led you to the kitchen, and I made you sit there at the table. You were like a little boy, you couldn't wait. You kept crossing and uncrossing your legs. You would get up and follow me around the room while I cooked, pull at the strings of my bathrobe. But I said, "Wait."

When I was done, I put the plate before you. I sat down, lit a cigarette, pointed at you with the burning end. "Eat," I said, and you did.

You ate and ate, and when you were done, you lifted the plate to your mouth and licked its whole face clean. And I smoked my cigarette the whole time, pretending like it was nothing, but feeling only something joyful inside.

So for your first meal back, I put a plate before you and a plate before me. I have some champagne: the good kind with the cork, not the bottle cap. I put two candles on the table, and I light them, let their flames burn against the weak morning sun peeping under the blinds. I put a glass in your hand, and I toast you. And I look to you, to your face, but it's off. It's wrong. So I put down my glass.

I take the candle in my hand.

I hold the flame under your chin.

I look at you, full into your eyes, which I only did once in a while, before you left me. I look at you until I see the tiniest beads of sweat form on your upper lip.

Then I set the candle down. I take my thumbs gently to your face; mold your lips until they're set a little softer, until they look right. Then I pick up my glass again, and I toast us. And I start to cry. I cry harder than I did when you died. I cry, and cry, with only your pretty wax face, with the glass eyes I asked Bobby to put in, watching me.

• • •

When my mother found out I was going to marry you, she said, "A man like that, you'll always end up sleeping at his back. He'll never sleep at yours." And I was ashamed, because how did she know it was already like that with you, that that was how we slept every night together? Our first night lying side by side, you slept with your smiling, open face to the wall, and I was the one who curved to your back, stuck too close for comfort.

We met at a show, of course. I was there with my cousin Morris. He was trying to get into your band, and I stood up at the front of the crowd with him. He said, "Delmore's nickname is the Emperor of the Universe," and I laughed and said, "Who gave him that one? He make it up himself? I'm the Queen of Sheba, if that's the case."

And then you came out on stage. You'd just started wearing the blue tux in the act. You stood at the front of the stage and looked down at the crowd, and after about the fourth or fifth song, you sang only to me. The hit, your only hit, had just come out. You sang it ten times in a row, and each time you sang it, you made the words dirtier. I was a grown woman when we met, or at least, I thought I was, but still the things you put in that song were so dirty they made me blush. To this day I can't hear it on the radio without my face getting hot. The band at your funeral played it, and our youngest granddaughter, Isis, she danced to it, and it made me laugh and it made me cry and it made me blush all over again to see her in the middle of St. Claude Avenue, four-year-old shoulders shaking to a love song.

When my mother told me I would end up always sleeping at your back, I knew I had to prove her wrong. The hardest part about loving you was pretending I didn't care so much. So many girls cared about you. Before you married me proper, in the house on Barracks Street, there lived Anita and Mary and Maureen. You knew enough not to mention their names, and the other names, to me. But I knew who they were. I saw them at the bar when we went out, late at night. They would look at me, and then they would look at you with burned-out eyes. They loved you so much it burned the life out of them, and who wants a woman like that? It scared you away from them to me. So I taught myself to keep my eyes cool, to look as if I didn't care so much, so you would love me best.

All over town you knew you'd get a warm welcome, but with me, you were never sure if I would grab your face and kiss your cheeks or blow smoke in your ear and only half listen to your stories. When you'd come home from a long tour, I'd be sweet at first, maybe for an hour, maybe two, just so you'd know what you were missing. But then it was work. Fix the porch. Change the light bulb. Play bass and sing at my mother's church, because I'd already promised you would.

I said, "I don't care if you got hundreds of girls scream-ing your name two weeks straight."

I said I didn't care if you lived your life away from me in a baby-blue tuxedo and a fancy mustache.

I said, "All I care about is you being a good man to me," and I never let you see how surprised I was that you sub-mitted. That you gladly submitted. You laughed and took off your tuxedo and put on work pants. I would have been so happy if you kept your tuxedo on forever, but you took it off for me. You fixed the porch. You took your bass and picked up every solo in my mother's choir. I wasn't in the habit of ever saying that I loved you. I said it to you only three times when we were married, the day each of our sons were born, though you told me you loved me often enough.

And when I wouldn't say anything back, when I would just smile, you'd wink at me and call me a cold woman.

Your family wasn't fooled. It's why they hated me. They saw through it, and they were frightened. When you told your sister Betty you were going to marry me, she said it would end badly. That I loved you too fiercely. That my kind of love is wrong. She said women like me ruin the things they love. They will draw the breath of life out of a man, till his heart stops. And when they're done, when they've ruined his very lungs, she said women like me go down one of two paths. They either get hysterical for what they've lost, flinch at the empty air around them, fall apart at the lightest touch. Or they go the other way. They look at the love they've ruined, and they become petrified, airless as a stone. Betty said, "When it's all over, Delmore, when she's ruined the both of you, Lillian will go the hard way. Just you wait."

You told Betty she was crazy. That she didn't know what she was talking about, and then you told me what she said.

And I knew then that your family understood me perfectly. They recognized the darkest part of me: that I've got a weak and greedy heart. And because of this, I was ashamed. I decided then and there that your family was my enemy and I had to get better at hiding my heart from you.

I'm talking to you about my heart, but you know, if you cracked my chest open, where my heart should be, you'd only find a hungry mouth, tongue moving, teeth gnashing, ready to eat the world and you who live in it. Nothing is ever enough for my heart.

So our whole married life became me hiding my heart from you. I knew if you ever saw it for what it was, what it really was, the empty, gaping maw of it, you couldn't love me anymore.

I tricked you into loving me best. And every night for the thirty years we were married, it was you who wound yourself around me, you who stayed close to my back. You fitted your chin into the hollow of my neck and put one arm around my hip, curled the other around my shoulder, held a loose fist over my lively, sleeping heart.

. . .

You died Mardi Gras morning. We woke up before dawn. You had to get ready early because you're Skeleton Crew. You and your boys get up when it's still dark, and you dress up like ghouls, and you meet on St. Claude Avenue at dawn, to creep up and down the streets and scare everyone else, all the other crews and all of our neighbors: You scare them into parading out on Mardi Gras morning.

I heard you get out of bed before me. You washed and put on your suit of bones and your smiling skull mask. The boys came to pick you up just as the light was starting. I answered the door while you got yourself together. You came up behind me, and I turned and saw that even at fifty-eight, you were the best-made skeleton there. But I didn't say it. Rex handed you a cow leg bone, a big one, long and thick and still red from the butcher, and you took it and slung it over your shoulder. You kissed my cheek, and I kissed the starchy canvas of your skeleton mask. And then you and the boys were gone, and I went back to bed, to sleep and wait for you for the rest of Mardi Gras morning.

And you came back to me, you did, you crawled into bed beside me after the sun was up and the room was full of light. You put your arms around me and you said, "I got Bobby real good."

"What'd you do?" I said.

"He was coming home, he was still nice from last night, you know? And I got him as he came out of the bar. I made Rex and his boy, the little one, crouch down on one side, and I hid behind a mailbox. And we followed Bobby for maybe two blocks, and then we got him." You laughed. "You should have seen his face," you said.

And that's when you started to leave me. Your arms went heavy on me, your skin went hot, and your mouth stretched wide, too wide, and I got out of bed. The biggest mistake of my life. I got out of bed while you were dying to call a damn doctor. So you didn't die with your arms around me, like you should have. When I came back, I knew it was too late. You'd left me. I climbed back in bed. I turned you on your side and pressed into your back to try to make you warm again. I cried and cried but it wasn't any use. You weren't ever coming back.

• • •

I got the idea during your funeral. We'd just walked you to the grave, we'd just put you in, and we were starting the long walk back. Our oldest son held my arm. He said, "Mommy, you'll be all right." Your sisters were there, and even though they were crying too, even though it was death, they still took the time to give me the cold once-over and whisper about my shoes. So I walked with our first son at my side and your family hating me, and I thought how much I wished they were you. How I wished everyone there were you. We were walking through the cemetery and I looked at the tombs around us, all those marble tombs standing up over the ground, with the fancy stone angels on top. And that's when I got the idea.

I waited a few weeks before I told anyone my plan. I knew if I said it right away, they'd say I wasn't serious, that I didn't know what I was talking about. That it was grief talking. As if grief is a temporary thing, like being drunk. As if I'll wake up in a few days' time with a dry mouth and a sore head and fading regrets. My grief is a bone. It grew inside me when I touched your cold skin, and it got muscles and ligaments and blood when I watched them put you in the ground. And now my grief's like a sixth finger or a tail on my behind: embarrassing to other people maybe, maybe something rude, but a part of me just the same.

When you first left me, I wanted to find the god who allowed this to happen and reach inside his chest and rip his heart out. Set it on fire and blow the smoke that came up out of it into his watering eyes. I thought a lot about which god I could get at, which one I'd have a good chance at scrabbling with. Not Jesus. He'd give it up too easy. He'd pull the skin on his chest back and hand me his heart and probably the match too. I wanted a fair fight. I wanted the god to lose. The Holy Spirit doesn't have a heart. And God god, the one in charge, I didn't even let myself think about. That's blasphemy. I'd take a little bit of god, maybe, maybe one of the saints. I'd take one of them and put a hurt on him so deep, he wouldn't even know it. He'd be hollowed out by the time I was finished with him.

A month after the funeral, I asked Bobby over for dinner. He came right away. He said, "Of course, Miss Lillian. How you holding up?"

I didn't make rice and beans. For Bobby it was spaghetti from the can. I hadn't cooked in weeks. I said, "Bobby, you know I like to get straight to the point."

"Yes, ma'am, that's the truth."

"Bobby, I want Delmore back," I said.

"I do too, Miss Lillian."

"So we're gonna bring him back."

Bobby stopped eating. He opened his eyes wide. He said, "What do you mean, Miss Lillian?"

"I want you to make Delmore for me."

"What do you mean?"

"Just that. I want you to make Delmore for me. You gotta make him like this," and I pointed to my T-shirt. I was wearing your memorial T-shirt, the one the kids had printed for the funeral. It has your picture and the words "Sunrise" beside your birthday and "Sunset" beside the day you died: March 3, 1998. The picture on it is of you from two Mardi Gras ago. You're sitting on the coachman's seat of a horse and carriage. You have on your gold crown and purple cape and you have a scepter in your hand and your arms are open wide to the camera. The kids also had "Emperor of the Universe" printed above the whole thing. Since the funeral, I've worn this T-shirt every day. Mine is fluorescent yellow, and I think our boys skimped a little on the price because the ink is already starting to flake off. It's OK. I got more shirts when this one fades. I told the kids to give me all the extras.

I said, "When you make him, you gotta match him to this picture. This one here. I'll get you the original."

"I don't understand," Bobby said.

I asked Bobby because he's the best. He's an artist. But he's not too bright. He's kinda slow on the uptake. He makes all the costumes for the crews. I've seen him thread a square of cardboard the size of a stop sign with beads as small as a grain of rice in one afternoon: just when he's sitting around with the boys, drinking beer and watching girls on TV. His hands do beautiful things, so I knew he could make you right.

"Bobby, you're gonna make me another Delmore. I'll pay, don't worry. I'll pay for your time and materials. I was thinking wood, maybe. Like a nice sycamore or oak. And you could stain it a good brown. Maybe you could do him in brass."

"Miss Lillian, you are talking crazy," he said. He kept saying this, but eventually I talked him around.

Once he got used to the idea, he told me wood was all wrong. Too expensive, first of all, and it would take a long time to carve. And then, we would have to hollow you out so that I could manage you: so that you were light enough to lift and dress and carry. "Your best bet is wax," he said.

He did do it to that picture I wanted, that one exactly. Bobby made you so your legs are always bent. You are always sitting down. Your head he was able to do right away: He had a friend who worked at the department store downtown who let him borrow mannequins to practice on. He filled the hollows of their necks with hot wax, let it cool and harden, then split the domes of their plaster skulls to get at the base wax head he wanted to work with underneath.

His first try, he got your profile pretty good, but your eyes were wrong. He painted two black pupils and two pools of white where they should be. When I saw them, I said, "Those don't look like my Delmore's eyes. I need them real when he looks at me." And I gave him more money for glass.

The money was the hardest part. The wax, Bobby's labor, all of that didn't come cheap. He wanted to use chinchilla for your hair and eyelashes, but I barely had enough for the glass eyes. To an out-of-town collector, I sold your only gold record and an autographed picture of you with all the greats. It was hardest to see the record go. It's true you had it before we met. But after we started going together, you took it off the wall one night and scratched my name and yours on one of the metal ridges, the one up closest to the center. I didn't care about selling the photo. In that, you're in the back, behind the greats. You're straining your neck to be seen, and your face is too eager. I don't ever remember seeing you that way when you were alive.

Since you've left me, your things are mine to do with as I please, but your sisters don't think so. Betty heard about the sale, and she called me up, sniffing around. "What you need cash for, Lillian?" she said. She knows it's greed at the root of it, but she thinks I'm greedy for money. I said, "Betty, kindly mind your own." I made Bobby swear not to tell anybody what he was doing for me.

Bobby got a special brown wax to match your color just right. And for your hair, I knew you had to wear it how you always wore it: in a conk. I found a wig at a store downtown, long and curly, the tag in the bag said it was a mermaid cut. I trimmed the ends so it would hang right on your head.

And then he brought you, all of you, to me this morning, and we ate our reunion meal, and I cried because it was so good, finally, to look into something like your face again.

• • •

After breakfast, I take off the memorial T-shirt for the first time in a month. I put on my tightest dress, the white one with the gold flowers that you like. And you, I put you in one of the blue tuxedos, and I even get your crown and scepter down from the closet and put those on you. Your wedding band is in your casket, so in its place, I slide a ring with a red glass stone onto your left ring finger. And then we sit.

I hadn't thought about this part. I had been so excited just to have you with me, I didn't think about what we would do all day together. We sit like that, all dressed up, until I lose my nerve. I get up, leave you on the couch, go about my day dressed to kill with you sitting stiff on the sofa. At night I get my nerve back.

We eat dinner together again, and another bottle of champagne, and this time I drink your glasses as well as mine. So I am ready. At ten at night, I lift you in my arms, and I walk the few blocks to the bar. I push the door open with my shoulder, and then I carry you over the threshold. I know what we look like: a mixed-up bride and groom, but I try not to care. I carry you anyways. I carry you safely into the smoke and the clinking glasses and the soft hum of the radio, and I sit you on the barstool and I say, "A bourbon for him and a whiskey sour for me," to Nate behind the bar.

Nate says, "Lillian Brown, you have lost your mind."

And I say, "All the more reason to make me a drink."

He pours for me and he pours for you. The first hour we are there, everyone leaves us alone. The men at the end of the bar huddle together and watch me drink but pretend that they aren't looking. In the bar, in the shine of the Christmas lights stretched all over the place, your wax doesn't look so harsh. It looks almost like the flesh of you. As I drink, my eyelids get heavy. You know how liquor makes me sleepy. When we were first going out, you told me you could tell I was a good girl at heart, despite my painted nails and fancy dresses, because two hard shots of liquor and I was asleep on your shoulder. So I drink and we sit in the warm gloom of the bar, my eyes half closed, your eyes sometimes catching the light.

As the night picks up and it becomes clear I'm not going to make much trouble, everyone ignores us. The men drink. A few women come in. I hold your hand in mine, but you, of course, can only look straight ahead. I watch us both in the mirror behind the bar.

I think we've had enough. I'm waiting for our tab when one of the younger men comes up to us. It's one of Rex's kids, the older one, Man-Man. He is drunk by now, and he comes up to the two of us. His smile is too big.

"Miss Lillian," he shouts. "What is wrong with you, girl? You are crazy. What is this?"

I hold my back straight, but my insides are flinching.

"You know who it is," I say. "This here is Delmore. And you better show him some respect."

Man-Man laughs at that. "This is Delmore? This doll is Delmore?"

And then he picks you up from the barstool. Too easy. I told Bobby to make you heavier, that I needed a weight on you, but he seems to think my arms are too weak, or will be soon, to carry you.

Man-Man picks you up and holds you in his arms, and then he starts to dance with you. The other men laugh: his friends outright, the older ones nervously. The ones that are still sober watch my face, looking to see what I will do. Man-Man isn't watching. He is holding you in his arms and waltzing with you, dipping you here and there, spinning. Then he holds you against his front and does a lewd grind. And I keep my face absolutely still. I keep murder in my eye. I sip my drink while Man-Man dances with you, and inside of me, the bone of my grief is growing.

Man-Man is getting too boisterous. He goes to slip you through his legs in a dip, and he loses hold of your arms and you fall to the barroom floor. When he tries to pick you up, the wig catches on his watchband. When he finally gets you straight, you are bald-headed, the shame of your scalp flashed to the bar, your conk dangling from that fool boy's wrist.

Everyone stops talking. The bar is quiet except for the radio. Man-Man looks at the long silky hair caught up on his wrist, at your smiling, unchanging wax face. And then he looks at me, where I sit at the bar, my eyes all hard and shiny.

"Jesus, Miss Lillian," he says. "Sorry, Miss Lillian. I'm so sorry."

When he speaks, the other men join in. They start to scold him. "You're a fool, Man-Man," one of them yells at him, and even his friends, his own boys, boo him, call him stupid.

He holds you in his arms more gently now. He sits you first beside me, and then he very carefully picks each strand of the wig out of his wristwatch band. He makes sure not to break a single hair. When he's untangled the wig, he shakes it out a little bit, curves the bangs into a curl with a sweep of his hand, then sits it on top of your head.

Then he looks you in the eye and he says, "My apologies, Delmore. I didn't mean any disrespect to you or your woman. Nate," he calls. "Get Miss Lillian a drink. And one for Delmore too. It's on me."

After that, everyone wants to buy us a round. The men put cigars between your fingers. They want to light them, but I stop them. I don't want you melting.

Another young man comes through the bar door. When he sees you and me sitting at the bar, he makes a face, as if he is about to laugh or be sick. I see it and I steel myself for more. But Man-Man, who is beside us now, sees it too. He gets up and claps his hands around the young man's shoulders. He says, "What's your name, son?"

"Roy," the boy says.

"Well, Roy," Man-Man says. "I noticed you looking. And I can't help but ask, Have you ever met the Emperor of the Universe?"

Man-Man brings him over to your stool. He explains to the boy that you're a very special case: only the third man in history to come back from the dead, after Lazarus and Our Lord Jesus Christ, of course. The boy is looking from your wax face to Man-Man to me, trying to figure out what is up.

Man-Man explains that you've been granted this favor because you are the son of a lion and a woman. He's drunk again by this point, enjoying the confusion on the boy's face. He says that you managed to get a drink after death and the least us humans could do is pay you respect for it. He says that you love a good drink and a pretty woman so much you made your spirit wax so that you could enjoy them both again.

Man-Man saying all that stuff about me is sweet. Even in the dark of the bar, I can see where my skin is too soft, where the dress is too tight, where I wish that I could be like you are now, all hard and smooth.

Roy is looking around the room for his friends now. Man-Man sees he is getting restless, so he points to me and says, "You can't leave until you say hello to the woman the Emperor of the Universe came back for. Wouldn't you come back from the dead for pretty Miss Lillian?"

The boy, poor Roy, smiles nervously. But he says, "Of course." He says, "Of course I'd come back from the dead for Miss Lillian."

I smile wide at Roy, and this makes Man-Man happy. Relieved. He claps his hands, laughs loud, and says, "You know, you're all right, Roy. But you can't leave yet. You have to kiss his ring."

And so the boy obediently bows his head over your hand, purses his lips, and kisses the glass gemstone I've set on a ring there.

I never thought, in all our years together, I could walk with my heart out like this, with my heart dipped in wax and sitting beside me on a barstool, and be met with anything other than laughter or fear. I never thought somebody would like my heart enough to buy it a drink and give it cigars and kiss the false jewels I've stuck on it.

When we finally leave, there are four full glasses of bourbon on the bar in front of us. What we couldn't finish between us. Man-Man himself carries you to our front door and sits you back down on the couch. It is a good night after all.

Once Man-Man's stumbled out the door, I get up and put the kettle on. I sit and hold your hand while I wait for it to boil. When the water is ready, I get up and take three hot water bottles down from a shelf in the linen closet. I fill them up, wrap them in a towel so my hands won't burn on the rubber, and bring them back to where you sit. I slip one down the front of your shirt; a second I lay carefully in your lap; the third I place at your feet. I take your hand again, laugh a little at the belly you have now spread across your knees.

We sit like this for about twenty minutes. I think you're almost ready for bed when the phone rings. I haven't been answering my phone since you left, but I'm curious who it could be at this hour. I pick it up. Your sister Betty's voice is on the other end, furious.

"You stupid woman," she says. "You could never leave that man alone when he was alive. And now you can't leave him in peace. You've got some dummy of him dressed up and drinking with you? It's a disgrace."

Nate called her as soon as I left. He told her he was worried about me. But Betty isn't worried.

"It's harmless," I say. "It's a good time. We're not hurting anybody. That's all I can say about it, Betty."

But she won't accept this as an answer. She yells at me until I put the phone down. I stand up, ease the first bottle out of your shirt, take the second bottle out of your lap. I put them on the coffee table, then hoist you into my arms. Your wax is good and warm against me, your arms are slick. I overdid it with the heat.

I take you into our room and lay you on our bed. I ease off the tuxedo jacket, unbutton your dress shirt, pull the undershirt over your head. The boxers I have to force over your knees. I stand up, shrug off my dress, and then I get underneath the sheet with you.

It doesn't matter now, if I sleep at your back or you sleep at mine. You can't really sleep at my back anymore anyways. I curl myself around you where you make a C in the bed. I fit my arms under yours. I press the palm of my hand to the wax of your chest, then I curl my hand into a ball, knock on your chest once, twice, over and over again. I fall asleep to the sound of my knuckles beating your heart.

ANGRY BLOOD

Estella Gonzalez

When the Chilanga head housekeeper with the red hair and eyebrows like María Félix came around to inspect the floors, Merced didn't blink. Did the Chilanga think this was Merced's first time training a new hotel worker? She'd done this many times before. The only difference was that this time she was training her daughter Alma.

Under the Chilanga's watch, Merced showed Alma the best way to swipe down the toilet with the rags La Plaza had given her as part of her cleaning equipment. She polished the heavy imported furniture in a circular motion; slowly vacuumed the thick wool carpet, maneuvering the brush-topped hose into the dark corners; and dusted the silk lampshades by hand.

"Cuidado," Merced warned. "Supuestamente this furniture is from Italy, so you have to treat all these cochinadas like a baby." Alma's rag slowly wiped the top of the deeply carved desk, then the porcelain base of the lamp. Her hands shook so hard she nearly pushed it off.

One by one, Merced shared all of the standard rules for La Plaza's housekeeping staff, plus a few of her own. All the while, Alma nodded and blinked with the black eyes she got from her father, Donaciano. The Chilanga watched her with ojos de vidirio, as if Merced would give her daughter special treatment. As soon as the Chilanga left, Merced got down to the truth—puteando.

"You think I got these nice tips for just making the beds?" Merced snorted. "You think these desgraciados ask for me because I'm so good at cleaning toilets?"

Alma's black eyes grew wide, but she did not blush. The full blush would come some weeks later when Merced would lay down the rules of hustling along with a glass of Presidente brandy and the room number of a waiting john.

For now, Merced kept it simple. Fold the top sheet underneath the mattress tight and smooth. No wrinkles, no creases. Those will come later when the couple who rents the room has sex. Or maybe when one of those Fort Bliss soldiers with a weekend pass comes through with one of the cabareteras. Merced didn't mention how her eldest daughter, Norma, helped support the family with her job at the Tivoli cabaret in downtown Juarez. Merced spoke only of the soldiers and their whores, groping and whispering in the halls of La Plaza before slipping inside the rooms. It didn't matter now that the war was over, had been over for five years; these Bliss men had more money than ever, and they spent it all here at La Plaza.

Alma blinked as her mother talked and took it all in.

After the training period ended, Alma worked on her own, and one day simply rolled into the next for Merced. Beds, beds all the day long. So what if the hotel was installing these new mugreroros, televisions or whatever these chingaderas were called, in the penthouse suites. So what if people like the mayor of Juarez or the governor of Texas stayed here, supuestamente the finest hotel in El Paso. They were all the same.

"Pigs," Merced whispered to herself as her wet hair dripped onto her pinche rag of a uniform. She stripped the soft cotton sheets from the bed, and a used condom fell on her rubber-soled shoe.

"Pinche john," she whispered. "Whore," she said as she wiped the mirror above the dressing table and finger combed her wet hair. She barely had three minutes to wash her crotch and culo, but that was time enough to fog up all the mirrors in the penthouse suite.

Merced emptied the wastepaper basket quickly and rushed into the marble-floored bathroom. It was bigger than her rasquache presidio apartment in Segundo Barrio. She inspected the room quickly. Water puddled near the claw-foot tub, and the canvas shower curtain was a little ripped at the brass rings, but that wasn't her doing. Mold and God knows what else grew in the deep scratches. Merced sucked her teeth in disgust remembering she had put her feet down on that piece of porcelain just minutes before. She would have to scrub her body raw when she got home, then powder her toes with the athlete's foot remedy Victor had left behind three years ago. Merced quickly wiped down the bathroom mirror, and her plump arm flapped like a little wing.

She looked at the clock. In four minutes she had to meet Alma at the service elevator. She rushed to powder the tub with Comet, swiping it down with the set of rags La Plaza Hotel had given her when she started. High-class hotel, her nalgas. The green-speckled powder ate away at her hands, making them itchy and stink of chlorine. After all these years as a chambermaid at the hotel, all she had to show for it were cracked, bloody hands and a heart as empty as the money jar Victor had left in the middle of the wooden floor of their tiny apartment before he vanished down Highway 80 toward California. All the neatly rolled American bills in the mason jar had disappeared into his pocket. All the hard earnings from her paychecks and tips at La Plaza gone, and with it her dreams for a home of her own in the Sunset neighborhood.

With just a half day to make up six floors of rooms, Merced and Alma were in joda pushing their loaded carts down the narrow hallways and in and out of the service elevators. Sometimes, to get her mind off her blistering feet, Merced would pretend she was one of the high-priced whores she'd seen sitting on those high-class stools, stretching out their silk-stockinged legs in the windows of the cabaret she passed by on the way to the Mercado Cuahtémoc, their tight shiny high heels and peroxide blonde hair glowing in the sunlight. Juarez women had a name for that color—Juareña Gold. It was a harsh, yellow-orange color, but Merced wanted it for her own hair even if it meant being called a whore herself. Why not? she thought, smoothing out her thick black hair. These days she practically was one. Already she'd made ten dollars fucking one old man, a regular at the hotel who'd been waiting for her to knock. Room 303.

"There's my little spitfire," the old sin vergüenza had told her, pulling her into the room. "My little María. Que bonita."

Merced rolled her eyes at his reference to María Félix. She'd heard it before, mainly from the gabachos and once from Victor when they first met at the Mercado Cuahtémoc.

She had been selling her chiles and sweet potatoes along with the other vendors against the shaded wall of the giant Mercado when she first saw him in his white linen suit and matching fedora hat. He walked toward her, eyeing her like she was one of the ancho chiles laid out for his inspection.

"Mira, la mera María Bonita right here in Juarez," he told her, reaching for her hand.

She had seen María Félix on a movie poster at the Tivoli Theater across the street from the Mercado when she had come with her husband Donaciano. Her fair-skinned face set off her black hair and eyes. From then on, Merced closely read the movie star magazines, looking to see how La María wore her hair, clothes, and makeup.

Carefully, Merced stripped off her uniform and hung it over the chair. The Chilanga would kill her if she saw her working in a wrinkled or ripped dress. Worse, she would probably dock her pay just to have it pressed. Javi the bellhop was docked one time after his mother forgot to iron his fancy suit covered with brass buttons and satin trim.

"Ama has to get up a half hour early just to finish ironing this chinagdera," Javi told her once after one of the Chilanga's lectures. "Pobrecita."

Luckily for her and Alma, they wore the same brown-gold potato sack with plastic buttons every day. Merced looked over at her flat uniform as the old man split her legs open and entered her. Of course fucking the old man was nothing like when she was with Victor. For him, she took her time caressing his face, kissing him. How she loved to look into his eyes and trace the outline of his lips, stopping at the mole dancing above his upper lip. Afterward, if there was time, she would refry some beans with the

leftover bacon grease and make him some fresh flour tortillas with lard.

"Just like my grandmother's," he would say, sopping up
the last of the beans with the fluffy, warm tortilla. And then
Victor would laugh and talk about Los Angeles. "Everybody
from El Paso is going there," he told her. "There's work
in the shipyards. I'll go ahead, and as soon as I find a place in
El Este, I'll send for you and the girls." But Victor sent no
word and no money. Merced had to come up with a way to
support her daughters. She considered herself lucky to have
met a young soldier when she did about five years ago, a
Bliss man hungry for love. And then it came to her one day
as she worked her rags and cursed under her breath. If she
could make ten dollars in a morning off these rich gabachos,
then her daughters should be making fifty dollars a night.

"No se rajen," she told them one morning while they
each ate the last of the beans and corn tortillas in the cold
kitchen. "You're big girls now, grandetotas."

"Ay, Mama," Norma started. "It's too early for this." But
when Merced narrowed her eyes and stepped toward her,
Norma stopped.

"You're not even pulling in half of what you're worth in
the cabaret," whispered Merced as she scraped the last handful of beans out of the olla into Alma's bowl. "With the war
over, lots of those soldados have a lot of money saved up.
You should sleep so you can look fresh for them tonight."

Norma blinked her mascara-smeared eyes. "I'm too
hungry to sleep." Before she could dip her spoon into her
bowl, Merced had emptied part of her beans into Alma's bowl.

"Cometelas," Merced told Alma. "You're going to need
your energy today."

Norma nodded. The smell of cigarettes and beer danced around her as she shook her thick gold hair, trying to wake up a little. "Today you'll need the brandy too."

"Sí," Merced sighed as she opened the kitchen sink cupboard and pulled out a half-filled pint bottle. "El Presidente has to come too."

"¿Por qué?" Alma asked as she looked at Norma, but her sister had covered her eyes with her hands. Merced cursed Victor again under her breath and motioned for Alma to eat.

With the rebozo tightly wrapped around her shoulders, Merced walked to the hotel with Alma. The shawl was a gift from Victor during their first year in El Paso. She pulled it tighter across her shoulders and thought about the ones she had left back home in Chihuahua pueblito with her husband Donaciano. In the distance, the Franklin Mountains glowed in the pink dawn. It wouldn't be long before snow covered them in thick blankets. She needed a coat. And so did the girls. They needed so many things. And now there was a way to get them.

Merced had experience with selling love. She was thankful to the first Bliss soldier she met. After the tenth john, it wasn't so bad anymore. And today Alma would learn. Today would be her first day earning real money just like Merced and Norma. As soon as they reached La Plaza Hotel's supply room, Merced and Alma began loading their carts. La Chilanga stood by, eyeing them while mentally counting the cleaning supplies. They headed to the elevator and saw Javi carrying heavy leather-bound suitcases behind a pair of men dressed in thick long coats. They nodded a greeting to each other before Javi went through the revolving doors. As the elevator pulled Merced and Alma up to the fifth floor, Merced shut her eyes and remembered what she had learned during the last five years.

First, you ask for the money right up front or the cabrón could take off on you. Second, make sure he takes off all of his clothes first, just to check he isn't armed. Third, don't eat or drink anything he offers you. You never know when these men will try to poison or drug you. You had to be safe.

Fourth, the moment he's done, you put your clothes on right away and shower in the next room you had to clean. That's the only time you can do this because later on as you cleaned more hotel rooms and maybe fucked more men, you want to be a little fresh but didn't want your skin to get all dried out with rashes. For the past five years, Merced had repeated these rules every day like a prayer. She shared this prayer with her daughter as they walked down the carpeted hallway to their next rooms and she watched as Alma just nodded her head and stared at her feet.

"And ask them for twenty mija," Merced said. "You're young enough you can ask for more. How old are you telling them?"

"Eighteen."

"Tell them sixteen. These descarados want to feel like they're young studs again."

Merced could tell her daughter was biting the inside of her cheeks.

"And you better not cry," Merced told Alma, pulling out the little brown bottle of brandy. "That'll scare them away. Here."

Merced took the brandy and twisted the cap open. Even after a week, it was still strong. "Take two long gulps," she told her. On such a skinny girl, Merced knew the alcohol worked much quicker.

Alma didn't spit it out like Norma did the first time she gave her some of the Presidente. Maybe Alma already drank on the side, sneaking after hours into the hotel's fancy Dome Bar like Merced did sometimes. Maybe Norma had already warned Alma. Whatever it was, Merced was glad. It made her life easier having at least one experienced daughter who liked to drink.

"Y no te rajes," Merced warned her. "If I hear any screams and he's not killing you, me la vas a pagar."

Merced looked into her daughter's nodding face and saw her ex-husband Donaciano's black eyes. Ese cabrón. He would pay for sticking her with his escuincles. He was the one who wanted the children, not her. But what did she know? Merced had only been fifteen when she married old man Donaciano. They had lived in a proper house in El Sauz, right across from the town plaza, and he had wanted a family of sons to fill it. But the son wouldn't come no matter how early she rose to make tortillas, to boil the beans, and to wash the clothes against the rocks of the tajo. God just continued to curse her and her old husband with two daughters. Ni modo. The only time she rested was when she rode in her comadre Rufina's old Chevy truck the thirty miles between El Sauz and Juarez to sell Donaciano's chili and sweet potato harvest. Finally, when she met Victor, rest would come when she slept with him.

But Victor was gone now, and the mason jar that once lay under the wooden floorboards of their brick presidio apartment was cleaned out. With the money gone, she had to fend for her daughters and herself while Victor, that drag-ass good-for-nothing, was in Los Angeles doing who knows what except sending for her and the girls.

"One day we'll leave El Paso too," Merced told Alma. "As soon as we get enough money to buy a house."

Alma pulled the Presidente brandy from behind the linens and drank a long drink. As she leaned her head back, Merced saw herself tilting back her first brandy at La Plaza Hotel's Dome Bar on a date with Victor. Her eyes watered when she remembered her burning throat and the way Victor gently stroked her face as she coughed.

"Not so quickly," he said. "You're not a man."

"But it burns."

"Pobrecita," he said, holding her hands. "Your hands are so cold, but the brandy will warm you up."

He cupped her hands, then blew on her fingers. Then he kissed her throat, tipping her head back again. Up above, she saw a glass dome made by some famous New York company. Pieces of stained glass fitted in iron whirled above her.

"Tifanis," the bartender had told them. He had meant Tiffany's, but they didn't know.

Against the night sky, purple and blue glass glowed with moonlight. A jungle of green leaves reached toward the center of the dome, making Merced feel like she could almost fly through the center into the stars. That night she had thought Victor would take her to his little brick apartment in Segundo Barrio. But instead, he drove her back over the bridge, back to Chihuahua. Back to Donaciano.

"Don't get drunk," Merced told Alma. "Men want you awake and doing something."

Merced did the sign of the cross over her head before Alma walked into the room.

"Think of me," Merced told her. "Y apurate. We don't have much time."

Merced watched the door close behind her daughter, then pressed her body up close, waiting until she heard Alma's muffled cries blend in with the john's murmurs.

"OK . . . OK . . . OK?" the john kept asking.

Con una jodida, Merced thought, pounding her fist into her thigh. Just fuck her and get it over with. Didn't the john know the rules? Why was this gabacho so soft on her daughter? He should just break her into submission and be done with it. Just like her first time with one of those traveling salesmen, a viejo who'd just come out of the shower. He was quick. No questions. No answers, just money.

Merced walked over to her cleaning cart and pulled out the bottle of brandy, drinking until she heard the elevator announce its arrival on the fifth floor. Before Javi the bellboy and the gabacho couple could reach her, Merced slipped the bottle back into the front pocket of her cleaning cart where she kept the rags and industrial cleaners. Wrapping her fingers around the cold wooden handle, Merced leaned into the heavy cart and pushed. The cart rolled slowly down the carpeted hallway, passing doors with little wooden "Do Not Disturb" signs hanging on chains. Their doorknobs gleamed like giant diamonds under the hallway lights.

"Cabrones," Merced whispered. "Cabrones."

The couple, a man in a long wool coat and a woman in fur and silk, passed by Merced, leaving behind a trail of perfume and cologne. The man winked at her as he passed. The perfume lingered then faded as Merced kept pushing her cart back and forth over the same one hundred yards of carpet.

"Ese gabacho," Javi said when he caught up with Merced. "The wife's a bitch. But he's a good tipper."

Merced stopped pushing her cart and stared at the bill in his hand.

"Not really."

Javi's face fell. "¿Como que no?"

"You're only twenty," laughed Merced. "What do you know about tipping?"

"I know a dollar is better than fifty cents," Javi said, snapping his bill. "Que bueno his wife came with him this time."

Then he started batting his eyes, putting his hand on his hips in imitation of the woman with the fur stole.

"I don't want these Mexicans stealing from me, so you better tip him good," Javi screeched. Merced and Javi's laughter could be heard down the hallway, making one guest poke his head out of the room.

"We better leave," Javi giggled. "Before they catch us."

"You're such a payaso," Merced sighed as she went back to pushing her cart.

Merced took the brandy bottle from her cleaning cart once more and tilted her head back. Even before she unscrewed the cap, she felt her blood warming up, rushing like love. She'd have to get more bottles now that Alma also drank, she thought. The bottle's heat throbbed through the cotton of her dress with every step down the carpeted hallway. When Alma came out of the john's room, she looked ghostly, her black eyes now a gunmetal gray.

"How much?" Merced asked, holding out her hand.

Alma put a tightly folded paper money square into Merced's palm.

"What is this?"

Alma reached over and unfolded the tight little square until three ten-dollar bills fanned out, almost covering her outstretched hand. Merced nodded at the money. She had never earned this much in her life. She carefully rolled the bills up and slipped them into her front pocket where the roll hung heavy like a gun.

"Let's finish up the last room together," Merced told Alma, who barely nodded and floated down the hallway in front of her.

The brandy banged against Merced's thigh, reminding her to finish it up before they left the hotel for the night. She hoped the guests in their last room had left behind a pack of cigarettes. They would go well with her drink. Once inside, she went straight to the nightstand and found a pack of Pall Malls next to two tumblers half filled with golden water and nearly melted ice. One whiff and Merced knew. Tequila. Expensive tequila. She gulped both glasses down and pulled the bottle from her apron.

"Go shower while I finish the room," she told Alma.

The brandy burned her throat. Merced reached for the pack of cigarettes and the book of matches, but before she could light up, Alma called from the bathroom with a voice that was low and desperate.

"Ama. Come here."

"¿Que?" Merced was ready to pour the brandy.

"I can't do it," Alma sobbed.

Merced rolled her eyes. Now what? She entered the bathroom and looked down into the toilet water.

"Just flush it mensa," Merced told Alma, who tried to squirm away from the blood.

"I can't."

Merced grabbed Alma's hand and pushed it toward the handle. But Alma pushed back, knocking Merced into the sink. Her quick footsteps brought her only as far as the door and no farther. Warm liquid covered Merced's eye, dripped into her mouth, and mixed with the tequila's bitterness.

Merced made her way to the edge of the bed. She grabbed the pack of Pall Malls and unwrapped it like a belated gift.

"My tip," she laughed out loud, feeling the brandy. The match made a nice, sharp cracking sound as it ignited into a tiny flame, and she took a deep breath. The cigarette smoke burned deep and long in Merced's lungs. Alma slid down the wall and sat on the carpet with her back against the patterned wallpaper.

Before she knew it, Merced felt herself falling back on the bed, the sheets' musky smell rising and mixing with the cigarette smoke. A deep, wet sob shook her body until a wail broke out of her. Choking and coughing with smoke and spit, she pushed herself up on one arm. A small string of smoke rose from the bed and spread toward the ceiling. Alma's dark eyes spread wide like a child's.

"Chingado," Merced yelled as she jumped up. She yanked the bedspread, threw it to the floor, and stomped on it until the smoke stopped. The hole, with its burned edges, looked like a burned-out eye socket. Merced knew the hotel wouldn't care, especially if she told the Chilanga it was the hotel guest who had burned the hole. But she also knew that she couldn't keep this life up. Sooner or later the hotel would figure out her little side job. Quickly, she rolled up the bedspread and tucked it under her arm like a baby.

Then she turned to look at Alma. She looked pale, her eyes dull black. Merced took the cigarette from her mouth and slowly began burning holes in the white cotton sheet, one by one until the sheet looked like it had a dozen bruised eye sockets and the room smelled of burning cotton and tobacco. The smell followed Merced into the hallway, where she kept burning holes until the perfumed couple's door opened. Merced didn't look down. Her eyes followed the couple walking toward her, their perfumed smell mixing with the smoke.

Before they could reach her, Merced threw her cigarette on the floor and rubbed it down into the thick carpet with her rubber-soled shoe. She kept staring at the couple, especially at the woman, who looked back at her with raised eyebrows and a red mouth frozen into an "O." Then Merced snapped open the sheet with its many eyes and laid it on the carpet in front of the couple, who looked down at her and then the sheet and then at her again.

"Mama," Alma said as she looked down at the sheet. Merced followed her gaze. The burned-out eyes stared back at Merced, bruised and empty.

"A la chingada con este hotel," Merced told the couple. The man stepped out in front of the woman, her blonde head peeking over the man's shoulder every third or fourth step.

"We're leaving," Merced told Alma as she grabbed the bottle of Presidente out of the cart and headed away from the service elevators. "Today."

By the time she and Alma reached the lobby, the couple had already called housekeeping. Merced wished she had taken the pack of cigarettes from her last room because at that moment she felt every eye in the world looking at her. From behind a stack of suitcases, Javi's gaze winked a goodbye. The Chilanga yelled out to her, but Merced never looked back. Instead she drank the last of the Presidente and dropped it with a crash in front of all the gabacho and Mexicano guests and workers.

Outside the sun glared down on her, on Alma, and on everybody walking toward and away from La Plaza. A car honked, and the smell of taquitos from the restaurant next door filled Merced. Somewhere out in Los Angeles, Victor was waiting for her, and she had to get to him soon or she would kill somebody. Merced looked at her daughter, still and silent under the white-hot sunshine. For a moment she saw Donaciano and then herself, still fifteen and stupid.

"Let's go get Norma," she told Alma. "We have to start packing for tomorrow."

"Pero . . ." Alma started, but Merced just kept walking away, her eyes on the horizon of brick and white stone buildings, the Franklin Mountains between her and the pulsing sky.

Thank you for supporting The Kweli Journal*'s mission to nurture emerging writers of color and foster a vibrant literary community.*

For more information about The Kweli Journal*'s offerings, such as our Fellowship Program, our Mentorship Program, and our Reading and Conversation Series, please scan here or visit www.kwelijournal.org.*

ACKNOWLEDGMENTS

Thank you to all the contributors who trusted *Kweli* with their art from day one: Princess Joy L. Perry, Reem Kassis, DéLana R. A. Dameron, JP Infante, Daphne Palasi Andreades, Jennine Capó Crucet, Naima Coster, LaToya Watkins, Ivelisse Rodriguez, K-Ming Chang, Susan Muaddi Darraj, Nicole Dennis-Benn, Kaitlyn Greenidge, and Estella Gonzalez; Victoria Sanders for your beautiful vision and for helping us keep the lights on; Robin Desser for your brilliant "third eye" and for helping my words truly sing; Madeline McIntosh, Nina von Moltke, and Don Weisberg for all your light and enthusiasm; and Rose Edwards, Andrea Bachofen, and JoliAmour Dubose-Morris for all your joy and careful attention. Thank you to the entire Authors Equity family for all the time and effort you put into *Sing*. And thank you to Edwidge Danticat and Honorée Fanonne Jeffers for all your love and for always saying yes to *Kweli*.

PERMISSIONS ACKNOWLEDGMENTS

"A Hard Bed" originally appeared in *The Kweli Journal*, December 2009.

"Farradiyya" originally appeared in *The Kweli Journal*, November 2019.

"Work" originally appeared in *The Kweli Journal*, April 2020. Excerpt(s) from REDWOOD COURT (REESE'S BOOK CLUB): FICTION by DéLana R. A. Dameron, copyright © 2024 by DéLana R. A. Dameron. Used by permission of The Dial Press, an imprint of Random House, a division of Penguin Random House LLC. All rights reserved.

"Without a Big One" originally appeared in *The Kweli Journal*, May 2018.

"Panagbenga" originally appeared in *The Kweli Journal*, April 2019.

"Magic City Relic" originally appeared as "Send a Dozen to Get One Through" in *The Kweli Journal*, October 2011, and was later expanded into the novel *Make Your Home Among Strangers* (St. Martin's Press, 2015).

"Cold" from *What's Mine and Yours* by Naima Coster, copyright © 2022. Reprinted by permission of Grand Central Publishing, an imprint of Hachette Book Group, Inc. "Cold" originally appeared in *The Kweli Journal*, June 2016.

"Straight Dollars or Loose Change" originally appeared in *The Kweli Journal*, January 2012.

Ivelisse Rodriguez, "La Hija de Changó" from Love War Stories. Originally published in *The Kweli Journal* (December 2009). Copyright © 2009, 2018 by Ivelisse Rodriguez. Reprinted with the permission of The Permissions Company, LLC on behalf of The Feminist Press, feministpress.org. All rights reserved.

"Jenny's Dollar Store" originally appeared in *The Kweli Journal*, August 2020.

"Cleaning Lentils" originally appeared in *The Kweli Journal*, May 2022.

Nicole Dennis-Benn's short story "What's For Sale" became part of her novel *Here Comes the Sun*, copyright 2016 (Liveright). "What's For Sale" originally appeared in *The Kweli Journal*, May 2014.

"Emperor of the Universe" originally appeared in *The Kweli Journal*, October 2014.

A re-edited version of "Angry Blood" appears in her novel, *Huizache Women*, Arte Público Press 2024. "Angry Blood" originally appeared in *The Kweli Journal*, May 2012.

CONTRIBUTORS

Daphne Palasi Andreades is the author of the debut novel *Brown Girls*, which was named a *New York Times* Editors' Choice, an Indie Next Pick, and a finalist for the Carol Shields Prize for Fiction, the Center for Fiction First Novel Prize, the New American Voices Award, and the VCU Cabell First Novelist Award. She graduated from the City University of New York, Baruch College, and Columbia University's MFA fiction program. She is the recipient of an O. Henry Prize; scholarships to the Bread Loaf Writers' Conference, the Sewanee Writers' Conference, and Martha's Vineyard Institute for Creative Writing, where she won the Voices of Color Prize; and other honors. Her fiction explores diaspora, immigration, family, and hybrid identities and draws from disciplines such as poetry, history, visual art, and more. She lives in New York City and is at work on several projects, including her second novel.

K-Ming Chang is a Kundiman fellow, a Lambda Literary Award finalist, and a National Book Foundation 5 Under 35 honoree. She is the author of the novel *Bestiary*, which was longlisted for the Center for Fiction First Novel Prize, the PEN/Faulkner Award, and the VCU Cabell First Novelist Award.

Naima Coster is a *New York Times* bestselling author of two novels and a recipient of the National Book Foundation's

5 Under 35 honor. Naima Coster's most recent book, *What's Mine and Yours*, was a pick for the *Today* show's Read with Jenna book club, a Book of the Month Club pick, a state-wide read for One Maryland One Book, and longlisted for the Mark Twain American Voice in Literature Award. It was named a best book of the year by *Kirkus Reviews*, Amazon, *Esquire, Marie Claire, Ms. Magazine, The Millions*, and Refinery29. Her first novel, *Halsey Street*, was a finalist for the Kirkus Prize for Fiction and a semifinalist for the VCU Cabell First Novelist Award. It was also named a must-read by *People, Essence, BitchMedia, Well-Read Black Girl, The Skimm*, and the Brooklyn Public Library. In 2018, she was named New Author of the Year by Go On Girl! Book Club, the largest national book club for Black women. Her stories and essays have appeared in *The New York Times, Elle, Time, The Kweli Journal, The Cut, The Sunday Times*, and *Catapult*, among other publications, and in numerous anthologies. She earned her MFA at Columbia University and has taught writing for over a decade in community settings, youth programs, and universities. She lives in Brooklyn with her family.

Jennine Capó Crucet is a novelist, essayist, and screenwriter. Her novel *Make Your Home Among Strangers* won the International Latino Book Award, was named a *New York Times* Editors' Choice, and was cited as a best book of the year by NBC Latino, *The Guardian*, and the *Miami Herald*, among others; it is an all-campus read at over forty US universities. Her story collection, *How to Leave Hialeah*, won the Iowa Short Fiction Prize, the John Gardner Book Award, and the Devil's Kitchen Reading Award. Her essay collection, *My Time Among the Whites: Notes from an Unfinished Education*, was longlisted for the 2019 PEN America / Open Book Award. She is a recipient of a PEN / O. Henry Prize, the Picador Fellowship, and the Hillsdale Award for the Short Story. Her writing has appeared on *PBS NewsHour* and NPR and in publications such as *The Atlantic*, *Condé Nast Traveler*, and *The New York Times*, among others. Her most recent novel, *Say Hello to My Little Friend*, was a finalist for the Kirkus Prize for Fiction and the *Los Angeles Times* Book Prize. Born and raised in Miami, she lives in North Carolina with her family.

DéLana R. A. Dameron is an artist whose primary medium is storytelling. Her first work of fiction, *Redwood Court*, was a Reese's Book Club pick. She is a graduate of New York University's MFA program in poetry and holds a BA in history from the University of North Carolina at Chapel Hill. Her debut poetry collection, *How God Ends Us*, was selected by Elizabeth Alexander for the South Carolina Poetry Book Prize, and her second collection, *Weary Kingdom*, was chosen by Nikky Finney for the Palmetto Poetry Series. Dameron is also the founder of Saloma Acres, an equestrian and cultural space in her hometown in South Carolina, where she resides.

Edwidge Danticat is the author of numerous works of fiction, including *Breath, Eyes, Memory*, *Krik? Krak!*, *The Farming of Bones*, and *Claire of the Sea Light*. She has written seven books for children and young adults; a travel narrative, *After the Dance*; and two collections of essays, *Create Dangerously* and, most recently, *We're Alone*. Her memoirs are *Brother, I'm Dying*, a National Book Award finalist and a winner of the National Book Critics Circle Award for Autobiography, and *The Art of Death*, a National Book Critics Circle Award finalist in Criticism. Her story collection *Everything Inside* was awarded the Bocas Fiction Prize, the Story Prize, and the National Book Critics Circle Fiction Prize. A MacArthur fellow, she is currently the Wun Tsun Tam Mellon Professor of Humanities in the African American and African Diaspora Studies Department at Columbia University.

Susan Muaddi Darraj is an award-winning writer of books for adults and children. She won an American Book Award, two Arab American Book Awards, and a Maryland State Arts Council Independent Artists Award. In 2018, she was named a USA Artists Ford Fellow. Her books include her linked short story collection, *A Curious Land*, as well as the Farah Rocks children's book series. She lives in Baltimore, where she teaches creative writing at Harford Community College and Johns Hopkins University. Her most recent novel, *Behind You Is the Sea*, received praise from *The New York Times*, the *San Francisco Chronicle*, and *Ms. Magazine* and was named a Best Book of 2024 by *The New Yorker*.

Nicole Dennis-Benn is the author of *Here Comes the Sun*, a *New York Times* Notable Book of the Year and a Lambda Literary Award winner. Her bestselling second novel, *Patsy*, was a Lambda Literary Award winner, a *New York Times* Editors' Choice, a *Financial Times* Critics Choice, a Stonewall Book Awards Honor Book, and a pick for the *Today* show's Read with Jenna book club. *Patsy* was named a Best Book of the

Year by *Kirkus Reviews*, *Time*, NPR, *People*, *The Washington Post*, Apple Books, *O, The Oprah Magazine*, *The Guardian*, *Good Housekeeping*, BuzzFeed, and *Elle*, among others. She received a National Foundation for the Arts Grant and was a finalist for the National Book Critics Circle John Leonard Award, the NYPL Young Lions Award, and the Center for Fiction First Novel Prize, longlisted for the Pen/Faulkner Award in Fiction, and shortlisted for the Aspen Words Literary Prize. Her work has appeared in *The New York Times*, *Elle*, *Electric Literature*, *Lenny Letter*, *The Rumpus*, *Catapult*, *Red Rock Review*, *The Kweli Journal*, *Mosaic*, *Ebony*, and *The Feminist Wire*. Her *New York Times* Modern Love essay, "Who Is Allowed to Hold Hands," was narrated by Alicia Keys. She was born and raised in Kingston, Jamaica. She graduated from Cornell University and holds a master of public health from the University of Michigan and an MFA in creative writing from Sarah Lawrence College. She is the founder of the Stuyvesant Writing Workshop and lives with her wife and two sons in Brooklyn.

Estella Gonzalez is the author of the acclaimed short story collection *Chola Salvation* and the novel *Huizache Women*. Her work has appeared in *The Kweli Journal*, the *Acentos Review*, and *Huizache*. Her fiction and poetry have been anthologized in both *Daughters of Latin America: An International Anthology of Writing by Latine Women* and *Nasty Women Poets: An Unapologetic Anthology of Subversive Verse*.

Kaitlyn Greenidge's debut novel, *We Love You, Charlie Freeman*, was one of *The New York Times* Critics' Top 10 Books. Her writing has appeared in *Vogue*, *Glamour*, *The Wall Street*

Journal, *Elle*, BuzzFeed, *The Kweli Journal*, *Transition Magazine*, *Virginia Quarterly Review*, *The Believer*, *American Short Fiction*, and other venues. She is the recipient of fellowships from the Whiting Foundation, the National Endowment for the Arts, the Radcliffe Institute for Advanced Study, the Lewis Center for the Arts at Princeton University, and the Guggenheim Foundation. She is currently the features director at *Harper's Bazaar*. Her most recent novel, *Libertie*, was a *New York Times* Notable Book and a Best Historical Fiction Pick and was named a Best Book of the Year by *The Washington Post*, *Time*, the *Los Angeles Times*, and *Christian Science Monitor*.

JP Infante is the author of *On the Tip of Your Mother's Tongue* and *Aquí y Allá: un retrato de la comunidad Dominicana en Washington Heights*. He is the winner of PEN's Robert J. Dau Short Story Prize and Thirty West's Chapbook contest. His writing has appeared in *The Kweli Journal*, *The Poetry Project*, *Rigorous*, *A Gathering of the Tribes*, and elsewhere. He has been awarded scholarships and fellowships from the NY State Writers Institute, PEN America, and the Center for Fiction. He holds an MFA from the New School.

Reem Kassis is a Palestinian writer whose work focuses on the intersection of food with culture, history, and politics. Her writings have appeared in *The Wall Street Journal*, *The Kweli Journal*, *The Washington Post*, the *LA Times*, and various academic journals. She is the author of *The Palestinian Table*, an acclaimed cookbook that won the Guild of Food Writers First Book Award and a Gourmand World Cookbook Award and was a James Beard Best International

Cookbook Award finalist as well as one of NPR's Best Books of the Year. Her second book, *The Arabesque Table*, is a collection of contemporary recipes tracing the rich history of Arab cuisine. She grew up in Jerusalem, then lived in the US, France, Germany, Jordan, and the UK. She now lives in the Philadelphia area with her husband and three daughters.

Laura Pegram, founding editor and publisher of *The Kweli Journal*, is a multi-hyphenate artist whose work is influencing a new generation of writers. She is an author, educator, and jazz vocalist who teamed with acclaimed jazz pianist Donald Smith in cabaret performances. She is also a painter whose richly hued murals are part of several private collections. She was mentored by the poet-activist June Jordan, who taught her that the sky was her ceiling. She lives in Manhattan.

Princess Joy L. Perry is a master lecturer of composition, American literature, and creative writing at Old Dominion University in Norfolk, Virginia. A 2010 Pushcart Prize nominee, her fiction has appeared in *The Kweli Journal*, *Harrington Gay Men's Literary Quarterly*, and *African American Review*. She was a Tobias Wolff Award in Fiction finalist and garnered an honorable mention from *The Common Review*'s first annual Short Story Prize. She is a past recipient of a Virginia Commission for the Arts Fellowship and a winner of the Zora Neale Hurston / Richard Wright Award.

Ivelisse Rodriguez is a fiction writer born in Arecibo, Puerto Rico, and raised in Holyoke, Massachusetts. Her debut short story collection, *Love War Stories*, is full of cautionary tales of characters on the cusp of romance who covet, wrestle with, and fight to subvert their familial and cultural legacies of suffering from and for love. *Love War Stories* was a PEN/Faulkner finalist and a Foreword Reviews INDIES finalist. She is a 2022 Letras Boricuas fellow and a Tanne Foundation award winner. Her fiction has appeared in the *Boston Review*, *Obsidian*, *The Kweli Journal*, *The Bilingual Review*, *Aster(ix)*, and other publications. She was a contributing arts editor for the *Boston Review* and the founder and editor of an interview series focused on contemporary Puerto Rican writers, which highlights the current status and the continuity of the Puerto Rican literary tradition. She was a senior fiction editor at *The Kweli Journal* and is a Kimbilio fellow and a VONA/Voices alum. She has taught creative writing at the University of Texas–Rio Grande Valley, the University of Arizona, the University of Missouri–St. Louis, and numerous writing centers across the country. She is an assistant professor and the Mary Rogers Field and Marion Field-McKenna Distinguished University Professor of Creative Writing at DePauw University.

LaToya Watkins's writing has appeared in *A Public Space*, *The Sun*, *The Kweli Journal*, *McSweeney's Quarterly Concern*, *Kenyon Review*, *The Pushcart Prize Anthology*, and elsewhere. She is a Kimbilio fellow and has received support from the Bread Loaf Writers' Conference, MacDowell, OMI: Arts, Yaddo, Hedgebrook, and the Camargo Foundation. She is the author of *Perish* and the story collection *Holler, Child*, which was longlisted for the National Book Award for Fiction.